PRAISE FOR RAGNAR JÓNASSON

'Enjoyed Ragnar Jónasson's *Snowblind* – a modern Icelandic take on an Agatha Christie-style mystery, as twisty as any slalom …' Ian Rankin

'A tense and convincing thriller; Jónasson is a welcome addition to the roster of Scandi authors…' Susan Moody

'Ragnar Jónasson writes with a chilling, poetic beauty – a must-read addition to the growing canon of Iceland Noir' Peter James

'Seductive … an old-fashioned murder mystery with a strong central character and the fascinating background of a small Icelandic town cut off by snow. Ragnar does claustrophobia beautifully' Ann Cleeves

'His first novel to be translated into English has all the skilful plotting of an old-fashioned whodunnit although it feels bitingly contemporary in setting and tone' Jake Kerridge, *Sunday Express*

'On the face of it, *Snowblind* is a gigantic locked-room mystery, an investigation into murder and other crimes within a closed society with a limited number of suspects … Jónasson plays fair with the reader – his clues are traditional and beautifully finessed – and he keeps you turning the pages. *Snowblind* is morally more equivocal than most traditional whodunnits, and it offers alluring glimpses of darker, and infinitely more threatening horizons' *Independent*

'Ragnar Jónasson's *Snowblind* is as dazzling a novel as its title implies and the wonderful Ari Thór is a welcome addition to the pantheon of Scandinavian detectives. I can't wait until the sequel!' William Ryan

'A truly chilling debut, perfect for fans of Karin Fossum and Henning Mankell' Eva Dolan

'Is King Arnaldur Indriðason looking to his laurels? There is a young pretender beavering away, his eye on the crown: Ragnar Jónasson ...' Barry Forshaw

'An isolated community, subtle clueing, clever misdirection and more than a few surprises combine to give a modern day Golden Age whodunnit. Well done! I look forward to the next in the series' Dr John Curran

'*Snowblind* brings you the chill of a snowbound Icelandic fishing village cut off from the outside world, and the warmth of a really well-crafted and translated murder mystery' Michael Ridpath

'The complex characters and absorbing plot make *Snowblind* memorable. Its setting – Siglufjördur, a small fishing village isolated in the depths of an Icelandic winter – makes it unforgettable. Let's hope that more of this Icelandic author's work will be translated' Sandra Balzo

'In Ari Thór Arason, Nordic Noir has a new hero as compelling and interesting as the Northern Icelandic setting' Nick Quantrill

'If a Golden Age crime novel was to emerge from a literary deep freeze then you'd hope it would read like this. Jónasson cleverly squeezes this small, isolated town in northern Iceland until it is hard to breathe, ensuring the setting is as claustrophobic as any locked room. If you call your book "Snowblind" then you better make sure it's chilling. He does' Craig Robertson

'If Arnaldur is the King and Yrsa the Queen of Icelandic crime fiction, then Ragnar is surely the Crown Prince ... more please!' Karen Meek, EuroCrime

'Ragnar Jónasson brilliantly evokes the claustrophobia of small-town Iceland in this intriguing murder mystery. Let's hope this is the first of many translations by Quentin Bates' Zoë Sharp

'Ragnar Jónasson is simply brilliant at planting a hook and using the magic of a dark Icelandic winter to reel in the story. *Snowblind* screams isolation and darkness in an exploration of the basic Icelandic nature with all its attendant contrasts and extremes, amid a plot filled with twists, turns, and one surprise after another' Jeffrey Siger

'A chilling, thrilling slice of Icelandic Noir' Thomas Enger

'A stunning murder mystery set in the northernmost town in Iceland, written by one of the country's finest crime writers. Ragnar has Nordic Noir down pat – a remote small-town mystery that is sure to please crime fiction aficionados' Yrsa Sigurðardóttir

'*Snowblind* is a brilliantly crafted crime story that gradually unravels old secrets in a small Icelandic town … an excellent debut from a talented Icelandic author. I can't wait to read more' Sarah Ward

'An intricately plotted crime novel, *Snowblind* is a remarkable début. Ragnar Jónasson has delivered an intelligent whodunnit that updates, stretches, and redefines the locked-room mystery format. The author's cool clean prose constructs atmospheric word pictures that recreate the harshness of an Icelandic winter in the reader's mind. Destined to be an instant classic' EuroDrama

'*Snowblind* is a beautifully written thriller, as tense as it is terrifying – Jónasson is a writer with a big future' Luca Veste

'It sometimes feels as if everyone in Iceland is writing crime novels but the first appearance of Ragnar Jónasson in English translation (itself a fluid adaptation by British mystery writer Quentin Bates) is cause for celebration' Maxim Jakubowski, Lovereading

'*Snowblind* has given rise to one of the biggest buzzes in the crime fiction world, and refreshingly usurps the cast iron grip of the present obsession with domestic noir … a complex and perplexing case, in a claustrophobic and chilling setting …' Raven Crime Reads

'The intricate plotting is reminiscent of the great Christie but the setting is very much more modern and darker. There is an increasing tension and threat, which mirrors the developing snow storm and creates a sense of isolation and confinement, ensuring that the story develops strongly once the characters and scene are laid out' Live Many Lives

'A brooding, atmospheric book; with the darkness and constant snow there is a claustrophobic feel to everything, which is heightened to the nth degree when there is an avalanche and the one road in and out of the village is blocked' Reading Writes & For Reading Addicts

'It is surely only a matter of time before *Snowblind* and the rest of Ragnar's Dark Iceland series go on to take the Nordic Noir genre by storm. The rest of the world has been patiently waiting for a new author to emerge from Iceland and join the ranks of Indriðason and Sigurðardóttir and it appears that he is now here' Grant Nichol, Volcanic Lilypad

'Jónasson's prose throughout this entire novel is captivating, and frequently borders on the poetic, constructing something that is both beautiful and uncomfortable for the reader … a simply stunning piece of prose that will certainly put him in the thick of the crime genre in the United Kingdom' MadHatter Reviews

'*Snowblind* uses its stunningly beautiful yet brutally remote setting to create a chilling, atmospheric locked-room mystery. Ragnar Jónasson is an outstanding new voice in Nordic Noir' Crime Thriller Girl

'Dark Iceland? This man not only invented it, he rules it. From the opening page, the tension and chilling horror is there. The idyllic snow angel image is no longer full of childhood innocence and the "snowblind" of the title covers your eyes with white flurries and clouds of mist that shroud the mystery and intrigue' The Booktrail

'*Snowblind* is a subtle, quiet mystery set in the most exquisite landscape – a slow burner that will suck you in and not let you go until you finish the final page' Reading Room with a View

'Just when I think I've had enough of the frozen north, another promising author shows up. This is a truly enjoyable debut, hinting at much more to come. A charming combination of influences, which feels very fresh and will appeal to those who find cosy crime too twee and Scandinavian noir too depressing' Crime Fiction Lover

'The writing is clear, evocative and fraught with tension and the descriptions of the unforgiving nature of an Icelandic winter are executed brilliantly. The overbearing landscape enhances the increasing sense of claustrophobia and isolation Ari Thór feels to the point where it is palpable' Salboho

'*Snowblind* is the first in a series of novels labelled as "Dark Iceland". Read the first page and you will immediately understand why – it is dark, it is gripping and it is fascinating' The Welsh Librarian

'*Snowblind* epitomises exactly this sort of exciting, new cross-genre fiction. It is a fusion of Nordic Noir and Golden Age detective fiction, with Christie-esque plotting, characterisation and narrative techniques' Vicky Newham

'This is an excellent debut novel … like reading a modern-day Icelandic Agatha Christie novel. I look forward to meeting Ari Thór again soon' Victoria Goldman

'A deliciously old-fashioned mystery' Crime Worm

'For a debut novel, *Snowblind* is startlingly confident and sure-footed. The characters and dialogue all ring true, the plot is original and packed with plenty a surprise. Perhaps most pleasingly of all, Jónasson steers clear of hackneyed plot devices and reveals' Mumbling About …

'A damn good thriller' OMG That Book

'The plot twists and turns as the investigation uncovers a plethora of old deceits and current intrigues. Festering wounds are opened spilling secrets as dark as the days, as shocking as the blood on the suffocating snow' Never Imitate

'There is something almost hauntingly melancholic about this story. The claustrophobia felt by Ari Thór is palpable. You can almost feel the walls of snow caging you in and the sense of almost perpetual winter darkness makes you reach for the light switch' From First Page to Last

'Jónasson has bestowed his characters with unique, more importantly believable, personalities, and has made sure that their interactions throughout serve mainly to play on readers' mind and psychology' Book Fabulous

'Ragnar Jónasson's debut *Snowblind* is a brilliant new thriller with storytelling that is clear and crisp … The plot twists and turns as the tension and intensity builds and we are treated to an excellent ending' Liz Loves Books

'The small town mentality juxtaposes with the vastness of the landscape and lends an eeriness to the overall narrative. The prose is delightful with moments of exceptional clarity' Bleach House Library

'If you like cold and claustrophobic settings as I do, then this might just be the book for you. Jónasson does a wonderful job placing you right there in the small snowed-in town' Rebecca Bradley

'A tiny, segregated town is a superb setting for a crime novel, and Jónasson exploits it well. He builds a layered mystery featuring a series of unhealthy secrets, and past crimes buried deep in the sheltered, almost claustrophobic recesses of family life, which Ari Thór will pay a high price for unravelling' Thriller Books Journal

'If the rest of the Dark Iceland series is as accomplished as *Snowblind*, Ragnar Jónasson's name is poised to become as common place as that of Stieg Larsson's. Don't be fooled into thinking Jónasson is a mere imitation. By deconstructing the Golden Age traditional mystery within a foreign setting, Ragnar Jónasson has practically created his own genre. For lack of a better term, let's call this Cosy Noir' Bolo Books

'Siglufjördur is a thriller writer's dream location – a tight-knit community, encircled by mountains, almost round-the-clock darkness in midwinter, cut off from the rest of the country by the harsh weather; it all adds to the brooding menace of having a killer at large!' Our Reviews Blogspot

'*Snowblind* – a masterclass in scene setting and subtle tension building … Where Agatha Christie created a murder mystery with a small suspect pool on a fast moving train or within a large country house, Ragnar Jónasson creates the same feel in a whole town' Grab This Book

'Siglufjördur is a wonderfully evocative setting; encircled by mountains and cut-off in the winter when the roads are impassable, as the complex web of secrets becomes ever more enmeshed, its small-town, suffocating darkness heightens Ari Thór's increasing paranoia at being an outsider in his own land.' Claire Thinking

'This is a first outing in English for Ari Þór, bolstered by a pin-sharp translation by Quentin Bates. Jónasson evokes an almost timeless feel to his narrative, with only mobile phones and computers reminding us that this is the 21st century. It's no surprise, either, to discover that Jónasson has translated fourteen Agatha Christie novels into Icelandic, as *Snowblind* has echoes of Golden Age stories. Siglufjördur may be light years away from St Mary Mead, but villagers here have secrets to hide' Sharon Wheeler, Crime Review

'*Snowblind* is as atmospheric a murder mystery that you could find' For Winter Nights

'An entertaining – and curiously thought-provoking – addition to Icelandic Noir. The writer manages the feat of keeping the prose quite pacey while getting across the ennui of the town's bleak existence during the harsh winter' Café Thinking

'Ragnar Jónasson is a new name in the crime writing genre and I urge anyone who is a fan of Nordic crime noir to rush out and get yourself a copy of *Snowblind* … you will want to add this to your collection. It is really that good … a tense, gripping novel' The Last Word

'This truly is a crime novel to tamper with your thoughts and send them skittering off in all directions. Ragnar Jónasson writes with a bitingly sparse, to-the-point style, and Quentin Bates has translated his words skilfully, ensuring the story flows. With several menacing stories, creeping and melding into one, *Blackout* is a wonderfully gripping and gritty novel' Lovereading

'*Blackout* is Ragnar Jónasson's darkest book yet … the plot is far more complex than that of the previous Dark Iceland books, with various different strands that at first seemed unrelated. The suspense and intrigue built up gradually with many surprises along the way. And as the jigsaw pieces slotted into place, there were several breath-holding final chapters' Off-the-Shelf Books

'*Blackout* is an excellent addition to the already fantastic Dark Iceland series. Wonderfully translated by the talented Quentin Bates, Jónasson manages to capture the rugged beauty of Iceland, the safest place in the world; and drags you into the dark underbelly' The Bandwagon

'What I absolutely love about this author's books is the mesmerising setting … and the story line is yet another web of mystery and suspense. A wonderfully atmospheric read that is very different from your usual crime books. It's Icelandic Noir at its best' By the Letter Book Reviews

'Once again it is a gripping, atmospheric mystery packed with fascinating, complex characters with plenty of secrets to uncover' The Owl on the Bookshelf

'Succinct and Spartan, atmospheric with elements of stark beauty. This is another enjoyable installment in an excellent crime fiction series that is gripping but never formulaic' Never Imitate

'Whenever a new book by Ragnar Jónasson is released I drop everything to read it. I know I'm going to get a gripping and atmospheric novel written with such style and grace that I will feel as if I am in Iceland living through the story myself … Jónasson's powerful narrative transports you into his rich and dangerous world' Crime Squad

'Weaving together all the sub-plots of such a multifaceted story could prove challenging yet Ragnar Jónasson makes it seem effortless – while his history of translating Agatha Christie novels into Icelandic means he's no stranger to mystery writing, it's his own voice and skill that makes *Blackout* and the Dark Iceland series one of the most compelling and rewarding additions to the thriller genre' Mumbling About …

'It's official, Jónasson has written himself into my heart and onto my list of great crime writers' This Crime Book

'Many strands and many timelines are interwoven in the book. The stories can seem a bit disconnected, but you have to have faith that all will be revealed in the exciting denouement – which it absolutely is (and in some style). One of Ragnar's great talents is bringing together disparate strands into a convincing and thrilling finale' Trip Fiction

'*Blackout* is a tense, fast-moving narrative with some grim secrets at the heart. I'm looking forward to the remaining books in the sequence: the darkness is definitely gathering ...' Blue Book Balloon

'Ragnar Jónasson is a bright light in the dark, who is getting better with every novel he creates. *Blackout* is a work of stark beauty' Library Thing

'*Blackout* has more depth and complexity than the previous two books, with the myriad of threads and characters weaving together as the book progresses, all told in Ragnar's wonderfully sparse style ... Nordic Noir, eat your heart out. Icelandic Noir is where it's at' Espresso Coco

'There is murder, intrigue, and more than a little suspense as the story unfolds piece by piece and page by page. This book is character-rich ... I've always sung Ragnar's praises with regards to his use of location and descriptive atmospheric passages in setting the scene for his novels, and this one is no different' Bibliophile Book Club

'As always, Ragnar Jónasson excels in his characterization ... The plot is excellent, it's classic crime, with a twist, but the characters and Iceland itself are the stars of the show. An excellent crime story' Random Things Through My Letterbox

RUPTURE

Icelandic crime writer Ragnar Jónasson was born in Reykjavík, and currently works as a lawyer, while teaching copyright law at the Reykjavík University Law School. In the past, he's worked in TV and radio, including as a news reporter for the Icelandic National Broadcasting Service. Before embarking on a writing career, Ragnar translated fourteen Agatha Christie novels into Icelandic, and has had several short stories published in German, English and Icelandic literary magazines. Ragnar set up the first overseas chapter of the CWA (Crime Writers' Association) in Reykjavík, and is co-founder of the international crime-writing festival Iceland Noir. Ragnar's debut thriller *Snowblind* became an almost instant bestseller when it was published in June 2015, with *Nightblind* (winner of the Dead Good Reads Most Captivating Crime in Translation Award) and then *Blackout* following soon after. To date, Ragnar Jónasson has written five novels in the Dark Iceland series, which has been optioned for TV by On the Corner. He lives in Reykjavík with his wife and two daughters.

Visit him at www.ragnarjonasson.com or on Twitter @ragnarjo

Quentin Bates escaped English suburbia as a teenager, jumping at the chance of a gap year working in Iceland. For a variety of reasons, the gap year stretched to become a gap decade, during which time he went native in the north of Iceland, acquiring a new language, a new profession as a seaman and a family, before decamping *en masse* for England. He worked as a truck driver, teacher, netmaker and trawlerman at various times before falling into journalism largely by accident. He is the author of a series of crime novels set in present-day Iceland (*Frozen Out, Cold Steal, Chilled to the Bone, Winterlude, Cold Comfort* and *Thin Ice*), which have been published worldwide. He's currently working on translating the next title in Ragnar Jónasson's Dark Iceland series.

Visit him at www.graskeggur.com or on Twitter @graskeggur

Rupture

RAGNAR JÓNASSON

translated by Quentin Bates

ORENDA
BOOKS

Orenda Books
16 Carson Road
West Dulwich
London SE21 8HU
www.orendabooks.co.uk

First published in Icelandic as *Rof,* 2012

Exclusive hardback edition published by Orenda Books in
association with Goldsboro Books in 2017

B-format paperback edition published by Orenda Books in 2017

Second reprint 2018

HB ISBN 978-1-910633-59-5
PB ISBN 978-1-910633-57-1
eISBN 978-1-910633-58-8

Typeset in Garamond by MacGuru Ltd
Printed and bound in Denmark by Nørhaven

*The author would like to thank the people of the north of Iceland and Siglufjörður in particular
for the use of those places as the settings for this book. It should, however, be made clear that this
is a work of imagination with none of the characters portrayed here having any basis in reality.*

This book has been translated with financial support from

 MIÐSTÖÐ ÍSLENSKRA BÓKMENNTA
ICELANDIC LITERATURE CENTER

For sales and distribution, please contact *info@orendabooks.co.uk*

This book is dedicated to the memory of my
grandparents from Siglufjördur, Þ. Ragnar Jónasson
(1913–2003) and Gudrún Reykdal (1922–2005).

Author's note

This story is entirely fictional and none of the characters portrayed here exist in reality. Hédinsfjördur has been uninhabited since 1951. The tale of the people living on the western side of Hédinsfjördur after that is purely imaginary and I am not aware that there was ever a settlement in that particular location. I would like to mention that the narrative in the third chapter – the story of a woman's journey from Hvanndalir to Hédinsfjördur – is based on the account related by Thórhalla Hjálmarsdóttir of the journey undertaken by Gudrún Thórarinsdóttir in 1859, which my grandfather, Th. Ragnar Jónasson, recorded in 1986. This was included in his book *Folk Tales from Siglufjördur*, published by Vaka-Helgafell in 1996. The quotation on the next page is taken from his book *Siglufjördur Stories* (pages 91–92) which was published the following year.

Special thanks are due, for their expert assistance and for checking the manuscript, to Dr Haraldur Briem, a specialist in infectious diseases at the Surgeon General's Office in Iceland, Detective Inspector Eiríkur Rafn Rafnsson, Prosecutor Hulda María Stefánsdóttir and Dr Jón Gunnlaugur Jónasson. The responsibility for the final version, including any mistakes, rests with the author.

Pronunciation guide

Siglufjördur – Siglue-fyoer-thur
Hédinsfjördur – Hye-thins-fyoer-thur
Ari Thór – Ari Tho-wr
Tómas – Tow-mas
Ísrún – Ees-roon
Kristín – Kris-tien
Ívar – Ie-var
Sunna – Soo-nna
Kjartan – Kyar-tan
Hédinn – Hye-thin
Snorri – Snor-ree
Maríus – Marie-oos
Gudfinna – Guth-finna
Gudmundur – Guth-moen-doer
Jórunn – Yo-roon
Marteinn – Mart-eitn
Eggert – Eg-gert

Icelandic has a couple of letters that don't exist in other European languages and that are not always easy to replicate. The letter ð is generally replaced with a d in English, as in Gudmundur, Gudfinna, Hédinn and place names ending in -fjördur. In fact, its sound is closer to the hard *th* in English, as found in *th*us and ba*th*e. Icelandic's letter *þ* is most often reproduced as *th*, as in Ari *Thór*, and is equivalent to a soft *th* in English, as in *th*ing or *th*ump.

The letter *r* is generally rolled hard with the tongue against the roof of the mouth.

Icelandic words are pronounced with the emphasis on the first syllable.

'… Living in Hédinsfjördur was never easy and any
communication with neighbouring communities could
be fraught with difficulty. During winter, the coast, which
had no harbour, was often inaccessible by sea, and the
snow-covered mountains were always difficult.'

Siglufjördur Stories, Þ. Ragnar Jónasson (1913–2003)

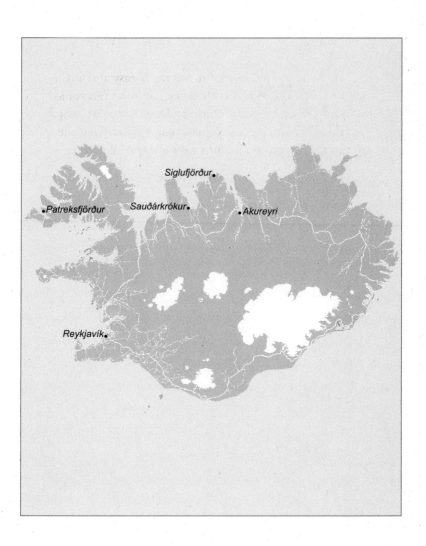

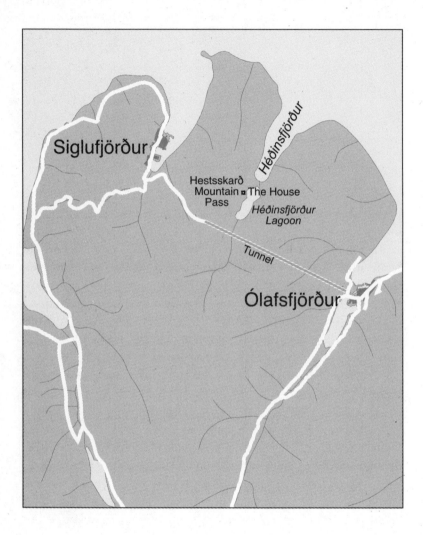

Siglufjörður

Héðinsfjörður

Hestsskarð Mountain Pass ▫ The House

Héðinsfjörður Lagoon

Tunnel

Ólafsfjörður

1

It had been an evening like any other, spent stretched out on the sofa.

They lived in a little apartment on the ground floor of an old house at the western end of Reykjavík, on Ljósvallagata. It was positioned in the middle of an old-fashioned terrace of three houses, built back in the 1930s. Róbert sat up, rubbed his eyes and looked out of the window at the little front garden. It was getting dark. It was March, when weather of any description could be expected; right now it was raining. There was something comforting about the patter of raindrops against the window while he was safely ensconced indoors.

His studies weren't going badly. A mature student at twenty-eight, he was in the first year of an engineering degree. Numbers had always been one of his pleasures. His parents were accountants, living uptown in Árbær, and while his relationship with them had always been difficult, it was now almost non-existent; his lifestyle seemed to have no place in their formula for success. They had done what they could to steer him towards bookkeeping, which was fair enough, but he had struck out on his own.

Now he was at university, at last, and he hadn't even bothered to let the old folks know. Instead, he tried to focus on his studies, although these days his mind tended to wander to the Westfjords. He owned a small boat there, together with a couple of friends, and he was already looking forward to summer. It was so easy to forget everything – good and bad – when he was out at sea. The rocking of the boat was a tonic for any stress and his spirit soared when he was enveloped by the complete peace. At the end of the month he'd be heading west to get the boat ready. For his friends, the trip to the fjords was a good excuse to go on a drinking binge. But not for Róbert. He had been dry now for two years – an abstinence that had become necessary after the period of serious drinking that began with the events that had unfolded on that fateful day eight years earlier.

It was a beautiful day. There was scarcely a breath of wind on the pitch, it was warm in the summer sun and there was a respectable crowd. They were on their way to a convincing win against an unconvincing opposition. Ahead of him lay training with the national youth team, and later that summer the possibility of a trial with a top Norwegian side. His agent had even mentioned interest from some of the teams lower down in the English leagues. The old man was as proud as hell of him. He had been a decent football player himself but never had the chance to play professionally. Now times had changed, there were more opportunities out there.

Five minutes were remaining when Róbert was passed the ball. He pushed past the defenders, and saw the goal and the fear on the goalkeeper's face. This was becoming a familiar experience; a five–nil victory loomed.

He didn't see the tackle coming, just heard the crack as his leg broke in three places and felt the shattering pain. He looked down, paralysed by the searing agony, and saw the open fracture.

It was a sight that was etched into his memory. The days spent in hospital passed in a fog, although he wouldn't forget the doctor telling him that his chances of playing football again – at a professional level, at any rate – were slim. So he gave it all up, and sought solace in the bottle; each drink quickly followed by another. The worst part was that, while he made a better recovery than the doctor expected, by the time he was fit, it was too late to turn the clock back on his football career.

Now, though, things were better. He had Sunna, and little Kjartan had a place in his heart as well. But despite this, his heart harboured some dark memories, which he hoped he could keep hidden in the shadows.

It was well into the evening when Sunna came home, tapping at the window to let him know that she had forgotten her keys. She was as beautiful as ever, in black jeans and a grey roll-neck sweater. Raven hair, long and glossy, framed her strong face. To begin with, it had been her eyes that had enchanted him, closely followed by her magnificent figure. She was a dancer, and sometimes it was as if she danced rather than walked around their little apartment, a confident grace imbuing every movement.

He knew he had been lucky with this one. He had first chatted to her at a friend's birthday party, and they'd clicked instantly. They'd been together for six months now, and three months ago they had moved in together.

Sunna turned up the heating as she came in; she felt the cold more than he did.

'Cold outside,' she said. Indeed, the chill was creeping into the room. The big living-room window wasn't as airtight as it could have been, and there was no getting used to the constant draughts.

Life wasn't easy for them, even though their relationship was becoming stronger. She had a child, little Kjartan, from a previous relationship and was engaged in a bitter custody battle with Breki, the boy's father. To begin with, Breki and Sunna had agreed on joint custody, and at the moment Kjartan was spending some time with his father.

Now, though, Sunna had engaged a lawyer and was pressing for full custody. She was also exploring the possibility of continuing her dance studies in Britain, although this was not something that she and Róbert had discussed in depth. But it was also a piece of news that Breki would be unlikely to accept without a fight, so it looked as if the whole matter would end up in court. Sunna believed she had a strong enough case, though, and that they would finally see Kjartan returned to her full time.

'Sit down, sweetheart,' Róbert said. 'There's pasta.'

'Mmm, great,' she said, curling up on the sofa.

Róbert fetched the food from the kitchen, bringing plates and glasses and a jug of water.

'I hope it tastes good,' he said. 'I'm still finding my way.'

'I'm so hungry it won't matter what it tastes like.'

He put on some relaxing music and sat down next to her.

She told him about her day – the rehearsals and the pressure she was under. Sunna was set on perfection, and hated to get anything wrong.

Róbert was satisfied that his pasta had been a success; nothing outstanding, but good enough.

Sunna got to her feet and took his hand. 'Stand up, my love,' she said. 'Time to dance.'

He stood up and wrapped his arms around her and they moved in time to a languid South American ballad. He slid a hand under her sweater and his fingertips stroked her back, unclipping her bra strap in one seamless movement. He was an expert at this.

'Hey, young man,' she said with mock sharpness, her eyes warm. 'What do you think you're up to?'

'Making the most of Kjartan being with his dad,' Róbert answered, and they moved into a long, deep kiss. The temperature between them was rising, as was the temperature in the room, and before long they were making their way to the bedroom.

Out of habit, Róbert pushed the door to and drew the curtains across the bedroom window overlooking the garden. However, none of these precautions stopped the sounds of their lovemaking carrying across to the apartment next door.

When everything was quiet again, he heard the indistinct slamming of a door, muffled by the hammering rain. His first thought was that it was the back door to the porch behind the old house.

Sunna sat up in alarm and glanced at him, disquiet in her eyes. He tried to stifle his own fear behind a show of bravado and, getting to his feet, ventured naked into the living room. It was empty.

But the back door was open, banging to and fro in the wind. He glanced quickly into the porch, just long enough to say that he had taken a look, and hurriedly pulled the door closed. A whole regiment of men could have been out there for all he knew, but he could make out nothing in the darkness.

He then went from one room to another, his heart beating harder and faster, but there were no unwelcome guests to be seen. It was just as well that Kjartan was not at home.

And then he noticed something that would keep him awake for the rest of the night.

He hurried through the living room, frightened for Sunna, terrified that something had happened to her. Holding his breath, he made his way to the bedroom to find her seated on the edge of the bed, pulling on a shirt. She smiled weakly, unable to hide her concern.

'It was nothing, sweetheart,' he said, hoping she would not notice the tremor in his voice. 'I forgot to lock the door after I took the rubbish out; didn't shut it properly behind me,' he lied. 'You know what tricks the wind plays out back. Stay there and I'll get you a drink.'

He stepped quickly out of the bedroom and rapidly removed what he had seen.

He hoped it was the right thing to do – not to tell Sunna about the water on the floor, the wet footprints left by the uninvited guest who had come in out of the rain. The worst part was that they hadn't stopped just inside the back door. The trail had led all the way to the bedroom.

Siglufjördur police officer Ari Thór Arason couldn't explain, even to himself, why he was looking into an old case on behalf of a complete stranger, especially at a time when the little community was going through a period of such chaos.

The man, Hédinn, had called him just before Christmas, when the police station's regular inspector was on holiday in Reykjavík. His request was that Ari Thór should look into a matter that had long ago been shelved: the death of a young woman. Ari Thór had promised to get to it when he had a moment, but it wasn't until this evening that he had finally found the time.

Ari Thór had asked Hédinn to drop into the station that evening, having, of course, confirmed that he hadn't left the house for two days and was therefore not infectious. Hédinn himself sounded dubious about seeing Ari Thór face to face, given the current circumstances, but he eventually agreed to a meeting to discuss the old case.

The infection had hit the town two days earlier – in the wake of a visit from a wealthy traveller. He was an adventurer from France, who had flown from Africa to Greenland, and while there had decided to take a quick trip to Iceland, where his light aircraft had been given permission to land at the remote Siglufjördur airstrip so he could pay a visit to the town's Herring Era museum. He'd only planned to stay for twenty-four hours, but on the night of his arrival he'd been taken violently ill.

To begin with he'd been diagnosed with an unusually virulent dose of flu, accompanied by a raging temperature. But his condition had rapidly deteriorated and the man had died the following night. A specialist in infectious diseases concluded that this was a case of a haemorrhagic fever, which the man must have picked up on his travels in Africa, and hadn't shown any symptoms of until now. The illness was considered to be highly contagious, and it was possible that any number of people could have been infected as his fever had developed.

The National Civil Defence Authority had been alerted to the situation, and tests carried out on samples from the deceased confirmed that this was the haemorrhagic fever that they'd feared. There was no practical way of dealing with it.

Not long after the man's death the drastic decision was taken to place the little town under quarantine. Efforts were made to trace anyone who had been in contact with the dead man, and everywhere he had been was painstakingly sterilised.

Soon there were rumours that the nurse who had been on duty that night had also been taken ill. She had been put under observation, and Ari Thór had heard that, earlier that day, when she began to experience mild symptoms, she had been placed in isolation.

Every effort was being made to establish where she'd been and with whom she had been in contact, and the process of sterilisation had begun all over again.

For the moment, though, everything was quiet. The nurse was still in isolation at the Siglufjördur hospital, and contingency plans were being made to transfer her to intensive care in Reykjavík should her condition become any worse. According to the information the police had been given, the town could expect to remain in quarantine for at least a few more days.

While there was little actually happening, Siglufjördur had been gripped by panic, stoked, of course, by the extensive media coverage. The townspeople were understandably terrified and the politicians and pundits laboured the point that no unnecessary risks should be taken.

The haemorrhagic fever had already been dubbed 'the French sickness', and the town was a shadow of its usual self. Most people chose to remain behind locked doors and to rely on their phones and email for any communication. Nobody had shown the slightest interest in climbing the town's invisible walls to get in. Workplaces were closed and school was suspended.

Ari Thór remained healthy, and he had every expectation that he would be untouched by the infection. He had been nowhere near the unfortunate traveller, or the nurse. The same was true of the Siglufjördur force's senior officer, Tómas, who was now back after his break, and on duty with Ari Thór.

Ari Thór hoped that Hédinn's visit would give him something other than the wretched infection to think about. And he had a chilling feeling that it would.

'I was born in Hédinsfjördur,' Ari Thór's guest, Hédinn, told him. 'Have you been there?'

They were sitting in the police station's coffee corner, keeping some distance between them; they hadn't even shaken hands when Hédinn had arrived.

'I've driven through, after the tunnel was opened,' Ari Thór replied, waiting for his tea to cool. Hédinn had opted for coffee.

'Yes, exactly,' he said, his voice deep.

He seemed to be a reserved, quiet man. He avoided eye contact with Ari and looked mostly at the table or his coffee.

'Exactly,' he repeated. 'Nobody stops there for long. It's still the same uninhabited fjord, even though people drive through it all day long, now. In the old days you'd never have imagined it could be possible to see so many passers-by.'

Hédinn looked to be close to sixty and it wasn't long before he confirmed Ari Thór's judgement.

'I was born there in 1956. My parents had moved there the year before, after the fjord had already been abandoned, because they wanted to keep it inhabited a little longer. They weren't alone. My mother's sister and her husband moved there with them; they wanted to try and farm there.'

He paused and sipped his coffee cautiously and nibbled a biscuit from the packet on the table. He seemed slightly nervous.

'Did they have a farmhouse or land there?' Ari Thór asked. 'It's a beautiful place.'

'Beautiful …' Hédinn echoed, his voice distant, seeming to become lost in memories. 'You could say that, but it's not what springs to my mind. It has been a terribly hard place to live throughout the centuries. The snow lies heavy and it's extremely isolated during the winter – no shortage of avalanches off the mountainsides. The fjord is entirely cut off during winter, with the ocean on one side and high mountains on the others; it was difficult enough to get to the next farm in an emergency, let alone to the next town, beyond the mountains.'

Hédinn underscored his words with a shake of the head and a frown. He was a big man, somewhat overweight; his thin, greasy hair was combed back from his face.

'But to answer your question – no, my parents didn't own a farmhouse there. They were offered the opportunity to rent one that had been left empty, but was still in good condition. My father was a hard worker and had always wanted to be a farmer. The house was easily big enough for the four of them – my parents and my mother's sister and her husband; he had actually been in some financial trouble at some point and he jumped at the chance to try something new. Then I came along a year later, so there were five of us there …' He paused and scowled. 'Well, that's not entirely certain, but I'll come to that,' he added.

Ari Thór said nothing, leaving Hédinn to continue his tale.

'You said you'd driven through there. In that case, you've hardly seen anything of the fjord further out. What you'll have seen from the new road is the Hédinsfjördur lagoon. There's a narrow spit of land, Víkursandur, that separates the lagoon from the fjord itself, and that's about as far as you can see from the road, not that it makes a difference to what I have to tell you. Our house was by the lagoon; it still is, what's left of it. It's the only house on the western side of the pool; there's very little lowland there, you see. It's in the shadow of a high mountain, right at its feet, so, of course, it was madness to try to live there, but my parents were determined to try their best. You know, it's always been my belief that the conditions – the mountain and the isolation – played a part in what happened there. People can lose their easily minds, somewhere like that, can't they?'

It was a moment before Ari Thór realised that Hédinn was waiting for an answer to his question.

'Well, yes. I suppose so,' was the best he could manage. Although it could hardly be compared to the isolation of Hédinsfjördur, he had painful memories of his first winter in Siglufjördur. He'd hardly been able to sleep at night, feeling almost suffocated by the grip of the darkness and confinement, with the snow more or less closing Siglufjördur off from the rest of the world.

'You'd know more about it that I would,' he said, shivering at the memory. 'What was it like living there?'

'Me? Good grief, I don't remember a thing. We moved away after … after what happened. I was barely a year old, and my parents didn't say much about their time in Hédinsfjördur, which is understandable, I suppose. But it wasn't all bad, I think. My mother told me I was born on a beautiful day at the end of May. After I was born she walked down to the pool and looked out over the water – perfectly calm on that sunny day – and decided that I should be called Hédinn, the name of the Viking who settled in Hédinsfjördur around the year 900. They told me stories about beautiful winter days, too, although my father would sometimes talk of how those high mountains could loom over you during the dark winter months.'

Ari Thór was starting to feel uncomfortable again. He remembered vividly how the ring of mountains encircling Siglufjördur had affected him when he had first arrived there, two and a half years before. The claustrophobia was still inside him, although he did his best not to let it get the better of him.

'Getting from Hédinsfjördur over to Siglufjördur or Ólafsfjördur was a tall order back then,' Hédinn continued. 'The best way was by sea, but it's possible on foot – over the Hestsskard mountain pass and down into Siglufjördur. There's a story from the nineteenth century, about a woman from one of the Hvanndalur farms going to fetch firewood; she went on foot, taking an extremely difficult route – under the scree on the east side of the fjord. She was pregnant at the time, and on top of that had another small child tucked inside her clothing – all that way. Anything's possible, if there's the will. That's a story that had a happy ending. But mine doesn't.' Hédinn looked up with a bitter smile, and paused before speaking again.

'Our old house isn't far from the track where you'd come down into Hédinsfjördur if you arrived by foot from Siglufjördur, over the Hestsskard pass. People walk this route for the fun of it, now. Times change, don't they? And so do people. My parents are both dead. Mother went first and father followed,' he said ruefully and fell silent again.

'The others are dead as well, are they?' Ari Thór asked, to break the silence more than anything. 'I mean, your aunt and her husband.'

Hédinn looked astonished. 'You've never heard about all this, then?' he asked at last.

'No, not that I remember.'

'I'm sorry. I just assumed you'd know the story. Back then everyone knew about it. But it fades away after a while, I suppose; it's more than half a century ago now. Even the most terrible things are forgotten as the years go by. Nobody ever found out for certain what happened, whether it was murder or suicide ...'

'Really? Who died?' Ari Thór asked with interest.

'My aunt. She drank poison.'

'Poison?' Ari Thór shuddered at the thought.

'Something had been stirred into her coffee. It took a long time to get a doctor to her. Maybe her life could have been saved if she had received help sooner. Maybe she did it herself, knowing that there would be little chance of getting an ambulance or a doctor there in time.' Hédinn's voice was even deeper and slower now. 'The verdict was that it was an accident – that she had put rat poison in her coffee instead of sugar. That's a little far-fetched, to my mind.'

'You think someone may have murdered her?' Ari Thór asked straight out, having long ago given up packaging awkward questions in tactful ways. He had never been particularly considerate in that regard, anyway.

'That's the most obvious conclusion, to my mind. There were only three possible suspects, of course: her husband and my parents. So the suspicion has always been looming over my family, like a shadow. Not that people mention it. The most common theory was that she had taken her own life. But people have little to say about it these days. We moved to Siglufjördur after she died, and her husband went back south to Reykjavík and spent the rest of his life there. My parents never discussed what happened with me and I didn't fish for information. Of course, you don't believe anything bad about your own parents, do you? But the doubt has always been at the back of my mind. I think she either committed suicide or she was murdered by her husband. It wouldn't have been the first time. Men have killed their wives before; and vice versa,' Hédinn said with a sigh.

'I imagine you can guess what my next question is?' Ari Thór said heavily.

'Yes,' Hédinn replied and was silent for a moment. 'You're wondering why I've come to you with this, after all these years, aren't you?'

Ari Thór nodded. He was about to sip the tea cooling in the mug on the table in front of him, but then the thought of the rat poison in the unfortunate woman's coffee made him stop.

'That's a tale in itself.' Hédinn squared his shoulders and thought for a moment, seeming to search for the right words. 'First of all, to be quite clear, I got in touch with you before Christmas because I knew you were taking over from Tómas. He knows the town and all the stories far too well; I thought you'd come to it with fresh eyes, even though I'm a bit surprised that you haven't heard the story before. But there's another reason. A friend of mine lives down south, and in the autumn he went to a meeting of the Siglufjördur Association, where people who moved away from Siglufjördur meet regularly. They had a picture night.'

Ari Thór raised an eyebrow.

'Yes, a picture night,' Hédinn repeated. 'They go through old pictures from Siglufjördur. Part of the fun of it is recognising people in the old photos and noting down their names. It's a way of maintaining a record of the people who've lived in Siglufjördur over the years.'

'And something happened there?'

'That's right. He rang me up that night – said he'd seen the photo.'

There was a sudden weight to Hédinn's voice, a darker undertone that prompted Ari Thór to listen more carefully.

'The picture was taken in Hédinsfjördur, right in front of where we lived.' He took a sip of coffee, his hand trembling. 'This was before my aunt's death, in the dead of winter; it was a bright day, but there was deep snow.'

The familiar feeling of unease gripped Ari Thór for a second; he pushed it to the back of his mind.

'There was nothing all that sunny about the picture, though. I must have been a few months old at the time, and it seems to show five of us there.'

'Well,' Ari Thór said. 'There's hardly anything strange about a family picture, is there?'

'That's just it,' Hédinn said in a low voice, and stared deep into his coffee mug before looking up sharply and straight into Ari Thór's eyes. 'The photo was of my mother, my father and me, and my aunt. Her husband, Maríus, must have taken the picture, or so I imagine.'

'So who's the fifth person?' Ari Thór asked, as a chill shot through him. His thoughts turned to old stories of ghosts appearing in photographs; was Hédinn about to imply something of that nature?

'A young man I've never seen before. He's there, in the centre of the picture, with me in his arms. The long and the short of it is that nobody at the picture night had any idea who this man was.' Hédinn sighed again. 'Who's this young man and what happened to him? Could he have been responsible for my aunt's death?'

4

Exhausted after a sleepless night, Róbert poured milk onto his cereal. Sunna sat opposite him at the kitchen table, looking like she'd slept well. The morning news muttered in the background; as far as he could make out, it was another mundane March morning, apart from the reports of the outbreak of a virus in Siglufjördur. A patient had died there during the night. Róbert felt a little anxious at the thought of a contagious disease; he hoped fervently that it would be possible to stop it spreading, that he would be able to keep his family safe. This morning, however, he had other, more pressing, matters than a distant outbreak on his mind.

Their home, as clean and smart as it was, now felt dirty – contaminated by the unwelcome intruder's night time visit. Who had been snooping around? Had he, or she, even, peeked through the bedroom window, seen them in the throes of passion and decided to break in? Was it some miserable Peeping Tom? Or was this something more serious? The back door had been locked; he was positive of that – absolutely positive.

There was, of course, the fact that Sunna had managed to lose her house keys. Had someone simply found them, realised whose they were and decided to break in? Or had the keys been deliberately stolen? That was certainly a very unpleasant thought. In any case, it was clear what the first job of the day would have to be: to call a locksmith and change all the locks.

He stretched for the radio and switched it off. For a moment there was silence in the cramped kitchen, apart from the rain continuing its relentless assault on the window. It was still coming down with a vengeance.

'Haven't found your keys, have you?' he asked, trying not to let his concern show in his voice.

'It's weird,' Sunna said, looking up from the paper. 'I can't understand where they are. I definitely had them at the rehearsal yesterday and I'm sure they were in my coat pocket. I'd left it in the lobby with everyone else's. Nothing's ever stolen there, but I suppose anyone could have put a hand in the pocket.'

'Anyone?' Róbert asked.

'Yes, I guess.'

'Someone coming in from off the street, even?'

'Yes, I suppose so,' she replied, looking at him hard. 'Why? Is everything all right?'

He forced a smile. 'Of course, sweetheart. I was just wondering …' He hesitated before continuing. 'I was wondering if we shouldn't get the locks changed, just to be sure.'

'Isn't that going a bit far?' she asked in obvious surprise. 'I'm sure I'll find them.'

'You know what I'm like … maybe I'm being overcautious. But it needs to be done anyhow,' he lied. 'The locks are getting stiff.'

'I hadn't noticed,' Sunna said, glancing at the clock as she got to her feet. 'But it's up to you. I'd better be going before I'm late.'

She hurried from the kitchen, turning in the doorway, to ask, 'Will you be here at lunchtime?'

Róbert had a lecture to attend, but he was determined not to leave the house until the locks had been changed. It had been no lie when he told Sunna that he was cautious by nature.

'I expect so,' he said.

'Breki will be bringing Kjartan. Is it all right if I'm not back by then?' she asked awkwardly.

He didn't have a high opinion of Sunna's ex.

'No problem,' Róbert replied. 'But, one thing …' he began as she was about to close the door behind her. 'He's been leaving you in peace, hasn't he?'

'Breki?'

'Yes. You know what the lawyer said – that you shouldn't be in touch with him about the dispute. From now on it's all between the lawyers.'

'Don't worry about Breki, I can handle him,' she added with a smile.

5

A knot of fear deep seemed to take up residence in Ísrún's belly as she took her seat in the aircraft that would take her home from the Faroe Islands to Iceland. The flight to the Faroes had been fine, but the landing was one that she would never forget, the plane on the approach threading its way between towering mountains that were terrifyingly close. Closing her eyes had only made things worse, boosting her imagination to new heights as sudden turbulence made the landing even more dramatic. As she left the plane, one of its crew wished her a pleasant stay, clearly noticing how pale she was.

'The flight was fine,' Ísrún had stammered. 'Apart from the landing.'

'The landing?' he had asked, sounding surprised. 'It was absolutely fine today. Good conditions and only a bit of turbulence.'

Now, as she strapped herself in, she told herself that the take-off had to be better than the landing.

Her few days in the Faroes hadn't been for pleasure – quite the opposite, in fact. She was deeply fond of the people she knew here, and had visited several times with her parents. This time, though, she had come by herself, to meet her mother, Anna.

Anna had been born in the Faroe Islands, into a fishing family. Her parents were both dead now, but she maintained close contact with her two sisters, who still lived on the islands. Anna had gone to Iceland at the age of twenty, having met an Icelander, Orri, who had been working in the Faroes one summer. Anna had told Ísrún that it had been love at first sight. They built a house in Kópavogur, moving much later out to the suburb of Grafarvogur. Anna had studied literature at the University of Iceland and Ísrún was born a few years after her mother had graduated.

Orri drove trucks and coaches for a living, while Anna, once her studies were over, had set up a small publishing business, with the intention of making Faroese books available in Icelandic. After a few of these translations had been published, she then expanded into children's books. And in the last few years she had tried her hand at travel guides, and these had also been highly successful.

While the books had made them financially secure, Anna and Orri's marriage proved less solid. Orri had decided to become involved in the travel business, aiming to make some money in foreign currency. This was particularly attractive at a time when most of Iceland was stuck with the currency controls put in place after the financial crash of 2008, which limited access to foreign cash. He was also hoping to hitch a ride on Anna's travel guides – using them to promote his own venture. He had bought a modest coach and had since added another one. The second coach was the straw that broke the camel's back. Anna was approaching sixty and had arranged to sell the publishing business on good enough terms for her to retire. Orri was seven years older than she was, but had no interest in slowing down, and was less than pleased by Anna's decision to sell her business. Ísrún had sat by and watched as the argument between her parents had escalated to a new level.

'Bought a new bus,' he had muttered over Sunday dinner.

'Isn't one enough?' Ísrún had asked innocently.

'Yep. But I've bought another one, ordered it from Germany.'

'Another coach?' Anna had asked sharply, staring at her husband and clearly trying hard to control her anger in their daughter's presence.

'Got it for a good price,' he had continued. 'A hundred thousand on the clock, but that's nothing. And it comes with *air conditioning*,' he said, exaggerating the last two words in English with the

American accent he had picked up during a year in the US in the eighties.

'And how much is that price?' Anna asked.

'It'll pay for itself soon enough, just you see,' he said, avoiding the question. 'I've figured it all out. There's so much demand for Golden Circle tours, it'll be an absolute gold mine,' he added with a sheepish smile.

'Hadn't we talked about taking it easy?' Anna had asked, and the conversation dried up.

They continued their meal in silence. But Ísrún knew that the argument must have flared up once she had gone.

Now, two months later, Anna had gone. Not only had she sold the publishing business and moved out of the family home, she had left the country and returned to the Faroes, where she was living in a large house owned by one of her sisters. Orri was devastated. He was doing his best to make his travel business work out, but Ísrún was concerned that he had stretched himself too far. With Anna gone, he was half the man he should have been; the energy seemed to have been sucked out of him.

It had been Ísrún's idea to use a break between her shifts on the news desk to fly to the Faroe Islands to try and persuade her mother to return to Iceland. The idea didn't make a lot of sense, but, these days, Ísrún was prone to making rash decisions. She was trying to focus on anything other than her inherited disease. A year and a half had passed since she had first sought medical advice about the possibility that she could be suffering from the same inherited condition that had caused her grandmother's death many years before, a disease that could result in dangerous tumours forming. Her suspicion had been true; she had received the worrying diagnosis, but the tumour they had found was fortunately benign. The doctor had left her in no doubt, however, that the illness could progress in a more serious direction. He told her to be optimistic, though, which she had tried to be. She did her best to live life as if nothing had happened, and told nobody about her illness, not even her parents. It had crossed her mind, just for a moment, to tell her mother about it – maybe as a way of bringing her back to Iceland. But she quickly dismissed the idea, deciding it would be unfair to all concerned. On the other hand, the end of her parents' marriage was adding to the pressure she was already under at work. The doctor had advised her to take regular exercise, to eat healthily and to avoid stress. He had effectively advised her to abandon journalism.

'You may as well just kill me right away,' she had told him carelessly, immediately regretting slipping into gallows humour.

The truth was that she revelled in the speed and excitement of the newsroom. She had worked in television news since her student years, with some breaks in between, and loved it. She'd made some good friends among her colleagues, although there were some who seemed not to wish her well. In fact, she was certain that one of her colleagues, Ívar, was systematically plotting to get rid of her. As he was the regular desk editor, he was also her boss most days, and it was generally up to him to decide what assignments came her way. For a long time he'd not given her anything challenging, but this had all changed the previous summer. She had been given an award for her report on people-trafficking in Iceland, and had instantly become a favourite with the news editor, María, and this had given her an edge over Ívar. From that point on he had been forced to be civil to Ísrún, most likely because he always went out of his way not to antagonise María, whose job, Ísrún was certain, he was after, and which she had her own eye on. Despite all this, it was obvious to everyone that he was being pleasant to Ísrún only through gritted teeth.

The trip to the Faroe Islands had turned out to be thoroughly unsatisfactory. Her mother was as stubborn as a whole team of mules – just as Ísrún herself could be – and was clearly determined to stay there, for the time being at least. Ísrún half regretted the cost of the flight and the time she had spent on the trip, but she knew now that she ought to spend more time on the islands. Her command of Faroese was almost non-existent, and she had given herself little time to get to know the place or its people, or to maintain contact with her relatives there, all of which was something that made her feel a deep sense of guilt.

'Your father and I just don't have anything in common any more, my love,' Anna had said to Ísrún. 'Not at the moment, anyway. Let's see.'

Then came the question Ísrún had expected: 'Did he send you?'

'No, of course not. Can't I come and see you on my own initiative?'

'I'm sorry … of course, my love,' Anna had replied in a subdued tone.

'He's not doing well,' Ísrún had said.

'I warned him, but he'll have to deal with it himself. We should be well off enough to retire. But this travel business nonsense of his is far too expensive.'

'You're not letting some tourists ruin a marriage that has lasted thirty years, are you?'

'It's not that simple. Every little thing was grating on my nerves, and I'm sure he felt the same about me. He had no interests other than work and those damned buses. I wanted to live a little, travel, work in the garden, go and see concerts and plays. But he had no interest in anything like that. I couldn't even read in bed as every light had to be switched off when he wanted to go to sleep. You know, Ísrún, you can build up a lot of fatigue in the course of a relationship as long as ours. It's not always easy. You'll find that out for yourself one day,' Anna had replied, making a veiled reference to Ísrún's single status.

Her mother was right – a few years had passed since Ísrún had last been in a serious relationship. Her illness had played a large part in this, as did the difficulty she had in coming to terms with another horrific experience she'd had a while back. It all meant she had little interest in, let alone energy for, searching out a new man.

The flight home from the Faroe Islands went perfectly and Ísrún hurried straight from the airport to work, arriving just in time for her shift.

'Ísrún!' Ívar yelled as she came through the door, his eyes on the clock.

She went over to him, doing her utmost to appear decisive and confident. Ívar hadn't won any awards; she knew it, and he knew it. And, what was more, María, the news editor, knew it as well.

She stared at him without saying a word.

'You're on shift the next few days, aren't you?' he asked after a short, awkward silence.

'Yes,' she answered.

'Can you keep track of this thing up in Siglufjördur? The killer virus? You were there last summer, weren't you?'

'No problem,' she said, without cracking a smile.

She went to her desk, switched on her computer and looked up the number for the Siglufjördur police. She remembered her time in the little town very well. Horrible events from her past had brought her there, but the place had in some ways inspired her to face the future head on. Now the people there had some serious dangers of their own challenging them, and she certainly hoped that she wouldn't need to go back there while the virus remained uncontained.

Tómas arrived at seven in the morning to relieve Ari Thór. The news that the nurse's condition had deteriorated had not long broken; she'd died before she could be taken to intensive care in Reykjavík.

Soon after Tómas arrived for his shift, he went onto a hastily arranged conference call with the hospital managers, a specialist in infectious diseases and the Civil Defence Authority. All face-to-face meetings had, naturally, been suspended. Nobody wanted to be the next victim.

Tómas did his best to appear unflappable during the call, trying to give the impression that duty came first and that his own health was a lower priority, although that wasn't the way he really felt. He was petrified by the thought of this wretched infection and as far as possible wanted to avoid going anywhere.

Tómas was given the task of producing a press release about the nurse's death. It seemed that the whole country had its eyes on the situation in Siglufjördur, watching from a safe distance. It was as if Siglufjördur and its people had become laboratory rats – locked away securely in a glass cage that nobody was even remotely tempted to open. The press release was a mere formality as the news had already spread rapidly and the nurse's death had been announced on radio long before Tómas had even put pen to paper to compose his state-ment. In the end his purpose was more to placate the townspeople and convince the rest of the country that the infection had been contained rather than to announce the nurse's death.

Physically Tómas himself was in fine condition. The infection had come nowhere near him. But he was tired. He and Ari Thór were taking alternate shifts as there had to be someone on call at the station at any time, day or night. Applications had been invited for the post of Siglufjördur's third police officer, but, under the current circumstances, the process had come to a standstill. Fortunately, there was an old camp bed at the station, so whoever was on the night shift could at least get some rest.

On the one hand Tómas truly wished that his wife was here to help him through this. On the other, he was, of course, glad that she was in Reykjavík, studying art history, a safe distance from the virus – for the time being at least.

Tómas had recently returned to Siglufjördur from a three-month sabbatical in the capital. His wife was living in a small apartment not far from the University of Iceland, and had seemed to have made herself comfortable there. It was at her suggestion that Tómas had moved south for a while to be with her. If he liked it, she said, they could try to sell their large house in Siglufjördur and buy an apartment in the city. He hadn't said yes right away, but had finally agreed to spend some time there with her. He missed her badly and had become tired of microwaved dinners.

It had been evening when he knocked at her door after the long drive south. She was expecting him, but, all the same, the place was packed with people; friends from university, she said – two men and a girl, all much younger than Tómas, sitting on a worn blue sofa in front of a coffee table that had seen better days. Tómas came in and awkwardly introduced himself. There were glasses of red wine on the table, a half-full bottle and another that had already been emptied.

'Would you like a glass of wine?' his wife asked.

He shook his head: 'I need to get some sleep after the trip,' he said.

He expected her to send her guests away as soon as she could, but that wasn't what happened; they sat and chatted until it was past two in the morning. Tómas lay and waited in the narrow bed in the apartment's little bedroom, like a prisoner in a tiny cell. The bed was only just big enough for one person, and it transpired that she intended to let him have it while she slept on the sofa. They could go and buy a bed if he decided to stay longer than the agreed three months. Of course, he offered to swap, and take the sofa himself.

It'll take a while for both of us to adjust, he decided. Nothing changed, however. Her friends continued to call at any time of the day, and her life seemed to revolve around lectures and exams, and staying up far into the night. For his part, Tómas found it impossible to connect with her fellow students, although he had to admit that he didn't put a great deal of effort into trying. Some evenings she spent studying in the library while he stayed on his own in the apartment. At the end of the three months, he'd completely failed to adjust to the rhythm of her lifestyle and still couldn't understand how someone who was only a year or two younger than him could live in such a chaotic fashion.

Returning home from his stay in Reykjavík, he'd at least been sure of one thing: she hadn't met anyone else. Instead – and almost as bad – he'd seen that she had fallen in love with her new life. As he approached the little town between the mountains, he was forced to recognise what other people – their friends and acquaintances – had undoubtedly been aware of for a while: their relationship was close to having run its course.

The timing couldn't have been worse – if there was such a thing as a good time to part company from your childhood sweetheart; Tómas was still struggling to come to terms with the death of his colleague, who had taken his own life the previous summer.

To make things worse, Ari Thór had suffered a knife injury the very same evening their colleague had died. Fortunately, the sharp steak knife had not done any serious damage, although it had narrowly missed some vital organs. The incident had been investigated and everyone present had insisted that it had been an accident. That was all very well, but Tómas was certain that there had been a struggle between Ari Thór and the man who had held the knife. The case had been closed and Tómas had acted as if nothing had happened.

Safely back in Siglufjördur, Tómas had immersed himself in work, if anything, to distract himself from the fact that his marriage was coming apart at the seams. Now, with the threat of the virus, he certainly had plenty to focus on.

It was Tómas's role to ensure that goods were reaching the town during the quarantine. He had been largely successful, although it had not been easy to find drivers prepared to come here; many of them seemed to imagine that the air itself was laden with killer germs, and had left their regular deliveries in stacks at the entrances to one or other of the two tunnels leading to Siglufjördur. On top of this, the townspeople were reluctant to leave their houses more often than absolutely necessary, and nobody was prepared to stand behind the counter at the local Co-op. In the end it had fallen to the Co-op's manager to deal with orders over the phone and then to deliver purchases to people's homes.

Tómas sighed. There was nothing for it but to push his worries about his marriage to one side, and focus on the current crisis. With the press release out of the way, his next job was to call the Co-op manager. But just as he was about to do this, the phone buzzed.

It was the young TV journalist, Ísrún – the one with a scar down one side of her face. She had shot to prominence the previous summer after she had been the first reporter on the scene when a man from Siglufjördur had been beaten to death in a nearby fjord.

She was calling to ask for information about the state of things in the town, now that a second death had been announced. Tómas was too busy to talk, but he wrote down her number and promised to call back.

He transferred the number onto a yellow post-it note and stuck it to the screen of Ari Thór's computer. He could deal with the media's pestering when he came in later for his evening shift.

7

Róbert was suddenly alert.

Had that been a knock on the window?

He sat up on the sofa. As far as he knew, he was alone in the apartment. He shivered as cold air ran down his back. And then he realised: he'd been lying under the open window and had fallen asleep.

A glance at the clock on the wall told him that it was almost midday. The chilly draught made him shiver again, catching at his throat and then his nose – he must be coming down with a cold, he thought.

Then he jumped; there was the knock again, sharp and clear, no longer part of an indistinct dream. It was far too real for that.

Looking up, a cold sweat spread in a wave down his body. A stranger was peering in through the window. For a moment he was so scared that he could not move. He had never been a sensitive type, but the night's events had left his nerves in shreds.

Then he shook his head at himself, remembering that he was expecting the locksmith.

He nodded to the man waiting outside in the rain, stood up and hurried to the hall, and let in a middle-aged man sporting a three-day beard and with hair swept back and wet with rain.

'I'd already tried the doorbell,' he said, with a note of reproach in his voice. 'So I tried knocking on the window and looked in to see if there was anyone here. Didn't want to be find myself on a fool's errand after driving thirty minutes downtown.'

'I'm sorry, come in,' said Róbert. 'The doorbell's so quiet you can hardly hear it. I'd dropped off for a minute, didn't hear a thing.'

The locksmith carefully wiped his shoes but made no sign of taking them off.

'What's the problem? Stiff locks?'

'Well, not exactly. We lost a set of house keys, so I'd really like you to change the locks – here and on the back door. Best to be sure, you see.'

The locksmith nodded and went straight to work; Róbert was sure he'd heard the same story often enough before.

Róbert made himself some coffee, sat at the kitchen table and waited. He was hoping that the steaming drink would kill the cold dead before it could get going, but he merely managed to burn his tongue instead. He was still tired. The truth was, the uninvited visitor the night before had only aggravated the difficulty he usually had sleeping. It was more difficult than he imagined it would be to come to terms with certain events from his past.

'You want security chains as well?' he heard the locksmith call from the hallway.

He thought, hesitated and then agreed. But not without a pang of guilt, as he admitted to himself that he was unable to guarantee his family's safety by himself.

The locksmith was quicker than Róbert had expected. After he left, he decided to lie down again, this time taking care to draw the curtains and slip the security chains into place on both front and back doors – not that the chains would be much help if someone was prepared to use force to get in. And anyway, Róbert still had the uncomfortable feeling of being watched as he lay down on the sofa and tried to empty his head of thoughts which was easier said than done these days.

Half an hour later Róbert was still awake when the doorbell chimed; this time he heard it clearly.

He didn't hurry to the door, certain that this time it would be Breki, Sunna's lousy ex, bringing Kjartan back. Róbert had always disliked Breki, although he had made no real effort to get to know him.

'You're alike in some ways,' Sunna had once said.

He knew what she meant: he wasn't one to give up and sensed that Breki was much the same.

He opened the door as far as the chain would let him, looked out and closed it again to unhook the chain.

'Hi,' he said in an unfriendly tone as he looked Breki in the eye.

They were much the same size – around six feet two. Breki had a shaved head, an unkempt beard and unusually large eyes. He nodded to Róbert and extended a beefy hand. Róbert ignored it.

With the other hand, Breki held a child's car seat, with Kjartan wrapped up and fast asleep inside. The boy was dressed for the rain and the insidious chill that accompanied it.

'Sunna home?' Breki asked, his eyes glancing around him.

'She's at work,' Róbert replied, taking the heavy car seat and placing it gently on the floor.

Breki shrugged, then turned and strode off towards the green pickup he had left in the middle of the narrow street.

'Hey,' Róbert called after him, sniffing. The coffee had done nothing to shift his cold. 'Hey,' he repeated. 'What were you doing here last night?'

He watched carefully to see how Breki reacted to this provocation; he turned and stared at him, his large eyes wide, and a perplexed look appearing on his face.

'What the hell do you mean? I was nowhere near here last night.'

Róbert waited. That was enough for now.

'I was sure I saw you,' he replied and slammed the door.

Róbert knew he shouldn't have made so much noise, but the little boy didn't seem to have woken up. He waited until Breki and his green rust bucket had gone and then moved Kjartan carefully from the car seat to the pushchair that they kept in the hall, before setting off around the block in the rain, the new keys in his pocket.

At the end of the street he stopped, turned and looked over his shoulder, almost without thinking.

There was nobody to be seen. But the memory of last night's unwelcome guest followed him like a ghost.

8

Ari Thór was ready for the night shift, despite feeling tired. He had tried to close his eyes during the day but hadn't managed to sleep properly.

There wasn't a great deal waiting for him, however. Maybe he'd be able to sleep for a few hours at home, with the phone at his side. He did need to call Ísrún, the journalist from Reykjavík, but he guessed she had probably gone home already, so that could wait until later in the evening.

He also needed to get in touch with the hospital and the specialist in infectious diseases that evening, to go over the situation with them. The second fatality had only ramped up people's fears about the virus. All across the media, descriptions of the nurse's symptoms were being discussed, from vomiting to internal and external bleeding. It was now obvious what kind of hazard they were now facing, and nobody wanted to be next. Speaking to the head doctor, it was clear to Ari Thór that the hospital staff were living in fear, even now that the most stringent contingency plans had been put into action.

The way he saw it, the media had only lit a fire under people's fears following the death of the nurse, while the authorities, on the other hand, were making every effort to assure the general public that the situation was under control, and were trying to get the message across that, taking all the circumstances into consideration, it was in fact a triumph that more people had not been infected.

This situation aside, Ari Thór felt he had reason to be cheerful currently, now that his relationship with Kristín, his former girl-friend, was improving. Having split up quite some time before, he had been unable to get her out of his head, and had ended up appearing unexpectedly at her door in Akureyri, only to find another man there. Jealousy had got the better of him and he had lost his temper. In the ensuing brawl he had been stabbed. He took the blame entirely on himself, but in some strange way it had served to bring him and Kristín closer together.

In January, though, there was yet more turmoil in his personal life. A surprise phone call had brought him news that was certainly not the uplifting kind he always thought he needed during the gloomy winter months near the Arctic Circle.

'Is that Ari Thór?' a woman's voice had enquired, hesitatingly.

'Yep,' he answered shortly, not recognising the voice. Being asked for by name during work hours was a rarity, so, to begin with, he had thought it was someone with a complaint; someone who felt that he should be doing his job better. If only that had been the case.

'You probably don't remember me,' the woman continued after a pause. 'We met in Blönduós.'

That was all she needed to say. Ari Thór had been as startled as if someone had slapped him. He remembered her, although not clearly; it was all he could do to recall her through the haze of that night's booze. This was the red-haired girl he had met at a country hop and had slept with that night, the autumn after he and Kristín had gone their separate ways.

'Yes, of course I remember,' he said.

'We need to talk.' There was a heavy silence before she continued. 'I was sort of in a relationship with someone else when we met; we were taking a break from each other … But soon after we … you know … I found that I was pregnant.'

It was a sentence Ari Thór had often dreaded.

'What? And you think the child might be mine?' he asked.

'I'm not sure. I've broken up with my boyfriend now. I let him think it was his baby to start with, and then I had to admit that I wasn't sure. We split up soon after that. I need to have a test done to make sure.'

Ari Thór realised that he had to agree to the test, however grudgingly. It wasn't as if he could say no, after all.

But before he ended the call, he asked: 'Is it a boy or a girl?'

'A boy,' she replied, the pride shining through in her voice. 'He's seven months. Would you like to meet him?'

Ari Thór had hesitated a little, giving himself time to think. 'No, let's not,' he said, at last. 'We'll make sure first, shall we?'

With the phone back in its cradle, he had been gripped by a blend of trepidation and excitement. How the hell was he going to tell Kristín about this? He had made a decision at the time never to mention that one-night stand in Blönduós to her. It was none of her business anyway – they hadn't been together then.

Over the few days following the fateful phone call, he had thought seriously about keeping the news of his potential fatherhood quiet, not saying a word about it to Kristín as their relationship developed, and letting her remain in blissful ignorance. But with the two of them becoming ever closer again, the idea that there was something like a lie sitting between them, preventing them finally being a true couple, became more and more uncomfortable.

So, finally, he had plucked up courage and told her the tale. She took it better than he had expected.

'There's no certainty it's your child,' she had said.

'I can't rule it out.'

'We'll cross that bridge when we come to it,' she replied, with a shrug and a little smile. Despite her attempt at a light tone, he had fully sensed – almost seen – the grave concern behind her nonchalant demeanour. But it was easiest to let the matter lie.

Blood samples had been taken from Ari Thór, from the little boy and the woman's previous boyfriend. It turned out that the boyfriend and Ari Thór shared a blood type, so the next step had been a DNA test. They were all now waiting for the results. They had been waiting for two months.

The phone rang on Ari Thór's desk, snapping him away from these thoughts about his turbulent personal life and back into the present.

On the line was an elderly lady who lived alone, even though she was well over eighty. She started by apologising for the inconvenience, but said she hadn't been able to get through to the Co-op all day and badly needed a few groceries; a fillet of fish, some rye bread and milk for both herself and the cat. Ari Thór promised to look into it, aware that the Co-op's manager was probably exhausted.

He said goodbye to the old lady and made a note to call the Co-op.

With nothing else to be done, he decided the peace and quiet of a town in quarantine gave him the perfect opportunity to take another look at the Hédinsfjördur file.

'I'm not promising anything,' he had told Hédinn, who had asked if he could look over the case and maybe try to locate the young man in the photograph.

First, Ari Thór had taken a look in the old police case files, but the ones they kept at the station went nowhere near far enough back to contain anything about this case, so all he had to go on was a file of material Hédinn had given him.

He took the slim folder out, and examined the photograph that lay on the top of the little pile of paperwork. It was a black-and-white snapshot, slightly faded. Someone, presumably Hédinn, had written some names on the back – everyone in the shot, apart from the young man, of course. The group of people were gathered on the steps of a low-slung masonry farmhouse. On the left stood Jórunn, the twenty-five-year-old sister of Hédinn's mother, the woman who had died after being poisoned. She had no idea how little time she had left, Ari Thór thought as he gazed at the photograph. It was difficult to tell precisely how long before her death in March 1957 the picture had been taken. The snow in the background told him that it was winter, but this far north it could just as easily snow in spring or autumn. The little boy, Hédinn, looked to be some months old

– no longer a newborn – so, based on Hédinn's birth date, Ari Thór guessed that the picture had been taken in the autumn or winter of 1957. There was a serious look on Jórunn's face, which was framed by short, dark hair. She was wearing a wool sweater and a jacket, her eyes on the ground in front of her and not on the person behind the camera.

The unknown young man stood at her side. Nothing about him looked unusual, but having heard Hédinn's story, Ari Thór couldn't help but feel there was something menacing about him. He saw in the picture a young man who was in the wrong place at the wrong time; an unwelcome guest. Nobody at the picture night had recognised him, according to Hédinn, which indicated that he wasn't from Siglufjördur. Ari Thór guessed that he was about fourteen or fifteen years old. He was dressed in working clothes, and the camera had caught him with his eyes wide open. He had a finely chiselled nose, his mouth was firmly shut, and his tousled hair stood on end in all directions. The baby was wrapped in a wool blanket, a thick hat on his head and the boy held him tightly in his arms. So why was he holding the baby? And what was his relationship with the family?

Hédinn's parents stood at the young man's side, at the far right of the photo. Hédinn's father, Gudmundur, looked to be around thirty. He was a tall man and didn't seem dressed for the conditions – in just working trousers and a checked shirt. He had a strong face, drawn in sharp lines, his eyes hidden behind fragile round spectacles. He didn't look cheerful at the prospect of being photographed.

Gudfinna, Hédinn's mother, looked as downcast as her sister. There was a strong resemblance between them, although Gudfinna was leaner and older than Jórunn, probably around thirty when the photograph had been taken.

Ari Thór couldn't put his finger on why, but there was a melancholy air about the people in the photo. It was only the small boy, lying innocently in the young man's arms, who didn't seem to sense the sadness that had affected everyone else.

Ari Thór looked at them all carefully once more: first Jórunn, then

the young man and baby Hédinn, and finally the couple, Gudmundur and Gudfinna. He couldn't help noticing that of all those in the
group, the young man was the only one whose eyes met the lens. The
two women were both looking down at the snow piled in front of
the house, and Gudmundur's odd spectacles completely obscured his
eyes. Whatever secret this photograph held, it was clearly well hidden.

Putting the photograph aside, he began to go through the newspaper clippings that had come with it. They dated back to long before
the days of red-top tabloid journalism and the unstoppable flood of
internet news. There were two short pieces from national newspapers,
each containing more or less the same details. A woman in her twenties had died after swallowing poison on a farm in Hédinsfjördur. The
news was being reported a week after the event, presumably based on
information made available by the police, and baldly stated that the
incident had been an accident. Both pieces left out the woman's name.

The third cutting was from the local Siglufjördur weekly paper,
which carried the lengthiest coverage of the woman's sudden death.
This one gave little more detail than the other reports, although it did
include her name and a black-and-white photograph from Hédinsfjördur. It had been taken during winter; the farmhouse was in the
centre of the picture, with the mountains on one side and the lake
on the other. Ari Thór felt a chill of discomfort as he peered at the
picture, similar to the feeling he had experienced during Hédinn's
account. The isolation of the place was almost palpable, the gloom
overwhelming.

Ari Thór wondered if he shouldn't take a drive through the new
tunnel to Hédinsfjördur to take a look at the place and look over
the ruins of the old house. He felt a need to absorb the atmosphere
of this empty fjord, which was now suddenly accessible via the new
tunnel, linking it directly with Siglufjördur and opening it up for
the first time to general traffic. But his conscience got the better of
him; he knew he couldn't disobey a direct instruction not to travel
outside the town's limits, even if it was only for an evening visit to
an uninhabited fjord.

The jangling of the phone shattered the evening's silence.

This time is was Tómas.

'How goes it, my boy?' Tómas asked, his voice betraying how tired he was.

Recently he had begun calling in the middle of Ari Thór's shifts to ask if everything was under control, although Ari Thór suspected the real reason was that he wanted someone to talk to.

'Not bad,' Ari Thór replied guardedly.

'You'll call me if anything comes up.'

'Of course. By the way ... where are all the old police files kept?' Ari Thór asked.

'What ...? How old do you mean?' Tómas replied, clearly surprised.

'Going back more than fifty years, 1957.'

'What do you want those for?' Tómas asked suspiciously.

Maybe it was as well to ask Tómas about the case. It wasn't as if Ari Thór had made a promise to keep things confidential.

'I'm just looking at an old case, while I have some spare time.'

'Really?'

'A woman who died after being poisoned – in Hédinsfjördur. Do you remember it?'

'I've heard of the case, of course, but I was just a lad when that happened. Hédinn's an old friend of mine and he was born there. His aunt was the one who died.'

'That's right. He was in touch in the winter, while you were down south, and I finally got to talk to him yesterday. He'd collected some old newspaper cuttings about the case and asked me if I could look into it. I promised I'd see what I could do. I'll tell you more later,' Ari Thór concluded, with unusual determination. Somehow he wanted to investigate this case by himself.

'Well, Hédinn digging up the past isn't a surprise, I suppose. He's an inquisitive sort of guy; he was a teacher for a long time. I should be able to find the files for you tomorrow.'

'Is there anyone other than Hédinn who knows the story?' Ari Thór asked.

'Maybe the priest, Eggert,' Tómas said after a pause. 'He knows the history of Hédinsfjördur very well. Go and see him. You can have a theological discussion while you're there.'

'Sure,' Ari Thór said shortly. He had been sure he'd heard the last of the jokes about his short dalliance with theology. It had taken him three tries to find his place in life, assuming he had now actually found it. First there had been philosophy, then he had switched to theology; he had given up on both.

'Before I forget,' Tómas added. 'Did you call the journalist back? It was Ísrún, the one who does all the crime reports.'

'Oops. You're right. I forgot,' Ari Thór replied.

As soon as the conversation with Tómas was finished, he dialled Ísrún's mobile number. She answered on the on the third ring.

'Hello?' she said, her voice sharp.

'Ísrún?' Ari Thór asked.

He rarely watched the news but he knew who she was. He had seen her occasionally reporting on various crime stories and he had read an interview with her in one of the weekend papers after she had won an award for her work on a people-trafficking case in Skagafjördur that both he and Tómas had been involved with almost a year before. She had a scar on her face, left by someone who had accidentally splashed hot coffee on her as a small baby – or so Ari Thór recalled from the interview.

'That's me,' she said, sounding defensive. 'Who might you be?'

'Ari Thór from the Siglufjördur police. There was a message to call you back.'

'You're remarkably prompt returning calls,' she said, the sarcasm clear in her voice. 'Maybe the phone lines up north also have a virus?'

'Up here everyone's doing their best to avoid a deadly infection so the police are about the only people in town who are still going to work,' Ari Thór said sharply. 'But it's good to know that not everyone takes the matter as seriously as we do.'

'Sorry,' Ísrún replied instantly. 'I didn't mean to cause offence. I just wanted to check what the situation is before the item we ran about it on this evening's news. We'll definitely run another one tomorrow, though, so anything you can tell me would be useful.'

'It's pretty miserable,' he said, his irritation prompting him to answer more directly than he would normally have done. 'We're doing our best here – there's always someone on duty; but the truth is we could be just one call-out from catching something fatal. That's the way it is right now.'

Ísrún was clearly taken by surprise.

'I'm sorry. I don't know what to say,' she said. There was a pause while she processed what he'd told her. Then she asked, in a more friendly tone: 'I'd like to do an additional item about this for later in the week. Could we record an interview over the phone tomorrow?'

'I'd have to run it past my superior,' he answered shortly. However, he admired the fact that she hadn't been knocked off balance by his abrupt manner. 'It shouldn't be a problem, though.'

'Sounds good,' she said cheerfully. 'Speak to you tomorrow, then.'

9

The basement flat Snorri Ellertsson rented in the Thingholt district of Reykjavík belonged to an elderly widow. She was now well over eighty but still lived upstairs. Her late husband, a psychiatrist, had fitted out the basement flat as his office sometime around the middle of the twentieth century, and when Snorri was bored, he amused himself by recreating the conversations that must have taken place there over the years – trying to sense the presence of their ghosts, using his vivid imagination. A strong imagination was essential for any artist, especially for a musician like him. What use was an artist without creativity?

Snorri was sitting at his keyboard in the half-darkness, trying to get a new composition to work. He found it hard to concentrate – he was too excited about that evening's meeting with a record company. At last, after all the years of struggling, the endless, poorly attended gigs in shabby bars, all the attempts to get airplay, he could finally see a brighter future ahead of him. He had been in seventh heaven after the phone call and this evening represented another step towards a recording contract.

There hadn't been much to be proud of in his short life, but now he was desperate to share the news with someone. He would have liked to have told his parents, but he knew that wasn't the right thing to do.

His father, Ellert Snorrason, was a well-known politician, now retired, with a long and successful career behind him, both in

Parliament and as a government minister. Ellert had always enjoyed the respect of both his own party and his political opponents, but he hadn't reached what Snorri knew to be his highest aspiration – to sit in government as Prime Minister. That looked to change, however, when, a little over two years before, the financial crisis had resulted in the decision to set up a national administration with all parties forming a coalition. There was little doubt as to who would be the most likely candidate to take the role of Prime Minister: Ellert was a remarkably uncontroversial figure, in spite of his long career, and also had more experience behind him than anyone else in Parliament. And, what was most important – other members of Parliament appeared to trust him.

For years Snorri had brought his parents one disappointment after another, as he sank deeper and deeper into alcohol and drugs. His dependence on the bottle and harder drugs had spiralled out of control just at the time when his father looked set to take the country's top job. His father's dream of being Prime Minister was snatched away, just as it was about to become a reality. Ellert had retired 'for personal reasons' and the real story was never made public.

Snorri's mother, Klara, had never gone out to work, yet she had still held all the political strands in her own hands. Snorri had no doubt that his father's success in politics was largely due to his mother's shrewdness and determination; and the dream of the Prime Minister's office had been Klara's as much as Ellert's. So when his career came to its sudden end, her disappointment was deep and unmistakeable.

Her reaction had been harsh. She closed every door on her son. On the rare occasions he called, she would not talk to him, and he had not been invited into his childhood home for more than two years. Snorri suspected that Ellert would be willing to welcome him back, but Klara had always been the one who ruled the household with an iron hand.

His mother's coldness towards him proved conclusively what he'd always suspected: politics was no place for the kind-hearted. That was why it had never even crossed Snorri's mind to follow in his father's footsteps.

So, his father had missed out on the opportunity to lead the government. What difference had that made, in the end? He still had a successful and unblemished career behind him. And the party had hung on to the Prime Minister's office without him. Its undisputed crown prince, Marteinn – a family friend and a childhood companion of Snorri's – had taken up the baton. The party had romped home in the elections that followed the coalition, with Marteinn at the helm – a leader for a new generation with a great future ahead of him. Snorri had every reason to believe that the old man didn't have the energy to go through another election campaign, let alone become as successful as Marteinn had been.

But perhaps Snorri did have reason to feel guilty. These bloody drugs.

Maybe he ought to speak to his sister, Nanna, about his success.

She was always so busy, but she'd talk to him sometimes; did her best to keep the peace with her brother, although that husband of hers wasn't always supportive. On one occasion, when Snorri had run into Nanna and her husband in the street, the conversation had been short and sharp, and as he walked away, he'd heard her husband comment – undoubtedly intended for his ears – that they shouldn't allow a dope-head like him anywhere near the family 'for the children's sake'. What a bastard.

But Snorri had now left all that stuff behind him, and his music career looked like it was about to take off.

He opened his laptop and typed a message to his sister, asking what was new, and telling her that he had some good news; he was hoping to get a recording deal. *Meeting tonight, in Kópavogur. We'll see what happens*, he wrote, knowing that Nanna lived in a large detached house in Kópavogur. *Thinking of you while I'm at the studio. Hope it all works out. Love to the family*, he added; he was fond of her two little ones, even though he rarely got to see them.

It would have been good to have been able to talk his news over with his childhood friend – and now Prime Minister – Marteinn; a chat over a coffee to reminisce and celebrate their successes. But getting to speak to the young man who now occupied the Prime Minister's office was easier said than done, particularly as their lives had taken such different paths.

They had both shown great promise as youngsters, but while Snorri had found himself in dubious company, Marteinn had never lost sight of his own objectives, showing an ice-cold shrewdness that was completely alien to Snorri. However, despite his ambition and focus, Marteinn hadn't given up on his old friend. When Snorri had fallen through the cracks into an underworld of drugs, Marteinn still took care to maintain contact with him through all those dark years. But while their friendship was no secret, like any conscientious politician, he was cautious, making sure that they didn't meet anywhere that might be crowded.

After those dramatic days in February two years ago, however, Marteinn had taken care to avoid Snorri. He could understand that – it was hardly fitting for the Prime Minister, even of a small country, to have a friend like him. And it made no difference that Snorri had done his best to straighten his life out – undergoing treatment, with the help of his sister; keeping himself dry; and going back to his first love: music.

It was past nine in the evening. He had called a cab as he had no car of his own and needed to get to a studio in an industrial area of the town of Kópavogur – a ten to fifteen-minute drive from the centre of Reykjavík. He had promised to be there at nine thirty.

He shivered at the prospect of going all that way. He felt most comfortable in town, and hoped that he'd be able to get a lift back.

Snorri glanced in the mirror on his way out, knowing that he needed to look the part. What he saw looked acceptable, he thought, running his fingers through his hair, which was starting to thin alarmingly for such a young man.

He dropped a CD into the pocket of his black overcoat and hurried out to wait for the cab on the corner. There was nobody to be seen on this damnably wet evening. He watched the raindrops pattering hard into a puddle in the street, the motif from a classical piece running through his mind – a beautiful waltz, although he wasn't sure who had composed it. Probably one of the Strauss family, he decided.

The cab turned the corner, water from the puddle spraying towards him from under its wheels; he managed to step back just in time to avoid being soaked. He felt this was his lucky night.

10

It was the middle of the night, but Róbert was still awake.

Nothing unusual had happened that evening. Kjartan had fallen asleep early and nothing seemed to be troubling Sunna when she came in from work. Over dinner – fragrant Arctic charr – Róbert told her that the locksmith had been. She nodded and smiled.

'And you weren't rude to Breki when he brought Kjartan home?' she asked.

'Of course not, sweetheart,' he lied.

She was soon asleep – tired after a strenuous rehearsal routine.

It wasn't just the thought of the unwelcome guest that was keeping Róbert awake. The same old nightmare had made a comeback. For some reason, it had been absent for a while; but recently it had returned with a vengeance.

Now he lay in bed, looking at Sunna where she lay, so peaceful and so beautiful, in between staring at the ceiling. Kjartan slept soundly in his own little bedroom down the hall.

Róbert decided to check on him, just to be sure. The peace and quiet of their home had been disturbed and he was struggling to come to terms with it.

He carefully got out of bed and went to the boy's room with sure, quiet steps, taking care not to touch anything in the darkness. The door was ajar but he couldn't see if the boy was in his bed or not. Suddenly, he had the oppressive feeling that the lad was gone, and hurried over to his bedside.

He felt a wave of relief as he saw Kjartan turn over in his sleep. Everything was fine.

Róbert padded back to the bedroom, and was just about to lie down when he thought he heard something breaking the silence – a movement outside their bedroom window.

The curtains were drawn, so he couldn't see anything.

Róbert stood still and listened. There was no mistaking it. There was definitely someone outside.

He went to the window, checking Sunna was still sound asleep, carefully pulled back the curtain and peered out.

While he had been sure he would see someone out there, what he saw still took him by surprise.

A figure in black stood in the middle of the garden. He, or she, was dressed in a raincoat of some kind with the hood pulled up; the person's head was bowed and their hands covered their face.

Róbert stood stock still, unable to move. His heart had almost stopped for a second, but now it was hammering. He was terrified.

Almost unable to control himself, he shut his eyes, convinced that his imagination was playing tricks on him. But when he opened them again the figure was still standing there. Róbert thought he could feel its eyes on him; or maybe even that was his imagination.

A few seconds passed – so slowly they felt like a lifetime. Finally, he began to think logically. His first instinct was to smash the window and hurl himself at the bastard. But he wanted to avoid waking Sunna and Kjartan; and he wanted to do something sensible and realistic. Something not governed by his fear.

The figure remained outside, as still as stone.

Róbert rushed from the bedroom, hurried to the front door and opened it as quietly as he could. But unhooking that damned security chain held him up before he could get out into the garden. It had taken him only a few seconds to get there, but that was enough. It was deserted.

He cast his eyes in every direction but could see nobody. The churchyard gate across the street, leading into the old Hólavellir graveyard, swung slightly as if someone had pushed it aside in passing.

For a moment Róbert was ready to run over the road and into the vast, dark cemetery, but he was well aware of just how much of a labyrinth the place was, and he had no intention of going that far from home.

He went back inside, shivering, every hair on his body seeming to stand on end.

11

Ísrún's old red banger of a car was still doing sterling service, although she knew that it could give up the ghost at any moment. It had managed to get her to work on this overcast March morning, at least.

The weather mirrored her mood – the constant lethargy that had dogged her since her illness had begun to take hold. It was undoubtedly a result of her constant worry about the progress of the disease, which preyed on her mind every single day. It was there while she was at work; it was there in the evenings; and even at night it lurked in her mind when she could not get to sleep.

After she had won the award for outstanding journalism the year before, there had been no shortage of interesting assignments. María, the news editor, had taken the decision, undoubtedly against the wishes of desk editor Ívar, that Ísrún should oversee any crime-related material.

However, having to deal with the endless series of horrific events that came across her desk had done nothing to help her low mood. At the beginning of the year there had been the news about an attempted murder in the north of Iceland in which the drunken, would-be killer had attacked an old acquaintance in a disagreement over an inheritance. After that a girl had been raped at a Kópavogur nightclub by an unknown assailant who still hadn't been caught. The victim hadn't been able to get a proper look at his face, which had been partly hidden behind a balaclava; she had only heard the vicious taunts he had whispered into her ear as he held her down. Ísrún found this story a particularly harrowing one to cover, having herself been a rape victim a few years earlier. She had done her best to live with the experience, but had only been able to talk about it with one person – a victim of the same man. She repeatedly tried to convince herself that she had finally got over it, that it was behind her, but flashbacks could appear from nowhere without any warning.

Only a week ago, a young woman had died after spending two years in a coma following a brutal and apparently motiveless attack with a baseball bat in her own home in Reykjavík. Her husband had been at work on the evening of the assault, so she had been in her house alone. This was yet another unsolved violent crime. Little Iceland was becoming more dangerous almost by the day.

Ísrún did her level best not to let it all get under her skin, but it wasn't easy. She tried to sleep as much as she could to keep up her strength. But this week wasn't going to be an easy one, with a late shift last night and day shifts the rest of the time.

She was ahead of the game, though – having set up an interview with the Siglufjördur police officer, Ari Thór. He came across as unusually open during the telephone call the night before, and it had been interesting to chat with him, even for just a few minutes. Out of habit, right after the call, she had looked him up on the internet, wanting to know what he looked like. But there was no search result; he was a real mystery man.

Ísrún's father had called as her evening shift was coming to an end. He had heard about her visit to the Faroes and wanted news of her mother. Too proud to ask straight out if Anna was coming home, he circled around the subject as cautiously as a fish circling a hook. Ísrún felt half sorry for him, and did her best to cheer him up by telling him she was sure it was a temporary situation, although she had nothing but her own conviction to base that assurance on.

Later that evening her mother had called from the Faroes, ostensibly asking how the trip home had gone. It was obvious to Ísrún that, in reality, she was fishing for news about Ísrún's father – although she didn't ask a single straight question about him. The two of them were so alike; they suited each other perfectly.

At Monday morning's editorial meeting, Ísrún was allocated her stories to follow up, including keeping tabs on the situation in Siglufjördur, as well as reporting on an assault that had taken place in Hafnarstræti during the night; one more police matter.

It wasn't until the editorial meeting was over that the day's big story arrived. Ívar and María called Ísrún in to talk to them.

'Something new for you to chase,' María said as soon as Ísrún had shut the office door behind her, as always, getting straight to the point.

Ísrún sat down and waited, her heart beating a little faster.

'It's sensitive,' María said. 'It's about Ellert Snorrason.'

Ísrún immediately had a vision of the elder statesman looking reserved and dignified. She had interviewed him once or twice. Had he become embroiled in some scandal late in life, now that he had retired?

'His son was involved in a hit-and-run incident last night,' María said, pausing for effect. 'In Kópavogur. On a quiet street in an industrial district. No witnesses and the driver didn't stop.'

'How is he – the son?' Ísrún asked.

'They reckon he was killed outright.'

There was a moment's silence. Ísrún felt that the victim deserved some respect.

'I'll get to work,' she said at last.

'The police are taking it very seriously,' María said. 'They reckon it was a violent collision, in a street where fast driving isn't easy. The road conditions weren't great last night, what with the rain, and the police aren't ruling out that it was done deliberately.'

'We're reporting this in tonight's bulletin?' Ísrún asked.

Ívar had stayed silent, but now his voice showed just what he thought of her question. 'Of course we are.'

'And we're going to name him?'

Unusually, Ívar hesitated and looked at María.

'I think we could,' she said. 'We can watch out for any other mention of his name today. He was well known – a regular face on the Reykjavík nightlife scene, until he got caught up in drugs. I gather he was something of a musician and had played publicly, although he hadn't been much of a hit. And we shouldn't forget that he was our honourable Prime Minister's closest childhood friend. That's a story in itself, practically a fairy tale. Childhood friends: one rises to prominence while the other gets caught up in drugs and gets himself murdered one rainy night.'

'Shall I try and get a comment from Marteinn? Is this something the Prime Minister's going to be prepared to talk about?' Ísrún asked, making sure she addressed her question to María.

'Do whatever you think works,' Ívar replied. 'I just want a decent story.'

Ísrún nodded. 'Before I forget, I was going to do a short piece about this virus that's hit Siglufjördur for our in-depth feature later this week. Is that OK?' she asked, again directing her question at María.

'Sounds good,' María said and smiled.

Ísrún enjoyed María's approval, and the look of envy on Ívar's face was enough to give her a warm feeling inside.

It had been a quiet night.

There had been time for Ari Thór to look through the folder of material Hédinn had brought, but when he felt his eyelids growing heavy, he decided to go home to sleep. He was due back at the police station later in the day.

As he walked back into the station, Tómas greeted him cheerfully. 'Welcome back, my boy,' he said, although his good humour seemed rather forced. 'I collected the documents you wanted,' he added, as if he were humouring a wayward child.

'Documents?' Ari Thór asked in surprise.

'That's right. The old police reports on the fatality in Hédinsfjördur.'

'Thank you. That's good of you.'

'It's in a folder on your desk. And I was going to tell you about … tell you about Sandra.'

'Sandra?' he asked, wondering if anything had happened to the old lady. He had met her twice during the investigation into the death of an elderly author in Siglufjördur two years previously; she had been both friendly and helpful.

After the case was closed, he'd continued to visit her regularly at the old people's home; he'd gone there at least once a month, and they had formed a strong friendship. Ari Thór had no immediate family of his own, so in a way old Sandra had filled a gap for him with her warmth and kindness. Visits to her were like taking a trip back to a past age, back when things weren't so damned complicated.

'She's been taken to hospital,' Tómas said.

'Hospital?' Ari Thór repeated, startled. 'Did she catch …?'

He could hardly dare think it through. He knew Sandra wasn't going to live for ever, but he wasn't ready to lose someone close, not yet.

'They're saying it's extremely unlikely,' Tómas replied. 'Just a normal flu, probably.'

'I spoke to that journalist last night,' Ari Thór said, anxious to change the subject. He didn't want to talk about Sandra's condition, it was better to pretend that she was OK. 'Ísrún. She wants to interview me about the situation here. Is that all right?'

'Up to you, my boy,' Tómas said, to Ari Thór's astonishment. Normally Tómas preferred to avoid the limelight and was always abrupt in his dealings with the media.

Ari Thór was surprised that he hadn't heard from Ísrún all day. Hadn't she said she'd call him? Maybe she had decided against the interview after all. It would be a shame if she had; it would have been nice to be able to call Kristín and tell her that he would be interviewed on television – even though it would only be on the telephone.

Kristín had called him that morning: 'I heard about the nurse who died,' she'd said. 'It's terrible, isn't it?'

'Yes, it really is.'

'Are you … are you scared?'

He had lied: 'No, not really. It isn't as bad as the media wants you to think, you know. It's easy to take the necessary precautions.'

'All the same, make sure you stay indoors as much as possible.'

'It doesn't matter much if I stay indoors or not,' he had replied. 'There's hardly a soul to be seen anywhere.'

Taking a seat at his desk, now, he started reading through the old police files Tómas had dug out for him. The short, factual sentences gave him no new ideas about the case, however. Jórunn had died on a March evening in 1957, having consumed rat poison mixed into her coffee. The weather was as bad as it could get that night and when her symptoms began to manifest themselves – in the bleeding typical of rat poison – there was no way to call a doctor. Everyone in the household had confirmed that there was rat poison in the house and that it had been kept in the kitchen in a jar that wasn't dissimilar to the sugar jar. By the time the police and the doctor arrived the following day Jórunn was already dead. She had told her family that she had stirred the poison into her coffee by mistake. At least, everyone's testimony agreed on that point.

Ari Thór practically flung the report away when he had finished it, hardly believing a word he had read, although he had no doubt that what was recorded was the information the police had received. He doubted its reliability, though. This was a far too easy and convenient conclusion to a difficult case. But he realised it must have been difficult for the police to deal with the lies, when nobody seemed to have been prepared to rock the boat, and all three witnesses had the same story to tell.

He was sure that the most interesting part of the report was the things that were missing from it. It was possible to work out that, on that evening of the death, there had been nobody there but Jórunn and Maríus, Gudmundur and Gudfinna, and of course their son Hédinn, who was then ten months old. The young man in the photograph seemed to have vanished – there was no mention of him at all.

After a brief search, Ari Thór found a number for the chairman of the Siglufjördur Association in Reykjavík. One phone call later, he was speaking to the man who had organised the picture evening. He introduced himself, but not as a police officer – rather, as someone with an interest in a certain picture. The man didn't seem surprised and asked which photograph.

'It's a group photo taken in Hédinsfjördur,' Ari Thór explained. 'Two women, one—' he began, but was immediately interrupted.

'Yes, yes. I remember it well. We don't see all that many pictures from Hédinsfjördur. It was a picture of Gudmundur and Gudfinna from Siglufjördur. They moved back to the town after they gave up trying to farm in Hédinsfjördur. That was right after the fatality there, if I recall correctly,' the man said, dropping his voice at the mention of a death.

Ari Thór waited for him to continue.

'Are you related to them?' the man asked.

'No, but I know their son. I was wondering where the picture came from?'

'So you know Hédinn?' the man asked, but didn't wait for a reply. 'He's a good sort.'

'They were a respectable couple, weren't they?' Ari Thór said. 'Gudmundur and Gudfinna, I mean.'

'Well, yes. Gudmundur wasn't someone everyone got on with. Nobody was keen on being at loggerheads with him. But he did well for himself. He started in the fishing business as a young man and he ran a company as well. Put it this way: he was well off enough to afford to make a mistake with that Hédinsfjördur adventure. Although it was an expensive way to put a foot wrong, I reckon. There must have been some ideas about the charm of isolation, the attraction of a deserted fjord, that kind of thing. Nobody has lived in Hédinsfjördur since.'

'And his wife?'

'She was from Reykjavík. Both of them were – she and her sister. The sister's the one who died. I can't recall her name …'

'Jórunn,' Ari Thór said.

'Exactly. Jórunn. I recall that her husband's name was Maríus and the picture came from him. I gather the sisters were much alike; and weren't too fond of that narrow, dark fjord. It's not a way of life that suits everyone. She drank poison, Jórunn did.'

'Is that certain?' Ari Thór asked.

'Well … as far as I remember – and I am getting on, you know – that was the explanation given at the time. I don't think there was much doubt about it. You can imagine how hard the winter must have been in a place like that, with no electricity. There had never been electricity there, in fact; no phone either. It was hard enough in Siglufjördur; I moved south a good while ago, so as to be closer to my family,' he said with regret in his voice.

'You said that the picture came from Maríus; but isn't he dead?' Ari Thór asked.

'He is. Two years ago. His brother took a while to go through everything. Last winter he got in touch; or rather a nurse at the old people's home he's in these days got in touch with us. She said that Maríus had left his brother two boxes of old photographs from the town, and the brother wanted to donate them to us. We included them in our collection and showed some of them at the picture evening the other day. You'd be amazed at how many people in these old photos can be identified,' he added, happily.

'Do you have Maríus's brother's phone number?'

'I'm sorry, I don't. But I know what the home is called; you can try and get through to them.' There was a pause, and then he read out the name of the old people's home. 'I think he's past ninety, the old fellow. His name's Nikulás Knutsson.'

13

The psychiatrist had done his best to help Emil.

'Emil. Tell me how you feel,' he'd said.

No response.

'Write it down, Emil, if that's easier for you,' he had said with paternal warmth in his voice.

Nothing.

It was as if he had been switched off. He neither wanted to speak nor could; at least, not about her.

Emil was twenty-seven years old. Born and raised in Kópavogur, he had left home when his application for a student apartment had been granted. Good with computers, it hadn't taken him long to decide that business studies was what he wanted to focus his energies on. He completed the course without any problems and then decided to take a break from studying after those three years; a BSc degree would do for the time being, he thought. He'd accepted a good offer from one of the large banks and was still employed by them, in theory. Right now, though, he was on a period of sick leave to which he could see no end.

Some of his colleagues had set up in business on their own accounts, using the skills they had acquired to establish their own new companies, but that was never a temptation for Emil. He didn't have the same energy, the pioneering spirit that such a venture demanded.

Once his studies had come to an end, he'd bought a small

apartment in Reykjavík; his parents had helped him scratch together the down payment and he'd taken out a mortgage for the rest. It was a year later that he met Bylgja.

She worked for the same bank as he did, and had been a year behind Emil in university. He'd noticed her at the university, but their paths had never really crossed. When they finally met at a staff party at work, they got on wonderfully. It seemed like only moments later that she was moving into his apartment. They were more than just lovers; they were partners and soulmates, spending every possible moment together and laying plans for the future.

And then she was gone, as if she had disappeared into the evening gloom.

It happened between a hasty dinner and sleep that never came that night; between the tattered old Ikea sofa and the replacement they had meant to buy; between his proposal on one knee and the wedding that never happened.

There had been overtime at the bank that night. In hindsight – and he'd had no shortage of that as he ran the same thoughts back and forth in his mind over and over again – the work could have waited. For a young man with a future ahead of him, he'd thought it was worth working overtime – being the last one to leave. Bylgja had been no less ambitious, but that evening she had been at home. She had been thinking of going back to university to continue her studies later that year and that night she was working through the reading list, months before the course was due to start. This fact had got her killed.

He was back living with his parents again. He had no interest in continuing payments on the apartment, although he knew his parents would see to them. They'd get him back on an even keel. They could hardly expect him to move back there, but at least it was something that could be sold to avoid bankruptcy on top of all his other troubles.

He'd stop seeing the psychiatrist. It wasn't helping. Emil told the man he no longer needed his assistance, although that was stretching the point.

He didn't talk much with other people, either – not even his parents. In the old days he had been more open.

But so much had changed. Now he only thought of revenge.

14

Ísrún sat, exhausted, in the newsroom, watching the evening bulletin on the big screen with her colleagues.

It was their habit to watch the news together at the end of the day, ready to answer the phone to anyone who felt like complaining – there were normally a few such calls every night – and then have a short conference to go over the day's events.

The first item on the evening news had been hers. There was a suspicion that Snorri Ellertsson had been run over deliberately, according to her police source.

There had been no way to keep Snorri's name out of the piece; María had taken the decision that the deceased's name was news in itself, as they were looking at a possible murder and the victim was both the son of a respected political figure and a one-time close friend of the current Prime Minister. María had justified releasing his name by saying that there could be a political opponent behind the attack who wanted to harm the government, or even Ellert in person. Ísrún had not gone so far as to repeat this wild conjecture in her report. On the other hand, her source had given her no other reason exactly why the police were not treating the incident as accidental.

Ísrún had been sure to contact the police and visit the scene with a cameraman. There hadn't been much to see, but they had to have some kind of footage for the evening bulletin. She had decided to show the family some consideration and called neither Snorri's parents nor his sister. She also preferred to leave the Prime Minister out of this for the time being. She knew Marteinn slightly, as did most journalists, and she was planning to see if she could talk to him either before or after the next day's cabinet meeting.

After all of the day's frenetic activity, she realised, with uncomfortable sudden-ness, that she had completely forgotten to call the police officer up north to follow up on the virus story. There probably wasn't much happening, and the story might be about to dry up. But there was always interest in a something as dramatic as this, and a good journalist would simply make an effort to find a new angle every day. It was practically unforgivable to have forgotten about it.

She stepped into a meeting room and called the Siglufjördur police station using her battered old mobile. There wasn't enough in the expenses pot to ensure that the news team had the latest phones.

'Police,' a sharp voice answered after a few rings.

Ísrún recognised it. 'Hello, Ari Thór, it's Ísrún,' she said. 'From the news desk,' she added after a moment's awkward silence.

'Yes, I know,' he rasped. 'What happened with that interview? I got clearance for it.'

'Thanks, that's great. It …' She hesitated before forging ahead, deciding – not for the first time – that a white lie was better than the truth. 'It didn't work out today …' *Didn't work out* – that sounded better than admitting she had forgotten.

'So it's not going to happen?'

'Sure it will. But I'll have to give you a call tomorrow, if that's alright? My shift's almost over now, and we need time to set up the recording.'

'No problem,' Ari Thór assured her in a more amiable tone of voice.

'But while I have you on the line, what's the situation at the moment? You haven't been infected?' she asked, taking a ballpoint from her pocket and reaching for a sheet of paper from the meeting-room table. If there was anything new, she could pass it on to her colleague on the late shift.

'No, nothing like that. I'm taking care,' he said. 'The only person I see at the moment is my inspector.'

'Fine. I hope you're still there in the morning.'

'I reckon so.'

Ísrún hoped that his answers wouldn't be so short in the next day's interview. She decided to push the conversation forward to see if she could gather any useful points she could expand on with him the next day. But she knew she had to be careful. More than once she had been caught out with a promising conversation before recording started, only to see the interview fall to pieces as the person being filmed hesitated and stammered. Sometimes it was as if people had no idea how to repeat what they had just said moments before when chatting off-camera.

'So what do the police mainly do in such a small place?' she asked.

'Not a lot.'

'What sort of thing do you have on your plate at the moment?'

He was quiet for a moment. 'I'm killing some time right now by going through old files.'

'Old files?' she asked with no real enthusiasm. 'Anything exciting?'

'I'm looking for a solution to something that happened over fifty years ago: the death of a young woman in Hédinsfjördur,' he said and his voice became more serious. 'This is between ourselves, isn't it? This is an old case that needn't find its way into the news.'

'It's not news unless you crack the case,' Ísrún said, finding that she was curious about it after all. 'Call me first, if you do, won't you?'

'Well … yes. But I don't expect anything like that. I don't imagine that I'll find out what really happened, or that there'll be much call to bring it to the media,' he said softly.

'Old cases like that are always popular. People love to see justice finally done, that kind of thing. You know what I mean?'

'Yeah, I know,' Ari Thór mumbled.

'We can do a programme about it if you solve the mystery,' she said, making an effort to appeal to his sense of vanity, but not expecting to keep her promise.

'That might be interesting,' Ari Thór said.

The bait had been taken. Now she just had to reel him in.

'What was the case all about?' she asked, feigning a lack of interest. 'I have to be quick. Our wrap-up meeting is about to start,' she said, to add a little urgency to the conversation.

'It's something that happened near here. A young woman drank poison in Héðinsfjördur in 1957 – or she was poisoned.'

'Héðinsfjördur? No one lives there, do they?'

'No, not anymore, but people used to. This woman was one of the last inhabitants. There were five of them. Two couples and the infant son of one of them – he was born in Héðinsfjördur. He's still alive. The others are all dead.'

'And why are you looking into this?'

'A few days ago a photograph showed up that was probably taken the winter before the woman died. There's a young man in the picture nobody can recognise. It poses a few questions in connection with the woman's death.'

'Intriguing,' Ísrún said. 'And you think there's a possibility of investigating this now? I don't imagine there are all that many people who could be interviewed fifty years on.'

'True … But we'll see. There's an old man in Reykjavík – the brother of one of the people who lived there; it would be interesting to talk to him. He inherited this picture, along with a lot of others, from his brother. But it'll have to wait.'

Ísrún now saw through the window that the evening wrap-up meeting really was about to start. These meetings were held at their desks or on foot and tended to be very short, making it easy to miss if you were even a few minutes late.

'Why's that?' she asked, curiosity overcoming her better judgement.

'The old boy's in his nineties and his hearing is so bad that he won't talk on the phone. But he's still as sharp as a knife, or so I'm told. I'll go and see him next time I'm down south, if I ever get let out of quarantine!' His tone hid determination behind its lightness.

Ísrún was just about to bring the conversation to an end, when Ari Thór asked a sudden questions.

'I don't suppose you could find time to go and have a chat with him? It shouldn't take more than a few minutes. He lives in a rest home down there. I would do it myself, but of course I can't make the trip south under the circumstances.'

'I don't really have …' Ísrún started to say when she thought again. It would do no harm to have a police officer owing her a favour. 'I'll see if I can get over to see him tomorrow, if there's time.'

She wrote down the old man's name and address on a sheet of paper, added Ari Thór's mobile number to it so she could definitely reach him for the interview, and brought the conversation to a close.

The wrap-up was over by the time she got to it. She picked up her coat, punched herself out and went out into the gloomy evening chill without a word to anyone.

15

The morning was refreshingly bright after the preceding damp days. Ísrún set off early from the western part of town for the Breidholt suburb of Reykjavík; it was as well that the weight of traffic was moving in the opposite direction.

After their conversation the night before, Ari Thór had sent her an email, giving her additional information about the Hédinsfjördur case, as well as his thoughts about it, questions for old Nikulás and a scan of the photograph.

Earlier that morning Ísrún had called the manager of the rest home where the ninety-three-year-old Nikulás lived, and was told that he was a lively character, although his hearing was failing. He had agreed to meet Ísrún whenever it was convenient for her.

It took longer than she had expected to locate the place, but she finally found it and still had enough time to talk to him before the morning meeting at the newsroom.

It was a sprawling, featureless building dating back to the eighties, encircled by well-kept grounds, although the trees were still looking forlorn this early in the year. Ísrún imagined that the gardens would look magnificent on a summer's day.

Nikulás was waiting for her in the rest home's lounge, gazing out over the bare gardens, a cup of coffee in his hand. He was heavily built and completely bald, with strong features. He was well dressed, in a dark-grey suit complete with a white shirt and a striped tie.

Ísrún explained what had brought her to him, reminding herself as they talked to speak loudly and clearly, and not mentioning that Ari Thór was a police officer. In every other respect she kept to the truth, telling him that they were looking into the case because the mysterious photograph had recently come to light. He simply nodded, and Ísrún asked his permission to use a voice recorder while they spoke. He nodded again.

'I'd like to ask you about the photograph, and about your brother,' Ísrún said, laying a printout of the photograph on the table in front of him. 'Have you seen this young man before?' she asked, her finger on the young man in the centre of the group, the baby in his arms.

'No. Never seen him. I imagine my brother must have taken this picture,' he said in a clear voice followed by a cough.

'Was this picture in a box with other photographs?' Ísrún asked.

'It was. He and Jórunn lived in Siglufjördur for a year or so. Her older sister had married a local, as I suppose you already know.' He sighed. 'Maríus discovered a passion for photography while he was in the town. As I recall, that was around 1954. The pictures in the box were mostly from Siglufjördur, apart from that one taken in Hédinsfjördur and a couple of landscapes from around there. I was wondering what to do with them all, as I don't have all that much space in my room here. An old friend who comes from up there said I should donate them to the Siglufjördur Society as they always have an interest in that kind of thing. That's the whole story.' He sipped his coffee and leaned closer towards Ísrún. 'I've seen you on television. You do a fine job.'

'Thank you,' she said, taking it in her stride. She took care to let neither praise nor criticism disturb her peace of mind. 'So you inherited all this from your brother?'

'That's right. There was nobody else, if you see what I mean.'

'And had he been well off?'

'Not really. He owned his apartment outright, which seems to be unusual these days, and there was some worn-out furniture. There were only a few books, as he wasn't much of a reader, the poor lad. He was a simple man. There was a bit of money in an old account that he hadn't touched for decades; but inflation had reduced that to not very much,' he finished, with a smile.

'Did you ever visit your brother in Hédinsfjördur?'

'Good grief, no. I've never been there. I wasn't interested in seeing the place, and anyway, I was far too busy. What business would I have in an abandoned place like that? Moving to that damned place destroyed my brother. He was never the same again after Jórunn took her own life. I'm sure it was the isolation that did it,' he said, brow furrowed.

'It wasn't an accident?' Ísrún asked.

'She took her own life. I think everyone knows that,' he said, certainty in his voice.

'You're sure?'

'Absolutely sure. Maríus often hinted at it when we talked. He said that the darkness had got to some of them very badly.'

Ísrún was taken by surprise by this half-revelation. Maybe it had been suicide after all? But she was determined to pursue her line of questioning all the same.

'How so?'

'He didn't go into detail; he didn't like to say much about that time in Hédinsfjördur. But he'd mention it occasionally, out of the blue. Now and then he told me that Jórunn shouldn't have chosen the path she chose. They had moved to Siglufjördur because Jórunn's sister Gudfinna had moved there. Maríus never did find what suited him in life. He was a simple soul, as I told you before. He was neither independent nor robust. He was easily influenced and wasn't strong physically, so he coped badly with heavy work. Gudfinna's husband, Gudmundur, promised him work in Siglufjördur. So Maríus worked in the herring there for a while; he was working there when I visited them there the following summer. He wasn't happy. And the work was too hard for him, although I believe he was given lighter work afterwards. I suspect that it was Gudmundur who supported them. He'd done well for himself – made his money in fish. All I can say is that he looked after my brother, helped put a roof over Maríus's head down south after he had lost his wife. The poor man had a tough life, but he's at rest now.'

'Were you both born in Reykjavík?' Ísrún asked after a pause.

'Good Lord, yes. Maríus and I were both born here. He should never have been tempted to move to the north. I've never wanted to move to anywhere else.' He shifted in his chair and straightened his back. 'Would you indulge a lazy old man and fetch me a drop more coffee?'

'Of course,' Ísrún said with a smile. She took the cup and refilled it from a thermos in the corner of the room.

Once he had taken a sip of his coffee, Nikulás continued seamlessly with his tale. 'He always struggled with work. I started as a young man, working in the coal, and was able to get Maríus a job there. He was supposed to be helping me but he wasn't much use. I managed to keep it quiet for a while, that he wasn't making an effort; but it was never going to work for long and so he was let go. I recall he took it badly. Then I went to work in retail; I worked for years in a gentlemen's outfitters on Laugavegur. You're so young you'd hardly remember it. The place closed down in the middle of the eighties, not long after I retired. I was never rolling in money; had enough for me and the family. Maríus had to look after himself.'

'Was that why he moved to Siglufjördur?' Ísrún asked.

'That's about right. They always struggled down here in Reykjavík. That was why they gave up their ...' the old man hesitated, glancing around him as if he were looking for an escape route.

Ísrún's news instincts had kicked in and she was determined to get to the bottom of the story.

'They gave up their ...?' she prompted, and then decided to finish the question with a guess. 'They gave up their child?'

She could visualise the young man in the picture. Nikulás sat silent for a while and then spoke in a low voice, avoiding Ísrún's eye.

'I suppose I can tell you; it was all such a long time ago. The boy could be still living, I don't know ...' He fell silent and Ísrún knew that it was best to keep quiet. 'This had nothing to do with Jórunn's death.'

'They had a child?' she asked softly.

'They did. Jórunn was just twenty and Maríus wasn't much older. They weren't able to support a child and had decided more or less right away to put it up for adoption. I … well, I encouraged them to go that way. I knew Maríus better than anyone did and I thought it would be too much for him, at least at that time. He didn't have permanent work and he was the type who matured late.'

Nikulás sighed and rubbed his eyes, maybe to hide tears or just because of tiredness. Ísrún had no intention of keeping him talking for too long. She was aware that time was not on her side, but was keen to get to the end of the tale.

'It was a very difficult decision for Jórunn to take,' he continued. 'But she stuck to it. She said it was best for the child.'

'And what became of the baby?' Ísrún asked eagerly after a moment's pause.

'Well … he – it was a boy – he was adopted, as I told you. I don't know where he went and they preferred not to know. Jórunn was adamant that it had to be people she didn't know. Good people from the countryside, was what she said. You see, she didn't want the risk of running into her own child on the street in Reykjavík,' he said and fell silent. His expression demonstrated the inner struggle that had gone into retrieving memories from long ago. 'She said that she was sure she'd recognise him, anywhere, any time.'

'They never had any contact with him – the boy?'

'No, not that I know of. He was formally adopted, all legal and above board. As far as I know, they never saw him again.' His voice had dropped almost to a whisper.

Ísrún looked at her watch. 'Can I get you some more coffee before I go?' she asked after a brief silence. 'I really have to run, I'm late for a meeting.'

'No, that will be fine,' Nikulás said. 'But thank you.'

'I'll be in touch if there's anything more I need to ask you,' she said.

'Of course. But you'll have to come here. There's no point trying to talk to me on the phone. I can't hear a thing through it,' he said, a smile returning to his face. 'Some of the others here, who are older than I am, even have internet in their rooms. They send emails! Can you imagine? I don't get on well with technology. That means there's no point sending me a message unless it's one that drops in through the letterbox.'

Ísrún gave him a smile as she said her farewells.

The youngster in the picture – the young man with the wide eyes and with the child in his arms – was all she could think about.

The old man had said that Jórunn's child had been born when she was twenty, and, according to Ari Thór's information, she would have been around twenty-five years old when the photo was taken. At that time, their boy would therefore have been a mere toddler, and certainly not been in his teens; so the young man in the photo had to be someone else.

Ísrún started her car and set off for the newsroom, unanswered questions fresh in her mind. Who was the young man in the picture? Then – what had become of Jórunn's and Maríus's son?

16

Already late for the morning conference, she tried to sneak in at the back of the meeting room but managed to knock over a colleague's cup of coffee as she sat down, making everyone clearly aware of her late arrival. Coffee was spread all over the table and those around her snatched up papers and notebooks, but nobody made any attempt to do anything about the pool of coffee. Apologising, Ísrún left the room to fetch a roll of kitchen towel, returning to an awkward silence as she mopped the mess up from the table.

'Thanks for joining us, Ísrún,' said Ívar who, as usual, was running the news desk that day.

'Sorry I'm late,' she replied and took a seat. 'I was chasing up a lead in the Snorri story.'

She felt no guilt about lying, telling herself that she was only lying to Ívar and he deserved it.

'And what sort of lead might that be?' Ívar enquired, eyes narrowing in irritation and scowling at her.

'I promised I'd keep it to myself for the moment,' she said with a smile. 'But I expect I'll have something soon for María … and you.' She paused. 'I'll look after the cabinet briefing as well, if that's all right. I want to see if I can get a comment from Marteinn about his friend.'

Ívar seemed ready to come up with an objection, so she hurriedly forestalled him.

'I'm keeping an eye on the situation in Siglufjördur as well. Hopefully something will come of it.'

Ívar looked sour and muttered something to himself. Ísrún had got her own way.

In revenge, Ívar gave her the task of going down to Laugavegur to ask people for their opinions on the rising price of petrol. They both knew how tiring and time-consuming it could be convincing passers-by to give an opinion on the issues of the day to a camera. But she just smiled, knowing that these little victories on his part had no bearing on the bigger picture. She was already on her way to being a bigger name in TV news than Ívar was, and could soon start to have realistic expectations of a promotion, or a decent offer from another station.

Her thoughts switched instantly to her health. Sometimes she could forget about the illness in the bustle of a busy day. Then it would slip into her mind when she was least expecting it and that was when all her ambition, all her hard work, would feel like it was worth nothing. Maybe she would no longer be living when the offer of a step up the ladder came, or that gold-plated offer from a rival station.

She tried to stifle the negativity, and – this generally worked better – to channel her energies in a positive direction in a way that helped her in this demanding environment.

To begin with, she called her police contact to check if he had anything new for her. After a few attempts, she managed to get through to him and the results were worth it.

'Snorri sent his sister an email the day he died. Check it out,' he said, but was unwilling to provide any more details. He seemed to have a penchant for cryptic sayings, keen to help her, but cautious about saying too much. Ísrún was sure that by doing this he was convincing himself that he was not breaking any confidentiality rules. She couldn't complain, she told herself. It was better than nothing.

She didn't think she should disturb Snorri's sister on a day like today, ideally she would leave it until tomorrow at least; but she decided to wait and see. She had shifts all week and needed to have something she could use, so an interview might work. The only problem with that was, some other journalist might beat her to the scoop.

The Laugavegur job, interviewing passers-by about fuel prices, turned out to be just as tedious as she had expected. If anything, it was worse; just as she was ready to start at ten thirty, the rain started to come down. There were very few people about and most of those she approached were tourists who were keen to make the most of their stay in spite of the weather. But there was little point asking them their opinions on rising Icelandic petrol prices, even though they probably had the same problems wherever they came from. The few locals who stopped, because Ísrún had practically blocked their paths, had no time to answer questions in the rain for a TV crew. Ísrún sent silent evil thoughts Ívar's way and finally gave up on the rain and nailed a couple of innocent victims in a bookshop and a post office. The answers were all much the same. Who was really likely to be happy to see petrol prices creep upwards? She did her best to squeeze more from her interviewees with extra questions – do you drive less than you used to? What's the best way to deal with the problem? But she knew that this wouldn't make the item any more interesting.

Once it was all over, it was hardly worth going back to the news-room as the cabinet briefing was due to start shortly. Ísrún and the cameraman decided to shelter in the car from the wind and rain, and parked not far from the Cabinet Office behind a row of polished ministry cars.

She decided to use the opportunity to make a call. After a wait, she was put through to a specialist in adoption practice at one of the government agencies – a polite and, judging from his voice, young man.

'Good morning,' she said, without introducing herself. 'I'm looking for information on an old adoption case.'

'Ah, yes,' he said and she detected a shadow of suspicion in his voice. 'Is this a case that you're personally involved in?'

'Well, not exactly. But it's an ancient case, from around 1950. A couple, people I knew but who are now both dead, had a child they gave up for adoption. They never saw him again, so I'm trying to find out what became of him. Could you find out for me?'

'You really think so?' the man asked with a chuckle.

The informality of his reply took Ísrún by surprise. Flustered, she introduced herself properly and added that she was working on a story connected to the adoption. She immediately realised that this was only going to make matters more awkward.

The young man's response fell by the wayside, however, as Rúrik the cameraman prodded her and pointed to the group of ministers leaving the Cabinet Office. She only half heard the young man's offended remarks about how she should make a formal application and his parting shot that the reply to such an application was unlikely to be positive.

She quickly ended the conversation and jumped out of the car with Rúrik close behind her. He had worked at the station for years, was never caught off guard and had little sympathy for overstressed reporters who acted as if each day was their last. He and Ísrún got on well together and she knew there was no point in chivvying him along; he worked at his own pace, was always in the right place at the right time, and never failed to produce top-quality footage. Normally he would add a few fill-in shots of the scene as well – things that Ísrún would never have thought to include, but which were always useful when it came to editing the final sequence, and filling two minutes of screen time with good material.

With no particular political issue hitting the headlines, there were only a few journalists waiting for the ministers to emerge. Marteinn, the Prime Minister, was on the steps, where he was being quizzed by a young woman from one of the daily papers. Ísrún held back and waited for an opportunity to speak to him without any of the other media overhearing.

Marteinn glowed with the self-confidence any politician is lost without. His short-cropped hair was starting to turn grey even though he was only in his early forties; he was a handsome man who clearly looked after himself. He wasn't tall, which had taken Ísrún by surprise when she had first met him in person, even though she knew how deceptive television images could be.

A politician to his fingertips, he nodded and smiled as he came towards her.

'Could I have a word?' she asked, returning his smile.

'Of course, Ísrún.'

She had noticed that he made a point of using her name every time they met. She knew it was all part of his polished performance, but it worked all the same; she found it difficult to withstand his charm. It was no surprise that it brought his party votes by the truckload.

She glanced at Rúrik to give him a signal to start shooting, but as usual, he was ahead of her. She turned back to Marteinn and let fly.

'I wanted to get your reaction to the death of Snorri Ellertsson.'

Marteinn stood stock still and she could not avoid seeing that the question had taken him by surprise. Normally he thought fast and his answers to even unexpected questions were quick and unerring. But this time there was a moment's hesitation. He looked like he was doing his best to remain unruffled for the camera.

'It's a difficult time for Snorri's family,' he said at last. 'I have already given Ellert and Klara my personal condolences.'

He stood in silence, his expression grave, and Ísrún realised that he was waiting for Rúrik to stop recording. Ísrún wasn't inclined to give way, though, and decided to try another angle of attack.

'The police have indicated that he may have been murdered. Has there been any discussion with you over increased security, considering this could have been a politically motivated incident?'

'I'm not prepared to comment,' said Marteinn; and right away both he and Ísrún appeared to realise that he had said the wrong thing.

'Thank you,' she said and turned to Rúrik. 'That'll do,' she told him and turned back to Marteinn. 'I didn't set out to ambush you with that question,' she lied, an amiable smile on her lips.

'That's alright,' he answered, with his own ballot-box smile.

'Were you close friends?' she asked.

Marteinn was cautious. The camera might have been turned off, but this was still a journalist he was speaking to.

'We knew each other well in the old days, before we went our separate ways. I hadn't been in close contact with him in recent years, but that doesn't mean to say that his loss is any less painful.'

Ísrún decided, however, that it hadn't take him long to distance himself from his old friend.

Marteinn looked at his watch. 'I'm going to be late. Good to see you, Ísrún.'

He smiled yet again and strode to the ministry car without a backward glance.

17

'Hello, Ari Thór.'

He recognised the voice of the girl at the other end of the line.

'Hello. Any news on the paternity test, yet?' he asked straightaway.

'No. Nothing yet,' she said.

It wasn't a surprise: the DNA sample had been sent overseas for analysis and it obviously didn't deserve any kind of priority treatment.

So, why the hell was she calling him, if there was nothing to tell him? He waited in silence for her to say something.

'Well, I … I just wanted to see how you were. I thought I'd check up and make sure you hadn't caught that fever. There's nothing about it in the news any more.'

'That's true. The media seem to lose interest in something once it stops being dramatic,' he agreed, suspecting that the girl had another reason to call but was reluctant to broach it. 'But don't worry. I'll take care of myself. There haven't been any new cases and we expect the town to be out of quarantine by the end of the week.'

He tried to sound confident, but in truth, his own fear of the illness was difficult to keep in check.

'Wasn't there a nurse who died?'

'There was, unfortunately. But the people who were in contact with her are being monitored carefully so that there isn't any further infection,' he said. He realised immediately just how cold-hearted that sounded, so he added, 'But it was a real tragedy that the poor woman lost her life.'

'Are you on duty at the moment?'

'Yes. Evening shift this time. The boss and I try and split the shifts between us.'

'We could maybe meet when this is all over,' she said in a dull voice. 'It would be fun for you to meet the boy.'

Ari Thór had no idea what to say, so he kept quiet. He felt that he had made it as clear as he could that he was not prepared to get to know the child before it was clear who the father might be.

'We'll see,' he said as politely as he could.

It wasn't worth cutting her off too abruptly, however much these calls got on his nerves. She could easily be the mother of his child. He felt a cold sweat on his forehead, and tried to push from his mind the thought that he could have a child he had never met in Blönduós.

'It's not easy,' she said, her voice still low. 'It's not easy to be alone.'

'I'm seeing someone else,' Ari Thór answered. 'If the boy is mine, then I'll do my bit bringing him up. But you have to understand ...' He tried his best to sound reasonable. 'You have to understand that it's best not to go into this until there's a definite result. We agreed before that I wouldn't meet him unless it's confirmed that I'm his father.'

'Yeah, yeah. I understand. Of course I do,' she said, and at the same moment he heard the sound of a child crying in the background. His stomach turned over. This could be his son. 'He's awake, so I need to go. Bye,' she said and put the phone down.

Ari Thór sat as if he were welded to the chair, imagining the little boy he had never seen.

Ísrún had called earlier in the day and told him quickly about the visit to the late Maríus's brother Nikulás. After that she had emailed him part of the recording she had made. The news of the adoption took Ari Thór by surprise. Somewhere, Hédinn had a cousin he knew nothing about, assuming the man was still alive. He knew that he ought to let Hédinn know about this development as soon as possible. He had asked Ísrún if the boy was maybe the young man in the photograph, but realised right away that he could not possibly be.

'That was my first thought as well,' Ísrún had said. 'But the boy in the picture is too old to be him.' Then she had come up with an interesting theory. 'The little boy in the picture ... is it possible that's not Hédinn?'

'What do you mean?' Ari Thór asked.

'We've assumed that the child in the photograph *is* Hédinn, and that's the most obvious explanation. But it could be another child and the picture could have been taken before Hédinn was born.'

'But there's no doubt that the picture was taken in Hédinsfjördur,' Ari Thór said doubtfully.

'Maybe before they had moved there. Even a couple of years previously.'

'So you're suggesting—'

'Yes,' she said, interrupting him. 'The baby could have been Maríus and Jórunn's son, the one who was adopted. He was born around 1950. There's nothing to say the picture couldn't have been taken then. The house in Hédinsfjördur was there at that time, wasn't it?'

'Yes, the house was there then,' Ari Thór replied. 'But it's not likely they would have travelled all the way to Siglufjördur and then to Hédinsfjördur with a small baby, is it? It could explain why the young man wasn't living with them when Jórunn died, though. Maybe he didn't ever live with them in Hédinsfjördur and never knew Hédinn at all,' he said. He was still doubtful but was grateful for any new possibility.

Ísrún then changed the subject, telling him that she was working on another story – a murder that seemed to have repercussions all the way to the top of the government.

'But you keep that to yourself,' she said playfully. 'It's all off the record, but be sure not to miss the news tonight,' she told him and added that, because of it, she would have to postpone the interview yet again.

Ari Thór was still smarting from his conversation with the red-headed girl, when he remembered Ísrún's recommendation. So he turned on the station's rickety old TV set just in time for the evening bulletin, and saw the unusual spectacle of the Prime Minister being taken by surprise. He had little interest in politics, but had often seen Marteinn Helgason on the screen – a charming and reassuring presence, always reasonable and always with the answers at his fingertips; a man born to be a politician. This time, however, he seemed to have little enthusiasm for talking about the death of Snorri Ellertsson, even though it was no secret that they had been friends.

Once the news had finished, Ari Thór made a call to the Reverend Eggert, Siglufjördur's priest. They knew each other slightly – the policemen and the priest in a little town would always have things to discuss. The first time they had met, Eggert had heard of Ari Thór's abandoned theology studies and the 'Reverend Ari Thór' nickname, and had assumed that he was a religious man with an interest in church affairs. He could not have been further from the truth. Ari Thór held to no faith, but instead held a bitter anger towards higher powers, if there were any, having lost his parents in his youth.

Ari Thór had never troubled to correct the priest's misunderstanding about him, and the Reverend Eggert often mentioned, with apparent surprise, that Ari Thór was never to be seen in church. In fact, Ari Thór had only once been inside Siglufjördur's church, and that had been to attend the funeral of the town's most famous son, Hrólfur Kristjánsson. Hrólfur had fallen to his death at the local theatre soon after Ari Thór had moved to Siglufjördur. Ari Thór had stubbornly refused to accept that it was merely an accident and this had marked the beginning of his first major case.

The Reverend Eggert seemed pleased to hear from Ari Thór and showed an immediate interest in his questions; he was always ready to talk about Hédinsfjördur, he said.

'You can drop by for a chat if you like,' he said.

Ari Thór thought for a moment. 'Sure. You're well, are you?'

The priest laughed. 'Perfectly fine. You think some virus is going to attack a man of God like me? I've never been better.'

Ari Thór decided to take him up on his invitation, leaving the police car parked outside the station and setting off for the priest's house on foot. It was a beautiful night for a walk; there was a chill in the air, but the sky was unusually clear. At this time of year, the weather was notoriously unpredictable, with some days bringing sunshine, rain and snow all together at once.

Siglufjördur had always been a peaceful place, but now it was too quiet. There was not a soul to be seen on the streets. It was as if Ari Thór was the only inhabitant of a ghost town. With nobody daring to go outside, there was no sign of life and the silence was so complete that it was disquieting. Ari Thór walked along the sea road – his favourite route, with its exquisite views over the fjord, calm yet majestic. The houses he passed were colourful, some quite old and some of them newly painted. He was pleased to see that the town was going through something of a rejuvenation.

The priest's house was on a hill not far from the town's hospital, a short walk from the police station. It was surrounded by trees, and, as Ari Thór approached, between the dark trunks and branches he saw a light switched on behind one of the windows. The priest had never married and, for the thirty-five years he had been Siglufjördur's parish priest, he had lived alone. Now in his sixties, he had been born and brought up in the town.

Ari Thór knocked and, as he waited for the priest to answer, gazed along the length of the fjord, the little town and its imposing church standing out against the surrounding darkness. The stillness was suddenly broken by a flock of birds – probably snow buntings – that came from nowhere, swooped into Ari Thór's line of sight, then vanished into the night as quickly as they had appeared.

The door swung open and the priest stood in the doorway.

'Come in, young man.'

The Reverend Eggert had aged well. He was a tall, slim man with a distinctive face under thick, grey hair. He was wearing flannel trousers and a checked shirt, the top button undone, and a pair of old-fashioned spectacles hung on a cord around his neck.

He showed Ari Thór to his office, sat at his desk and waved his guest to an old chair.

'Keeping busy these days?' he asked cheerfully.

'You could say that,' Ari Thór agreed, taking a seat.

'It seems to be almost over, I'm delighted to say,' the priest said. 'What happened to poor Rósa was terrible. Did you know her?'

'Not personally. But she'd been a nurse here for years, hadn't she?'

'She had,' Eggert said. 'But you know Sandra, don't you?'

Ari Thór nodded, aware that every snippet of news was passed on in a small community. 'I go and see her sometimes.'

'I met her today. She's down with normal flu, but serious all the same.'

It was certainly a relief to hear that Sandra had not caught the lethal infection.

'I hear there are few people who know as much as you do about Hédinsfjördur,' Ari Thór said, changing the subject.

'Yes,' Eggert said. 'What do you want to know?'

'I'm looking into an old case – in between other assignments,' he replied, hesitating.

'The death?' the priest asked. 'Jórunn?' he continued before Ari Thór could even nod his head.

'That's right,' Ari Thór confirmed. There was no need to encourage the Reverend Eggert to talk.

'I know about the case, of course. Gudmundur and Gudfinna were the last inhabitants of Hédinsfjördur. They had lived in Siglufjördur first and then they moved back here after that terrible event. The other people living there with them were Jórunn and ...' He paused and thought. 'Yes. Jórunn and Maríus, if my memory is correct.'

'They were sisters, Gudfinna and Jórunn,' Ari Thór managed to add.

'You don't need to remind me,' Eggert said sharply, but he smiled again. 'That's the thing about being interested in a place like Hédins-fjördur, somewhere few people have lived over the years – it didn't take long to get to know its history and stories about the people who lived there.'

'Did you ever live there yourself?'

'Good heavens, no. It's far too remote. Siglufjördur's isolated enough for me,' he laughed. 'I'd have died of misery and loneliness there, just as poor Jórunn did.'

Ari Thór was about to ask if the priest was sure of this, but kept quiet and let him continue.

'I visited Hédinsfjördur a few times before the tunnel was dug, normally on foot. It's an excellent hike. I went there by sea once, many years ago, when it was decided that a service ought to be held there. I was the parish priest here and so it fell to me. It was an unusual service because the fjord was deserted, but we thought it would be a good idea to do this to remember those who had lived there in the past and the priests who had held services there centuries ago. People from Siglufjördur flocked there by boat to attend the event.' He lapsed into silence to get his breath back.

The ceiling light was switched off but the bright light from the desk lamp was enough to illuminate the room, giving it a warmth and making it a comfortable place to be, especially when Ari Thór glanced through the window at the darkness beyond. Books were stacked high on the desk. He peered at the titles while the priest was speaking and saw that, while a few of the books were theological works, most covered other subjects. The shelves were also filled with books, most of them carefully bound. He wondered for a moment what would become of this collection once the priest had gone to meet his maker. The old man was a childless bachelor, a role that maybe he had chosen for himself. The thought of the little boy in Blönduós who might or might not have a rootless father in Siglufjördur came to mind, and his heart missed a beat.

The Reverend Eggert stood up quickly, and the expression on his face showed that rapid movement did not come easily to him, although he seemed to be a man in good health and fitness. Ari Thór was taken by surprise.

'Young man,' he said with a grin. 'We can't sit here where it's warm and light to talk about Hédinsfjördur. You have to experience it,' he said in a tone of voice that Ari Thór could imagine him using to address a full congregation.

Eggert took an overcoat from a hook on the back door, and swung the door open, letting the darkness creep in.

'Come on. We can take the jeep,' he said. Then he stopped and looked Ari Thór up and down. 'You're dressed warmly enough; it's not that cold tonight.'

The priest's jeep was fairly new and even in the dim lights from the house, Ari Thór could see that it was bright red. The dashboard thermometer showed it was just above freezing, but it felt colder. Ari Thór wished he was in bed, under a warm duvet; it was all he could do to avoid shaking. Maybe he was one of those southern types who feel the cold, still unused to the northern climate.

It was a starlit night, although the lights of the town left the stars indistinct in the sky. Ari Thór looked out of the car's window towards the mountains, but the slopes were nowhere to be seen, just the darkness and the stars. They were halfway to the Hédinsfjördur tunnel when a thought struck him.

'We can't go to Hédinsfjördur. We're not supposed to go beyond the town limits.'

The Reverend Eggert roared with laughter. 'Here we are: one of us God's representative and the other the representative of law and order. Who's going to stop us?'

Ari Thór had no argument with which to counter the priest's logic. And, as if to prove his point, Eggert put his foot down and they accelerated to a speed well above the legal limit. Ari Thór decided not to argue the assumption out with him; he knew that the Reverend Eggert was probably right.

They drove in silence for a long time. They were in the tunnel when Ari Thór next spoke. 'It's completely dark over there, isn't it? Did you bring a torch?'

The priest snorted. 'The car's lights will do,' he said. 'Don't you worry.'

Ari Thór was right. The only light in Hédinsfjördur emanated from the tunnels, spilling out from the entrances leading to Siglufjördur on one side and to Ólafsfjördur on the other. Shortly after they left the Siglufjördur tunnel, Eggert drove off the road and brought the car to a halt. A private road had been laid most of the way down to the lagoon, but it had been closed off. Eggert got out of the car, leaving the car's lights on.

Ari Thór stepped down from the jeep.

'Come on. We'll go over this way,' Reverend Eggert said, more used to getting out of the high wheelbase vehicle than his passenger was. He pointed to a set of wooden steps that led up and over the fence and was over them in a moment, with Ari Thór following behind.

The jeep's headlights illuminated much of the track, but not all the way to the lagoon, and nowhere near as far as the little point of land on its western shore where the ruins of the farmhouse stood. Ari Thór had never walked to the ruins before, but had often noticed the wreck of the house when passing through Hédinsfjördur. The new tunnels had been opened relatively recently. One carried the road from Siglufjördur into uninhabited Hédinsfjördur, and the other took it on to neighbouring Ólafsfjordur, a town of around 800 people. These new tunnels had made it much easier than before for the people of Siglufjördur to reach the largest town in the north of Iceland, Akureyri. And, naturally, this also meant that Siglufjördur had been opened up to many more tourists.

They walked side by side in the glare of the headlights, their shadows a step ahead of them, tall and menacing. Ari Thór listened as the priest spoke.

'Can you imagine it?' he asked gently. 'You don't even need to close your eyes. You can hardly see a thing anyway. We have the tunnels now, but those poor people – Jórunn and Maríus, Gudfinna and Gudmundur – they had to cross the mountain on foot.' He raised an arm towards the range of crags on the western side of the fjord. 'That's the Hestsskard pass up there. That's the best route out, but even on a mild winter's night like tonight, you'd think twice about making that kind of crossing.'

Ari Thór's eyes followed the priest's pointing finger. To begin with, he could see only vague outlines in places, nothing reminiscent of mountain slopes, just something that looked like shadowy creatures. The sight made it easy enough for him to understand how folk tales had had such a tenacious grip on the minds of Icelanders through the ages. Here he was, accompanied by a priest, with the lights of the car, as far as they reached, bright behind them, and an easy route out of this place to either Siglufjördur or Ólafsfjördur – yet still a heavy disquiet inhabited him. The cold hand of solitude rested on his shoulder, the gloom sent shivers down his back and the darkness made him want to shut his eyes rather than look around him. The certainty of the familiar blackness as his eyelids closed was more comfortable than whatever might be there in the unknown night.

The priest stopped at the fringe of the bright arc cast by the car's lights, the point where it no longer illuminated the track in front of them. The road ahead twisted and the next part of it was hidden from Ari Thór's sight, although he knew that if he were to carry on, he would come to the lagoon with the open sea on its far side.

The Reverend Eggert continued speaking.

'They were farming here, those two poor couples. People doubted that they would be able to do it. Some people are born farmers. Some aren't. There's some fishing in the lagoon. The fishing rights came with the land, as it borders the lagoon. It's a sport these days, of course. I know they had a small boat as well, so they could sail round to Siglufjördur if they needed to and weather permitting.'

'I don't suppose they had electricity,' Ari Thór said, to contribute something to the conversation, although the answer was obvious.

'Good grief,' the priest said. 'There's no electricity here, and no telephones. I gather they had a CB radio set in the house. It was a primitive setup, even though this wasn't that long ago, really. The whole thing seemed to have this sense of determination to have a damned adventure. That's all it was about, as far as I can tell.

Gudmundur could afford it. He was a wealthy man by the standards of the day.'

Ari Thór's eyes were starting to adjust to the darkness. He could make out the snow-covered mountainsides. Looking up, the sight of the star-studded heavens was before him, the twinkling Milky Way an unusual sight for someone who had rarely stepped outside urban areas.

He reflected that the starlight had travelled unimaginable distances to appear there for him, in an abandoned fjord on the most northerly coast of Iceland.

'You said earlier that Jórunn died of loneliness and fear of the dark,' he said, turning to the priest. 'What did you mean by that?'

'General opinion was that she took her own life,' Eggert said in a low voice, standing motionless just beyond the reach of the car's lights, his shadow eaten up by the darkness beyond.

Ari Thór's thoughts went back to the police report stating that Jórunn's death had been accidental; a convenient conclusion. The local gossip had decided differently – that it had been suicide. It was less palatable, but more plausible, he thought. The third possibility, murder, was a far more disturbing prospect, but Ari Thór felt that he could not rule it out. He hadn't forgotten Hédinn's words: that there had been nothing to confirm whether it had been suicide or murder.

'Heaven help me,' the priest continued. 'I can't bring myself to justify suicide. Life is sacred, whatever the circumstances, but maybe I can say ...' He hesitated for a moment before continuing, haltingly. 'I can say that maybe I can understand how she felt. I suppose that's why I brought you over here tonight, so you can put yourself in her position. You're a city kid, just as she was. Don't you feel uncomfortable here?'

Ari Thór made no reply. He felt far from comfortable, but didn't want to admit it. He was still cold, the night air made even more chilling by the enveloping darkness; it seemed almost to press on his chest, threatening suffocation.

Even in a place as remote as Hédinsfjördur, however, silence was absent. There was a distant mutter of surf, muffled but unmistakeable. It was as if the crash of waves on the shore was calling to him alone. He wanted to walk on further, out into the darkness, to see how far he could go.

Before he knew it, he had set off, with the priest hurrying after him.

'We ought to be careful. You don't want to fall down and hurt yourself in this darkness.' Eggert said in the same low voice, so that the sound of the surf almost swallowed his words.

'Suppose I told you they hadn't been alone here?' Ari Thór said.

'What do you mean?' The priest asked, his voice quavering. 'Gudfinna had a son, of course,' he added.

'I don't mean Hédinn,' Ari Thór said.

'Well, what on earth do you mean, then? This is hardly the time or the place for ghost stories.'

'It's no ghost story,' Ari Thór said grimly. 'Even though it sounds far-fetched. Do ghosts show up on film?'

They were close to the shore of the lagoon, the lights of the car far behind them. It was almost impossible to see anything so Ari Thór crept slowly forward, conscious that they were on a road and that there could be steep banks leading down on either side.

'Don't be ridiculous,' the priest said sharply.

Ari Thór decided to go for the facts.

'A picture has come to light of the two couples with little Hédinn in the arms of a young man, a teenager, more like.'

'Maybe someone who was just passing by,' Reverend Eggert said.

'I doubt that many people passed through here,' Ari Thór said coldly. 'And not everyone would be allowed to hold—'

But he was unable to finish before the priest interrupted him. 'Well, you're right, few people came this way. But I recall that Delía came here at around that time.'

They stood still. Ari Thór was really starting to feel the cold now. He would have liked to go straight back to the jeep. But he waited, wanting to give the priest a chance to finish what he was saying.

'Who is Delía?' he asked, guessing that the priest was expecting the question.

'She's a few years older than I am. Her father was a photographer and did some filming with a cine-camera as well. She never went on to study anything after leaving school, wasn't interested in anything but cameras. She stayed in Siglufjördur and spent a lot of time taking pictures and filming. She took over her father's photography business, but that fizzled out as more and more people moved away. She went to live in the south, and then moved back here to retire.'

'And she visited Hédinsfjördur?'

'I recall she once told me she came over here to make the most of the winter scenery. That's right – it's coming back to me now. She met Jórunn. You never know, she might still have some pictures. Go and see her tomorrow. And now I think we should be on our way, don't you?'

Ari Thór nodded and then realised that the priest probably couldn't see him. 'Let's go, shall we?' he muttered.

Eggert walked briskly towards the jeep.

Ari Thór made to set off after him, but then he stopped for a moment to turn and look back over the fjord and the star-bright sky, drinking in the beauty of the heavens. At one point, a few months earlier, Ari Thór had actually gone over to Hédinsfjördur in the dead of winter to look out for the northern lights. He had the good fortune to spot these elusive wonders and had stood stock still by the side of road, in total awe of this natural phenomenon, for a few breathtaking minutes. He could almost envisage them now.

When he turned back again, the priest had disappeared from sight.

Ari Thór knew that Eggert was not far away, but all the same, and against his own better judgement, he felt a chill of fear. He didn't want to call out to ask the priest to wait. He couldn't let it be known that he, a police officer, was afraid of the dark.

He crept forward slowly, and fished his phone from his pocket to try and make use of its light. But the glaring beam just made the surrounding darkness deeper.

The worst part was the lights of the jeep. They had been invaluable before, when they were behind him, but now they were dazzling, making it impossible to make out where the twisting track led.

He realised too late that he had stepped off the road. He lost his footing and fell, tumbling a few feet down the bank onto the cold earth. He had instinctively shut his eyes as he fell, and finding himself on the ground, he opened them and found himself staring at the mouth of a culvert that ran under the track. He thanked his lucky stars that he had not hit his head on it. He struggled to his feet with difficulty, sore and bruised, with a stinging pain in his knee. He climbed back onto the road and stumbled towards the car. This time he managed to keep to the track and found the priest already behind the wheel.

'I was wondering where you had got to,' he said, and looked at Ari Thór's hand. 'What on earth happened to you?'

Ari Thór hadn't noticed the blood seeping from the back of his right hand. He had put it out to break his fall and it had caught on the stones at the track's edge.

'I tripped and fell,' he said shortly.

The priest nodded as if he'd expected as much. The journey back to Siglufjördur passed in silence.

18

The call came from Sunna's sister.

Heida lived in Denmark, was ten years older than Sunna, and was single and childless. The two sisters had been brought up in Reykjavík. Sunna rarely talked about her sister, but Róbert had the feeling that Heida had never quite found a comfortable niche for herself in life. She had tried any number of professions, but had been unemployed and living in Denmark for a while.

Róbert had met her twice and both times he had found it difficult to form any kind of connection with her, feeling certain that she had no liking for him. He decided it was most likely that Heida thought Sunna could have done better for herself.

Now Heida had been in Iceland for two weeks. He was sure she was short of money and was scrounging from her parents, who had actually now left Iceland for a holiday abroad. She still hadn't found time to meet Sunna, Róbert and little Kjartan, but the sisters had agreed to meet at a downtown coffee shop that morning, taking Kjartan with them. After that, the plan was that the little boy would stay with Róbert at home while Sunna was at a rehearsal.

They still hadn't found anyone to look after Kjartan during the day, although they were considering it. So far it wasn't urgent. Sunna's working hours were flexible, as were Róbert's study times, and he didn't worry too much about missing the occasional lecture. The boy also spent time with Breki, so things generally worked out.

Róbert lay in bed. His cold was worse so he hadn't made the effort to go to his class. His instincts were also working overtime, telling him that their home had to be guarded against the unknown presence he was convinced now threatened it.

Now, though, after Heida's call, he realised that he had made a huge mistake.

He had let himself be fooled.

He should have put his energies into protecting his family, not their home.

'What the hell do you mean?' he yelled furiously as Heida, a woman he hardly knew, told him about the shocking turn of events.

'Kjartan's disappeared,' she said in a flat voice. 'Someone took him from the pushchair.'

'Disappeared? Where's Sunna?'

By now he was on his feet, pulling on his jeans and a shirt, with the phone still to his ear.

'She's right here, crying, screaming, waiting for the police. She's in no state to speak on the phone.'

19

Ísrún could feel her energy ebbing away with each day that passed. She longed for a break between shifts. The newsroom pressure was enough to test even people with robust health, with its long shifts and the constant activity from morning to night.

She pushed herself to do one more day, forcing herself out of her bed in spite of the temptation to call in sick, which would have only been the truth, but she couldn't bring herself to hand the Snorri Ellertsson story to someone else. The interview the previous day with the Prime Minister had attracted attention, with bloggers and social media going wild, followed by the Prime Minister's assistant, a young and talented woman with party connections, trying to contact Ísrún. She knew who was calling and let the phone ring, deciding to let the young woman sweat for a while.

Her illness was taking its toll, as it did most days. Occasionally, when she was drowning in work, she could forget it for a while, this damned sickness, or syndrome as the doctor called it. It was extremely rare, he had told her, as if that was supposed to be some kind of consolation. And it had turned out that her grandmother had suffered from this 'extremely rare condition' too. The old lady was thought to have died from cancer brought on by smoking. But the doctor had been through her medical records and had come to the conclusion that the cause of death was the same syndrome that Ísrún was now suffering from. The results of further research supported the theory that the disorder was genetic, and Ísrún had been offered counselling.

During these sessions, it became apparent that the illness could be inherited by her own children, if she should choose to have any.

The tumour Ísrún herself had developed was benign and had been removed with surgery. Somehow she had managed to keep her condition a secret from both her family and her colleagues. But it was impossible for Ísrún to predict how the illness would develop, whether or not more tumours would appear or what their effects might be; in addition to which, further side effects could also be part of her condition.

It was all too much to take some days.

Ísrún had turned up early for the morning conference but listened to the discussion with only limited interest, her mind on her own assignments. She found it a welcome relief to be under María's protective wing, with a free choice of assignments and without having to cater to Ívar's whims.

Following the meeting, she decided to try and finally set up a meeting with Snorri's sister, Nanna. She thought she should follow up on her police contact's recommendation, and take a chance on finding out what the email he had sent her on the day he died had been about. Nanna's phone was switched off, however, and as she had no registered landline number, Ísrún's best option was to knock on her door. It was maybe pushing things too far, but she had done worse things.

She enlisted Rúrik to be there with the camera, although she had him wait in the car while she walked up alone to the low block of flats in Kópavogur and rang Nanna's doorbell.

Ísrún tried to look away from the intercom so as not to be recognisable on camera. She waited and when there was no response, she rang a second time, but again with no reply.

'Are you alright to hang around for a while?' she asked Rúrik, getting back in the car.

'I don't really have time,' he replied. 'You're not the only one doing a report for the evening bulletin.'

The upshot was that he took a taxi back, while Ísrún continued her vigil in the news car. It was a bitingly cold day outside and even starting the engine and turning on the car's heater wasn't enough to drive out the chill. Some days the cold air felt refreshing, but today no amount of positive thinking could make the shivers go away.

She took the opportunity to move the car, clearly marked with the TV station's logo, further from the drive leading to the block.

She had been able to find pictures of Nanna online and watched out for any signs of activity at the block of flats, hoping to see her. But almost an hour passed before anything happened. In the meantime, Ívar had tried to call her, but she had decided that she had better things to do than reply to him.

Finally, an old black Mercedes came to a halt outside the block. Ísrún sat up, immediately recognising the man behind the wheel. She hoped that neither he nor his passengers had noticed the TV station's car.

As he got out of the Mercedes, Ísrún was able to see Ellert more clearly. It was as if he had aged dramatically – the respected statesman transformed into a grief-stricken old man. She recognised the woman walking behind him, her eyes puffy with tears, as his daughter, Nanna. He put an arm around her as they made their way to the door. Ellert's wife, Klara, who had occasionally made headlines back when her husband had been in politics, was last out of the car and hurried to catch them up, her face noticeably stony.

Ísrún decided to strike while the iron was hot, and was quickly out of the car, making her appearance in the lobby just as Nanna was trying to unlock the door to the stairwell.

The family looked at each other, and Klara seemed to be the first to realise that Ísrún was a journalist.

She frowned. 'We're not talking to the media,' she said in a harsh voice.

'It's not you I was hoping to speak to,' Ísrún said. 'I came here for a word with Nanna.'

Nanna stared back wordlessly.

'I'm alone, no cameraman,' she said, without mentioning that the recorder in her pocket was running.

'We would prefer some consideration,' Ellert told her in a friendly, almost fatherly, tone of voice. 'I hope you can appreciate that.'

His voice was low, but all the same, it filled the lobby and for a moment there was silence. There were good reasons this man had spent his life in politics. Everyone took notice when he spoke.

But Ísrún was not inclined to give up right away.

'I was hoping I might be able to help you. Someone ran your son down,' she said. And then, glancing at Nanna, 'Your brother. These cases are frequently solved more easily when the media play a part along with the police. Your brother sent you an email shortly before he died. I gather the message has given the police a trail to follow.'

Nanna nodded, her gaze distant. 'He was going over to Kópavogur,' she mumbled. 'Something about a studio. He was sure he was going to be offered a recording contract.'

'This is none of her damned business,' Klara snapped, turning to her daughter.

But Nanna continued as if she had not heard her mother's objection. 'The police couldn't find a studio anywhere on the road where the taxi dropped him off. Someone had brought him there to kill him.'

Now Klara's fury got the better of her. 'Snorri's always the victim, isn't he? Nobody killed him. He took his own life the day he decided drugs are more important than family.'

Despite herself, Ísrún couldn't help an inward smile as she stepped back into the knife-edged wind outside. That night's top story was in the can.

20

Róbert felt as if the earth was literally disappearing from under his feet.

He ended the call the second Heida had told him which coffee house they were at and rushed out, not even taking time to pull on a coat over his white t-shirt. The sharp wind stung his bare arms but he was so numb that he hardly noticed. He realised that he had left the keys to the car inside, but didn't trouble to go back for them. He could run to the café on Laugavegur where Sunna and Heida had arranged to meet. The café where someone had snatched Kjartan ...

He had practically become the boy's father, and now he felt nauseous at the thought that someone had taken an innocent child from his pushchair.

He ran down the slope beside the old graveyard and out onto Sudurgata with the wind in his face.

Breki.

That was the only thought in his mind. It had to be Breki. The bastard.

Róbert felt a sudden chill. He ran down past the city hall and was almost hit by a bus on Vonarstræti, when he remembered the cold he had been trying to fight off. Being outside in this weather was hardly going to help. But he didn't care, he had to get to Sunna as quickly as he could; he had to find Kjartan.

Maybe it would be just as well if it had been Breki who had taken the boy. Breki would never do him any harm.

Róbert had never expected the custody battle to go as far as it had. Breki and Sunna had fought bitterly, but Breki had always stayed within the law. They had accepted that the courts would have the last word. But now, maybe Breki was fearing the worst from the courts – that the judgement would go against him. The gnawing uncertainty could have been too much for him.

Róbert was starting to think more clearly, though. The adrenaline, the cold and the shock made him visualise another possibility – one that was infinitely worse.

21

It didn't take Ísrún long to come up with a draft of the story about Snorri. The angle was that he had been enticed to the scene of the crime, which was a fine scoop. The only problem was that she was short of visual material to go with it. There was no interview. She would have to use yesterday's footage again. The story was a good one, although it would have been more suitable for the front page of a newspaper than as a TV news item.

She decided it was as well to check it out with her contact in the police. It was likely he wouldn't want to say anything, but he might be able to warn her if she was on the wrong track.

He answered her call right away.

'I spoke to Snorri's sister,' she said, not bothering to say who was calling, and gave him the details of the conversation with Nanna. 'It'll be our lead story tonight,' she added proudly.

'I don't think so, somehow,' he said shortly, taking her by surprise.

Had Nanna lied to her, she wondered, frowning. *Hell.* It was just as well she hadn't mentioned the story to Ívar.

'Have I misunderstood something?' she asked.

'Not at all,' he replied. 'I'm not worried about what you have to say about Snorri.'

Ísrún sighed with relief. She knew her contact well enough to realise that this was confirmation, albeit indirect, that she was on the right path.

'What I mean is that someone kidnapped a small child on

Laugavegur this morning,' her contact continued. 'It's still unclear what exactly happened, but I reckon that Snorri Ellertsson pales into insignificance compared to that.'

'A child?' Ísrún asked in astonishment. 'You mean a baby's disappeared?'

'That's right.'

'Good heavens, I can't believe it! I mean, no one kidnaps a baby in Iceland ... This is really shocking. Do you know the details?'

'No, I can't tell you any more. It's not a case I'm involved with, but there's bound to be a statement later.'

'I'll look out for that, for sure. I hope it turns out well. The poor parents ...' Then she added: 'Any progress on Snorri?'

'Nothing, unfortunately. The taxi driver doesn't remember seeing anyone about. We've been going through CCTV footage from the district, but no luck so far.'

As soon as she put the phone down, Ísrún told Ívar about the child's abduction and the latest developments on the Snorri Ellertsson case.

He had also heard some vague reports about the missing child, and she told him she was working on both, leaving him no room to manoeuvre and give an exciting story like this to someone else. She had more than enough to do now, plus she was close to running out of time to get the interview with Ari Thór. She sighed as she booked some studio time for that evening.

On top of everything else she had to do, there were emails from both of her parents that were long overdue her replies. Each in their own way, was trying to use Ísrún as a go-between to get their marriage back on track. She was more than happy to help, but found herself short of both time and patience, tempted to forward the messages to each of them and encourage them to sort their affairs out for themselves.

Ísrún also had a doctor's appointment that day, something she had tried to avoid thinking about. She had almost thought that she might forget to go to it. It was a vain hope.

She used the time before her appointment to make enquiries into the missing child, all unsuccessful.

'Take a seat, Ísrún,' the doctor said as she entered his surgery with a sour expression on her face. She had been kept waiting for a quarter of an hour past her appointment time and was itching to get away – more so than usual when she had to go to the doctor.

'How are you feeling?'

'Not bad,' she said, giving him the same answer she always gave.

The place was colder than it needed to be, she felt, wondering if she really wanted to see a doctor who couldn't heat his surgery properly. Or maybe it was just the frosty atmosphere of the place that had this effect on her: the plastic film on the windows to ensure privacy in the ground floor surgery; the silver-grey desk; the tidy bookshelves; the cool, aluminium-framed chair and the shabby white bench.

The doctor had sent her for an MRI scan to check on the possible appearance of any more tumours. She waited nervously for the results to see if her condition was improving or worsening.

However, the results still weren't available, and his questions were the standard ones, asking whether or not she had been aware of any of the symptoms he had asked her to watch out for. She sat impassively and answered one question after another.

'Have you spoken to your parents about this yet?' he asked finally, as he always did. She knew where this was going to lead.

'No. I'm waiting for the right moment.'

'I'd like your father to come in for a check-up, as I've repeatedly told you. We need to know if he has this condition too.'

She muttered something inaudible.

The doctor waited for a proper response, but Ísrún also knew how to wait.

'Well, I'll bear it in mind,' she said at last. 'But, you know, he's getting old and I don't want to worry him. And if he has inherited this … condition … then it certainly hasn't done him any harm.'

The doctor nodded, stood up and placed a paternal hand on

Ísrún's shoulder. 'Think it over,' he said. 'You can book yourself another appointment at reception. I'll see you in a month and we'll see then how things look. But I'll call you as soon as I get the scan results,' he said. 'I'm optimistic, I can tell you,' he added when she had risen to her feet.

He always said that when she left the surgery, and she had no way of knowing if he said the same thing to every patient.

The doctor always asked her to take it easy, too, but she ignored that advice, hurried to the car and was back at the news studio shortly afterwards.

The story of the kidnapped child had broken and was all over the news outlets. There had still been no press conference, but the police had issued a statement: a young woman had been sitting in a café on Laugavegur with her sister, leaving her eighteen-month-old child asleep in its pram outside. The child had been removed from the pram sometime between ten and a quarter past. Witnesses were requested to come forward, and, according to the police statement, the investigation was making progress, supported by CCTV footage from the area. But the child had not been located.

Ísrún felt a shiver as she wrote the story. Was Iceland no longer the friendly, safe society it had once been? Would this particular Icelandic custom of allowing children to sleep outside in their prams now suddenly die out?

Even hardened newsroom colleagues seemed stunned by the news.

She tried time and again to reach her police contact, but with no success.

Eventually, with the time getting on for seven o'clock in the evening, he called her back. 'You're going to have to stop calling for a while,' he said. 'I'm tied up and I can't say anything.'

'Have you found the boy?'

'No.'

'Who are the parents? Do you have a suspect?'

'Sorry. I can't say anything. This is massively sensitive, Ísrún. We daren't take any chances, and we can't have any leaks. We have to find this child. That's an absolute priority.'

With that, he ended the call. That was something he rarely did – cut her off like that. There was no doubt that everyone was on edge.

The story would have to go out as it stood, as practically a rehashed police press release. It was something Ísrún had always disliked, but this time she agreed with her police contact. The little boy's safety was more important than any scoop.

22

Tómas had taken the night shift, so Ari Thór had finally slept well and arrived for his morning shift refreshed. People were starting to be seen venturing out of doors around the town. The most coura- geous ones, or the most foolhardy, had ignored the risk the infection posed and gone for a walk in the cold, fresh winter air. But there was no talking on street corners and the shops remained shut. People continued to avoid each other under the present conditions.

Ari Thór and Kristín had a talk on the phone that morning.

'You're doing well, Ari, aren't you?' she asked, clearly concerned.

'Of course, and you? Are they keeping you busy?'

'The workload is insane. Also, I try to do as many shifts as I can, you know, since you are not around. I feel quite lonely just sitting around at home waiting for them to take Siglufjördur out of quarantine.'

'It'll be soon, I'm sure,' Ari Thór said. 'There's more people on the streets today than yesterday, it's all becoming normal again.'

'Be careful, OK?'

'Of course.'

'And don't engage in any heroics, do you hear me, Ari?'

'I promise.'

There was little chance of him breaking that promise. His instincts for self-preservation were stretched to their limits and he was deter- mined to do as little as he could. He felt most comfortable at home, but when he had to be on duty, he tried to immerse himself in the

Hédinsfjördur files to forget about his other current worries. But his investigation into what had happened to Jórunn had ground to a halt.

He had tried to note down the main facts of the case as they appeared to him. A well-off couple from Siglufjördur, Gudfinna and Gudmundur, decided to try setting up home in Hédinsfjördur in 1955, hoping to inhabit the abandoned fjord once again. Jórunn and Maríus, who had lived in Siglufjördur for a year and who were not financially well off, moved with them to the house in Hédinsfjördur. Towards the end of 1956 or in early 1957, Maríus took a photograph of the group of them, plus an unidentified young man holding baby Hédinn – if the baby was Hédinn. The date of this photograph assumed that the child in the picture was Hédinn. The fjord was abandoned once more in the spring of 1957.

Ari Thór also knew that, before moving to the north of Iceland, Jórunn and Maríus had a son, born around 1950. Unable to support a family, they had no choice but to put the child up for adoption. There had clearly been no support from Gudfinna and Gudmundur, Ari Thór decided, even though they had been fairly wealthy.

There was no knowledge of where the child had gone after being adopted, but he would have been six or seven years old when the picture was taken, which ruled him out as the young man in the photograph.

Brought up in Reykjavík, Jórunn was unused to weather conditions in the north, and, according to the police files, she had found it difficult to cope with the snow and the isolation.

One evening in March 1957, during a heavy snowstorm, she drank poison and subsequently died. She admitted, according to the testimony of the others, to having put poison in her coffee by mistake. General opinion was that this version of events was unlikely, and the suicide theory was more widely believed.

This was a case that would in all likelihood never be solved. It was even possible that the original investigation had reached the correct conclusion; that Jórunn had taken poison by mistake, as unlikely as that sounded.

Ari Thór decided that the priest's suggestion – to pay a visit to Delía the photographer – was a good one. If she had travelled to Hédinsfjördur to take pictures of the winter landscape and had met Jórunn there, as Reverend Eggert believed, then she might have some nugget of useful information.

The priest had repeated his suggestion as they parted after their night-time visit to Hédinsfjördur a couple of days before, although Ari Thór wondered if it would be wise to go and see her with the town still under quarantine.

'Don't you worry about that,' the Reverend Eggert had cheerfully assured him. 'Delía is scared stiff and hasn't been out of the house for days. She lives alone and there's no chance of catching anything from her.'

The priest had told Ari Thór where she lived and that morning, in the middle of what would have been a routine patrol, if there had been anything that needed to be patrolled, he decided to knock on her door.

It didn't take long to find the place – a small, colourless house clad in corrugated-iron sheets. It stood between much larger and more imposing buildings, like a delicate flower surrounded by shrubs.

Ari Thór parked the police jeep in front of the house. The curtains were all drawn and there was no sign of life. He looked around, and saw that the town as a whole was lacking many signs of life, although a figure could be seen peering out of the window of one of the larger houses nearby, disappearing into the gloom inside as soon as Ari Thór made eye contact with them. There was nothing better than a visit from the police to start the gossip mill – apart from a visit from the ambulance, of course.

He rang the doorbell and waited. Nothing happened, so he hammered briskly on the door. The place was so small that it was unthinkable that anyone inside could not hear it. He waited a while longer and was about to give up when he heard movement behind the door.

'Hello?' a clear female voice enquired, the door still firmly closed.

He realised that the voice was reaching him through the letterbox. 'Who is it? I don't want any visitors,' the voice continued.

'I'm Ari Thór,' he said. 'From the police.'

'Go away, young man,' she grated. 'I don't want any infections.' The letterbox snapped shut.

Unwilling to give up so easily, Ari Thór knocked again, although not with the same determination as before.

The letterbox opened again. 'What do you want?' Delía asked, her voice less hostile this time.

'The Reverend Eggert suggested that I should pay you a visit,' Ari Thór said, speaking in a loud, clear voice, as he was unwilling to stoop to speak into the letterbox, certain that his visit had already attracted enough attention from the neighbours.

'Eggert?' Her interest appeared to have been piqued.

'That's right. He said that you travelled to Héðinsfjördur while it was still inhabited – to take pictures.'

'Eggert talks too much,' she said after a pause.

'Is that right?'

'It certainly is. So, young man, you want to see the pictures, do you?'

'I'd like that very much.'

There was another pause.

'Can't it wait? I don't want to catch that infection.'

'I'm in fine health, and never went anywhere near the people who died,' Ari Thór said. 'If there's anyone who's taking more precautions than you, then that's me. I haven't met anyone but Tómas these last few days, and we're both fine.'

'But what about Eggert? Didn't you say he sent you to come and see me? Didn't you meet him as well?' she asked, the suspicion plain in her voice.

Ari Thór was starting to become tired of this. He had no intention of standing outside all day, and the cold was starting to make itself felt.

'Yes, of course. I met him yesterday. I forgot to mention that. But he was happy to meet me and that speaks for itself.'

Delía sniffed. 'Eggert is as strong as an ox. It's as if there's a higher power watching over him and it goes to his head. It's shocking how careless he is in regard to his own health, always going to meet anyone who's sick and never catching as much as a cold,' she said and it was clear that in the priest's place, she would behave very differently. 'But, well, since you've not been around too many people, I'll give you the benefit of the doubt. But for heaven's sake don't come too close.'

The letter box clicked shut and the door swung open.

A short, elderly woman with curly grey hair stood before Ari Thór. She was smartly dressed, as if she had been on the way out; her appearance gave no indication that she had been practically a prisoner in her own home for the last few days.

'I'm Delía,' she said, gesturing for Ari Thór to go into a living room that was as diminutive as the house itself.

He felt as if he had stepped into an antique shop. The furniture was old but of the best quality, even though there was little spare space in the room. The walls were decorated with flower-patterned wallpaper, the shelves full of old books and what looked like photograph albums. There were photographs hanging on every wall – all monochrome prints of a bygone age, presumably taken by Delía or her father.

'Has this house been in your family for long?' Ari Thór asked as he sat down.

'Would you mind not sitting so close?' Delía asked. 'Over there, maybe.' She pointed to a stool in a corner. 'You can't be too careful with a dreadful disease doing the rounds.'

Ari Thór didn't trouble to remind her that the infection was far from 'doing the rounds' and repeated his question.

'The house? Yes, for a very long time,' she answered.

Eggert had told Ari Thór that Delía was some years older than he was and he guessed that she was in her mid-seventies, but she looked fit and healthy for her age.

'You're the one they call the Reverend?' Delía asked when he had sat down again further away from her.

He took a deep breath and nodded. Would he ever be rid of that nickname? But he needed Delía's help, so he took pains not to show his irritation.

'You're a theology graduate?' she asked.

'No,' he said and forced a smile. 'But maybe one day I'll go back and finish my degree.'

'I can't offer you anything. I haven't been able to get to the shops,' she added without a note of apology in her tone. It was a straightforward statement of fact before she got down to business. 'You want to look at old stuff from Hédinsfjördur, then?'

Ari Thór nodded again.

'May I ask why? I can't imagine much going on over there that could be police business.'

'I'm looking into an old case, on my own initiative. Partly to keep myself occupied while the situation here lasts.'

'An old case from Hédinsfjördur?' Delía asked in surprise. 'I can't recall any crime ever having been committed there.'

'You remember Jórunn, who lived there when you went to Hédinsfjördur?'

'Yes, I remember that she took her own life. There's hardly anything suspicious about that.'

'Are you sure she committed suicide?' Ari Thór asked. 'That's not what the police reports say.'

'Of course she did. Everyone said so. I don't remember what reason was given when it was reported in the papers, but it was a long time ago. I was around twenty back then, just a child,' she said and smiled at the recollection.

'Do you think you still have …' Ari Thór began, but Delía carried on as if he had not spoken.

'You know, young man,' she said in a low voice. 'I never really believed in ghosts, but I've always been sure that the poor woman, Jórunn, simply died of fright.' She leaned forward to give her words emphasis and then was silent for a moment. Ari Thór could hear only the ticking of the grandfather clock that stood in the living room and the whistle of the wind outside. 'Not directly, you understand,' Delía added. 'She just gave up, and drank poison so she didn't have to live with the ghosts there.'

Ari Thór tried to shake off the shiver that ran up his spine. 'What makes you think the place was haunted?'

'Well, he as good as told me that himself when I went over there.'

'Told you? Who did? Gudmundur, or was it Maríus?'

'No, the boy. The young man.'

23

'The young man?' Ari Thór stammered in astonishment. He could feel his pulse racing and he groped for the photograph in his jacket pocket before realising that he hadn't brought it with him. This piece of information had come like a bolt from the blue.

'That's right, the boy at the farm,' Delía confirmed placidly, apparently unaware of the effect her words were having on Ari Thór.

'What was his name?'

'I don't remember, young man. I didn't talk to him much. To be quite honest, I didn't get a warm welcome there.'

'How so?'

'I hadn't let them know that I was coming. I'd been sure they'd be happy to have a visitor. My father knew Gudmundur well – he and Gudfinna had lived in Siglufjördur before they decided to try their luck in Hédinsfjördur.'

Ari Thór nodded and Delía continued.

'The conditions were fine, with some beautiful, calm winter weather. That's why I decided to take the chance and go over the Hestsskard mountain pass. My father wasn't keen on the idea, but I was determined back then. I could see the house as I was coming down the mountain, and I saw a young woman standing not far from it. I went to talk to her; that was Jórunn. She was very friendly and was going to invite me in. Then Gudmundur appeared with a face like thunder. He seemed surprised to see a stranger. I suppose they weren't used to seeing visitors, especially not in winter.'

She sat in silence for a moment.

'Did you meet any other people there?' Ari Thór asked, desperate to know more about the young man. He could see the photograph in his mind; the thought of it had been with him night and day. The youngster had become an enigma, in spite of his innocent look in the photograph.

'No. I wasn't invited in, and didn't push myself on them. They had a small child at the time. Wasn't Hédinn born around that time?'

'Do you recall when this was?'

'It wasn't long before Christmas ...' Delía closed her eyes as she thought. '1957 ... no. 1956. That fits, yes. 1956.'

'Hédinn was born that spring.'

'You know him? Aren't you a newcomer round here?'

'I've been here three years now ...'

'That's right,' she said. 'A newcomer.'

'In fact, it was Hédinn who asked me to look into all this. He found an old photograph from back then that came from Jórunn's husband's estate. In the middle of the group in the picture was a young man, holding baby Hédinn. But Hédinn had never heard of anyone else having been present, other than himself and the two couples – his own parents and Maríus and Jórunn.'

'I had never thought about that before. Of course, I was young and thoughtless back then, but I didn't even wonder why this boy was there. I just assumed he was part of the family. Then, when Jórunn died, it was never seen as anything other than a tragic suicide. Are you telling me the boy wasn't there when that happened?' she asked, a frown on her face.

'No. I've read carefully through all the statements. There's no mention of him.'

'How strange.'

Ari Thór took a deep breath and let fly with the question that everything could hinge on.

'You said you thought he was part of the family. Do you know how he was related to them?' he asked and waited hopefully for Delía's reply.

'I'm sorry,' she said and appeared to regret deeply that she was unable to help. 'I didn't ask. He came out and asked me about the equipment I was using, so we chatted for a while. Then someone called him – I think it was Gudmundur – and off he went.'

'What did you talk about?'

'Now we get to the heart of the matter,' she said thoughtfully. 'That is, the reason I had such an uncomfortable feeling about that house. Ever since then I've been certain that the place was haunted.'

Ari Thór usually had little time for ghost stories, but now he wasn't so sure.

'I remember it clearly,' Delía went on, her eyes looking into the distance. 'Sometimes there's an incident or a conversation that stays with you for years. I asked him what it was like living there, told him I couldn't imagine it being an exciting sort of place. That took him unawares and he muttered something about it being not a bad place, and that was that. We talked about a few other things, I don't remember exactly what, and he finally admitted that it wasn't a comfortable place to be.'

Ari Thór jumped as the old grandfather clock chimed.

Delía ignored it and carried on talking. 'He said that he had seen something abnormal there; that was the word he used – abnormal. I was surprised.'

'What did he mean?' Ari Thór asked quietly, as if the young man were there in the wallpapered living room and he didn't want him to hear.

'He wouldn't say. Then he went rushing off. I reckon he had said more than he meant to,' she said thoughtfully. 'I can tell you that I didn't feel as safe going back home as I had been on the way over from Siglufjördur. You know, I never went back there again – not until the tunnel opened.'

'Do you still have the pictures?'

'Of course. I never throw anything away.'

'Are they here?' Ari Thór asked, indicating the albums.

'They're in the attic, but it's an easy job if you want to see them.'

'Are they damaged?' Ari Thór asked, hoping that wasn't the case. He was excited at the prospect of seeing these old photographs; there was a chance she had taken a picture of the boy.

'Not at all, but I have to set the projector up.'

'Projector?'

'Yes,' she said shortly, and seemed to understand his confusion. 'You thought I meant *still* pictures?' she said with a smile.

'You mean you have a film from Hédinsfjördur at that time?' Ari Thór said in surprise. 'Of this boy? And Jórunn?'

'Maybe,' she said. 'But I can't remember. It's years since I last looked at this footage. It wasn't all that successful a visit and I would have liked to have had more activity in the film – the people at the farm with that fantastic landscape behind them. But they weren't co-operative. I was obsessed with taking pictures back then. My father had bought an old eight-millimetre cine-camera and a projector, but he preferred to concentrate on taking still pictures and lost interest quite quickly. But I thoroughly enjoyed filming what was going on in the town. The developing bills my parents got used to mount up!' she laughed.

Ari Thór kept quiet, not wanting to interrupt, in spite of his excitement at the prospect of the film.

'I have all kinds of film from the herring years. Some of them are in the Herring Era museum; the rest are here,' she said, then hesitated a little. 'It's such a shame that it's all so disorganised. I used to love filming, but organisation was never my strong point. It'll be here somewhere, though.'

'In the attic?' Ari Thór asked with a courteous smile.

'I'm afraid so. It's all up there in boxes. I rarely go up there these days. Once you get to your seventies you lose the urge to climb ladders, and then there are the spiders up there that I'd prefer to stay away from,' Delía said with a grin. Ari Thór quickly picked up what she was hinting at.

'I'll go up there and fetch them if that's all right with you?' he suggested, dismayed at the thought of the spiders, but thinking they were a more enticing option than returning to the real world outside.

'Be my guest,' Delía replied. 'The projector's in the other room.'

Armed with instructions on just where the right boxes were to be found, and with an old but remarkably powerful torch in his hand, Ari Thór climbed the steps leading up into the attic from the hall. The house was small and there was hardly room to move in the cramped space under the roof. He quickly found what he was looking for, climbed back down and placed the dusty boxes on the living-room table.

'Let's have a look …' Delía murmured, going through the boxes carefully. 'This is it,' she said in triumph, shortly after, holding up a film canister. 'I hope the film is still all right,' she added.

Ari Thór fetched the projector from its home in the broom cupboard in the kitchen; it was a solid, green machine that didn't appear to have been affected by the passage of time.

'We need to set it up on the kitchen table,' Delía instructed. 'Point it at the wall over there. That's one of the only white walls in this place; we can use it as a backdrop.'

Her quick fingers skilfully threaded the film into the projector.

'I look at films occasionally, so the projector's fine,' she said, switching off the lights and drawing the curtains.

The projector clattered into life. For Ari Thór it was like being at the cinema for the very first time. The Hédinsfjördur of sixty years ago appeared in all its glory, as the past came to brilliant life. The brightness from the projector also illuminated every crack and lump in the kitchen wall, but that didn't make the show any less appealing.

The rhythmic clattering of the projector filled the room and Delía chuckled. 'There's no soundtrack. I used to record sound on tape if it was anything special – a concert or anything like that. Then I'd show the film and play the tape at the same time. But I didn't record any sound in Hédinsfjördur.'

A little disappointed, Ari Thór nodded.

The landscape of the remote fjord was breathtakingly beautiful, with sparkling white snow lying deep everywhere; the sight was almost unreal, as if from a different world – peaceful and picture-perfect. The first part of the film had been taken from the Hestsskard mountain pass. There was no tunnel and no traffic, just a white expanse and snow-clad mountain slopes, followed by a shot of the house and a woman looking out over the fjord.

'Is that Jórunn?' Ari Thór asked.

'That's her. You can see how peaceful she looks, standing still like that with her mind on her own thoughts. I let the camera roll for a while. She didn't notice me right away.'

Ari Thór wanted to yell the question that was on his mind: 'What are you thinking, Jórunn?'

Then she looked around, straight into the lens, as if she had heard his thoughts. From beyond the grave and across years and decades, she looked straight into Ari Thór's eyes.

He recognised her immediately from the photograph – her short, dark hair, and the clothes she was wearing were much the same: a coat over a thick, wool sweater. The only difference was that now she was smiling, while in the photograph she had been distracted.

She's smiling at me, Ari Thór thought. In some indiscernible way he felt that she had a message for him, or a task; a request to solve the mystery of her death at long last.

'It was quite a house in those days,' Ari Thór said, to try and steer his thoughts in another direction. It was a sturdy-looking concrete building – not too big, and similar to other farmhouses he'd seen around the country. Ari guessed, or maybe hoped, that it had been painted red, although the black-and-white film gave no indication.

'It was hit by an avalanche many years ago,' Delía said. 'Long after the fjord was finally abandoned. It's a terrible place to build a house; much too close to the mountain. Nobody would dream of building somewhere so dangerous today.'

Now the images that flickered across the kitchen wall were from a new viewpoint, over the magnificent lagoon and the sea beyond it. The water, the sea and the horizon all merged into one on the white wall. That wonderful moment fifty-five years ago had become part

of today and then retreated into the past as the girl with the camera
turned its lens elsewhere.

The Delía of half a century ago was behind the camera, gradually
turning in a circle, framing first the mountains to the east, and then
coming back round to the valley covered in snow and the majestic mountains sheltering it. Then she stopped abruptly as a figure
appeared in front of the lens.

Ari Thór started with the sudden realisation.

This was the boy.

The mystery figure had appeared, as large as life, on the kitchen
wall of an old house in Siglufjördur.

Ari Thór shuddered and felt a sudden chill. The boy was wearing a
hat, a scarf and some sort of an overcoat, but Ari recognised his face
right away; that innocent look.

It was only a brief glance; the boy disappeared almost instantly
from the frame, replaced by a view of the house where Hédinn's
family had lived. It stood to the west of the lagoon and was close
to the spot where Delía had stood to film her sequence of pictures.

There was some movement to be seen by the farmhouse; a man
appeared in the doorway and the camera remained focused on him. The
man waved a hand, and appeared to be calling to the boy and to Delía.
Then the viewpoint shifted again, back to the view over the lagoon.

'That was Gudmundur,' Delía said as the film continued to flicker
over the wall.

Ari Thór shook himself, and was back in the warmth of the
kitchen after the cold of the remote fjord.

'He called the boy in. As you can see, I just carried on filming,
but not for long. It wasn't easy to get about in that kind of snow, and
I had to use snowshoes to make walking easier,' she said and then
paused. 'He was something of a difficult character,' she murmured,
breaking the silence.

'Who? Gudmundur?'

'Yes. I remember him well from when he lived here. He was an
awkward, arrogant man who was used to getting his own way.'

'A dangerous man?' Ari Thór asked, hesitatingly.

'Dangerous?' Delía thought for a moment. 'I wouldn't go so far as to say he was dangerous. He never did anyone any harm, as far as I know; at least, he wasn't violent. But I'll tell you that he's not the kind of man I'd have wanted to quarrel with.'

The police four-by-four headed out of town with Ari Thór at the wheel, making for the Hédinsfjördur tunnel. He had appropriated the priest's philosophy, deciding that there would be no harm in venturing beyond the town's limits as long as he only went as far as the uninhabited fjord.

He glanced up at the peak of Hólshyrnan, looming over the town. As so often before, he found the ring of mountains encircling Siglufjördur overwhelming. There were certainly higher mountains elsewhere, but compared to the little houses on the spit of land, these sometimes seemed breathtakingly vast. The church was the most prominent building in the landscape, sheltering under the mountains, and the other houses, with their colourful roofs, made up the final but essential part of this glorious painting.

Hédinsfjördur welcomed him with bright sunshine. The previous visit in the dark was a distant memory. But Delía's ghost story still troubled him. What had the boy seen that was so 'abnormal'?

Ari Thór parked the four-by-four off the road and walked towards the lagoon, conscious of the difference between this and his previous night-time visit. He stopped at the water's edge, where the path came to an end, enjoying the cold, fresh, ocean air, which rejuvenated him every single day up here in the north.

The ruins of a building stood on a spit of land that jutted out into the water to his left. Ari Thór worked out that he was standing roughly where Delía had stood with her camera decades before, when Jórunn was still living and had all her life before her; back when the two families were living together in harmony. Or were there tensions beneath the surface even then – difficulties or disputes that led to Jórunn's mysterious death on that ordinary March day in 1957?

He decided to walk out to the ruins, picking his way between tussocks and holes, as there was no path, and reaching his destination with difficulty.

There was not much to see. The years and the forces of nature had not treated the place well. The whispering surf in the distance blended into the chatter of the brooks finding their way down the mountainsides. He gazed out over the water, which at this moment was so tranquil, it was hard to imagine that this remote place could ever be anything other than a spot where beauty thrived. Ugly brutality was far away. Or was it?

His thoughts turned again to Jórunn and he wondered if she had been so unhappy as to take her own life. He closed his eyes and was sure that he could sense her presence. He quickly shook the feeling off, determined not to let his own imagination run riot.

Almost imperceptibly, like a ghost appearing in broad daylight, the thought that he now realised had been at the back of his mind all along seemed to step forward. Could Jórunn have been the only one to meet her death in this lonely, abandoned fjord; or had the nameless, unknown youngster met the same fate?

He stared out over the water.

24

He was a minute into Rachmaninov's second piano concerto when his phone rang. Ari Thór was stretched out on the sofa in his Eyrargata apartment, doing his best to get some rest before deciding what to cook that evening. Not that there was much in the fridge; he would have welcomed the opportunity to order a pizza, but that was out of the question. The infection hung over the town like a curse.

Siglufjördur was still in quarantine. The opinion was becoming prevalent that it must be safe by now to lift the restrictions; no new infection cases had appeared in a few days, and a careful watch was being kept on anyone who had been in contact with the victims. However, the decision had been taken to delay the all-clear a little longer. Tómas had told Ari Thór that he had agreed with the decision. 'It would be unforgivable if more people became infected just because we lifted the quarantine restrictions too early,' he said, making it plain that closing off a small town for a few more days was not considered a major sacrifice.

Ari Thór sat up quickly when he heard his phone. He hated to interrupt a good piano concerto, whether in a concert hall or on a CD at home. This was a piece he had never heard played live, even though he had been a regular at the symphony orchestra's recitals when his mother had been alive and playing with the orchestra. Nowadays, though, he found that going to a live concert was accompanied by a sense of loss and too many old memories.

He looked at his phone's screen and turned down the music when he saw that it was the journalist calling. It was probably as well to take the call, as she had helped him out; although he'd given up on the interview ever taking place.

'Hello,' she said cheerfully. 'I hear it'll all be over up there soon.'

'There isn't anyone seriously ill at the moment,' Ari Thór replied, although Sandra came immediately to mind; he quickly stifled that train of thought.

'Pleased to hear it,' she said, although there was little sincerity in her voice. 'Ready?'

'Ready for what?'

'The interview,' she said with impatience. 'It'll go in the news bulletin tomorrow night. I'm promised a few minutes for an item – something with some human interest to it.'

'You mean something lightweight?' Ari Thór said sharply.

'Exactly.'

'Don't forget that two people lost their lives.'

'People die all the time,' she replied in a flat tone that made Ari Thór think there was something more serious behind her words – something unsaid.

'All right. Let's get on with it,' he said.

'Do you have another phone? A landline, maybe?'

'No, only the mobile.'

'Then that'll have to do,' Ísrún said after a pause. 'I can hear you fine and it won't be a long item. It's been frantic down here and I haven't had time to do this interview until now. A child disappeared down here today.'

'I heard. It's terrible,' Ari Thór replied. 'No news?'

'Your colleagues in the police won't say a word. There's been a very strange atmosphere here today – as if everyone's counting the seconds until there's some good news at last. But these things normally work out, don't they? This has to have a happy ending.'

Ari Thór said nothing; he had no answer to give.

'How is the search going for the boy in the picture?' Ísrún asked after a short, uncomfortable silence. 'Have you tracked him down?'

Ari Thór hesitated. 'Not exactly,' he said. 'But I saw him today.'

'Today?' Ísrún asked in clear astonishment.

'On an old film.' Ari Thór said, and explained about his visits to Hédinsfjördur and his conversations with Reverend Eggert and Delía.

'Maríus's brother didn't recognise the boy from the photo,' Ísrún said, more to herself than to Ari Thór. 'So it's unlikely he was family.'

'At least not related to Maríus and Nikulás,' Ari Thór said shortly, the piano concerto building into a crescendo in the background. He switched it off, unable to enjoy the music at the same time as holding a conversation. He told himself that next time he wanted to enjoy music, he would turn off his phone.

Ísrún was quiet for a moment. 'Maybe I can help you,' she said.'

'Really? How?'

'I could weave it into the story about the infection. The danger situation seems to be out of the way now, so we can make it into something about the life of a police officer under these strange circumstances. I can say that life carries on as usual, as far as possible, and the police still have to deal with minor things as well as major cases, such as investigating the whereabouts of people in old photographs.'

Ari Thór was about to interrupt: Ísrún's summary was some way from reality, after all. Daily life in Siglufjördur had practically come to a halt during the quarantine, and it certainly wasn't part of a police officer's role to enquire about people in old photographs. He would prefer that the interview showed that the job of a police officer, even in a small town, was more demanding than that. But he decided to let her finish.

'We can take it as an example of what you're doing. And if you can scan the picture with the boy in it and send it to me, we can show it,' she said, pleased with herself. 'I'll make sure the others aren't recognisable, apart from Hédinn; not that anyone is going to recognise him from such an old photo. Then we wait and see. This programme has a huge audience,' she added.

Ari Thór thought quickly. There was nothing to lose.

'Sounds good,' he said. 'But the film I saw disproved your theory,' he added cheerfully.

'What theory?'

'That the child in the photograph might not be Hédinn, but could have been the boy born around 1950, the son of Maríus and Jórunn. The young man was the same age in the film as in the photograph, and the film was taken in 1956. Delía has no reason to lie, so the photograph has to have been taken at around the same time. In a way, you could say that we're looking for two boys here: the teenager in the picture and the little boy who was adopted – Maríus and Jórunn's son.'

Ísrún was silent for a moment.

'Three boys,' she said quietly. 'There's the baby who was abducted this morning. I sincerely hope he's found before we work out who the other two are.'

25

Sunna had refused to accept that Kjartan had gone. She was screaming at the top of her lungs when Róbert appeared, out of breath, at
the coffee house.

'This can't be happening,' she had snapped. 'I can't have taken him
with me this morning. Wasn't he with you?'

Róbert tried his best to convince her that she had hardly gone into
town pushing an empty pram.

'Don't lie to me! Tell me he was with you, please!' she pleaded,
a wild, vacant look in her eyes. She made as if to run off down the
street, back towards their house.

He caught hold of her, and finally persuaded her to sit with him
in the police car, where she seemed to calm down a little. He held her
hand and did his best to be warm and encouraging. Her eyes were so
distant and filled with desperation that he felt as if knives were being
driven into his heart; he could hardy bring himself to look at her.

Finally accepting that someone had really taken the boy, his
support was what she sought. She immediately blamed herself.

'How could I leave him out there?'

The question was not directed at Róbert, but he tried to explain
to her that this was something that had never before happened in
Reykjavík. She could never have foreseen it.

'Why didn't I keep a closer eye on the pram? Why?'

He noticed her sister, Heida, had been quick to disappear.

'I'll go now,' she had announced as soon as Róbert had turned up.

That was just like her, he thought. The woman who had never taken responsibility for her own life and who made a habit of leeching off others couldn't even support her own sister at a time like this.

By the time Róbert and Sunna had reached the police station, Sunna had stopped accusing herself and had turned her invective on the boy's father instead.

'Breki must have taken him. To hell with him! How could he do such a thing?' Her voice became loud, as her anger grew. She made no attempt to keep her feelings to herself and seemed to be in a world of her own.

'How could he do it?' she shouted. 'Couldn't he just fight it out in court?'

Róbert held her tightly and said the first thing that came into his head. 'He'll be fine if it was Breki who took him,' he said and instantly regretted it.

Sunna suddenly seemed to be hit by the possibility that this was nothing to do with Breki, and that Kjartan could now be in the hands of a stranger. It was too much for her, she fell silent and perfectly still, and Róbert was unable to stop her collapsing onto the cold lino of the police station floor.

'He must be with Breki,' Róbert said under his breath.

They were in the interview room with the Chief Inspector, who informed them that the investigation was in his hands. He tried to convince them that this case had absolute priority and they would find the baby soon enough. But Róbert was sure that there was a quiver of doubt in the policeman's voice and hoped that Sunna had not noticed it.

She showed no response so he whispered to her again, 'He must be with Breki.'

Sunna's rage exploded with new-found energy.

'Have you found his father? Well? You have to find him,' she screamed at the Chief Inspector.

'Do you have reason to believe he might have taken the child?'

the Chief Inspector asked in a slow, careful voice, as if there were no urgency.

Sunna made a confused attempt to explain the custody battle that they were engaged in, with Róbert interrupting at intervals to provide details about Breki – his phone number, address and workplace. Bewildered, they both said that they had no idea of anyone else who might bear them a grudge.

'I don't normally take my eyes off him,' Sunna cried. 'But he was asleep,' she said. 'I didn't notice anything out of the ordinary. No one suspicious hanging around.'

The Chief Inspector asked for Heida's number and dispatched an officer to interview her and find out if she had seen anything.

'And you're sure nothing unusual has happened recently?' the Chief Inspector asked finally.

Sunna shook her head and glanced at Róbert.

He was silent. Should he mention the missing keys, the uninvited guest and the figure in the garden? An uncomfortable feeling had sneaked up on him during the day, as soon as he had heard of Kjartan's disappearance and had run as fast as he could to the coffee house. His theory could explain the sinister attention they had been getting, but he tried to convince himself that there was nothing in it; the simple thought of it being a possibility made him sick with fear. Calm and collected for a moment, he thought it through, weighed the advantages and disadvantages, and came to the conclusion that risking losing Sunna was not worth it.

'Nothing unusual,' he said and smiled at her.

'I lost my keys, though,' she said suddenly, taking him by surprise.

'Ah?' the Chief Inspector said sternly, and the look on his face told them that he smelt blood. 'Were they stolen? A break-in?'

Sunna seemed not to know what to say. 'No, I don't think so,' she said, as if that was the answer to both questions. 'But Róbert changed the locks, just to be sure.'

'Ah?' the Chief Inspector said, as if that were the only word he could find to convey his surprise. 'Any special reason for that?'

Róbert felt the man's piercing gaze. Now he would have to make a decision. Keep quiet or tell all? The last thing he wanted was to be caught out in a falsehood. He stopped to think – long enough, he knew, to arouse suspicion. His cold was again making itself felt, draining him of energy.

'I got up and found the back door ajar,' he admitted. 'The same night that Sunna lost her keys. I probably forgot to lock up, the door doesn't always close properly. It's an old place, you see. But it bugged me, so I decided to change the locks.'

'Why didn't you tell me?' Sunna demanded.

'I didn't want to worry you, sweetheart. It was probably nothing.'

'Interesting,' was all the Chief Inspector had to say as they left the room.

He returned a little later to tell them that Heida had been interviewed, and she had not been able to provide any further information. The police were already at work collating CCTV footage from the area.

'But we haven't been able to contact the boy's father yet,' he said.

Sunna and Róbert were again left in the interview room. Sunna was calmer – silent and staring into space. Róbert said nothing and waited, trying to convince himself that Breki had taken the child. He felt it was unforgivable to abduct the boy like that, regardless of how dark the outlook might be in the custody dispute. Róbert already feared that Breki was making plans to whisk Kjartan out of the country. He must have planned it in advance, he thought, certain that he could not have simply lifted the child from the pram and taken him home.

Róbert tried to force his thoughts elsewhere. Closing his eyes, he tried to visualise the ocean – sitting alone in the little boat, far away in the Westfjords, enjoying the stillness and the mirror-calm sea. It was so real he could almost smell it. But he could still hear Sunna's occasional sob. He opened his eyes but avoided looking directly at her. She was far away in a world of her own, silent in her chair as she wept.

There was a serious expression on the Chief Inspector's face when he returned. Róbert was startled by it; he wiped the sweat from his forehead and anxiously waited for him to say something.

'We've located Breki and he's up north. The police in Akureyri are speaking to him,' he said, then paused. 'He travelled there early this morning, looking for some temporary work, I understand. The airline has confirmed that he checked in for the flight first thing, so he seems to have been out of town when the boy disappeared. Now we're exploring other avenues of enquiry.'

His voice grave, he directed his next words to Sunna. 'We have a psychologist here, out front, who is going to talk to you. It's important that we look after you while we're waiting. The boy will be found. I'm certain of it.'

Sunna nodded and left the room with the Chief Inspector without a word.

Shortly after, the Chief Inspector returned. He looked straight into Róbert's eyes. 'Well, I think we need a chat, just the two of us,' he said, closing the door behind him.

Róbert could tell from his tone that this was going to be a less-than-friendly conversation. He could feel the sweat breaking out again. Had he become so weak that he was frightened of the police? That had never been the case before. Or was it just the cold that had been plaguing him, making him feel vulnerable?

'We think we're on the right track,' he said and sat down. 'Do you know someone called Emil Teitsson?'

It was a lightweight question and Róbert hoped that the strangled 'no' he managed to squeeze out was convincing.

It was true. He didn't know the man personally. But he knew *exactly* who he was. He recalled clearly the interview he had read; and the young man's picture was indelibly etched into his memory. For the first time, Róbert felt real fear.

'Well, let me share with you the theory I've worked out,' the Chief Inspector said.

*

Afterwards, Róbert sat outside in the corridor and waited for Sunna.

The conversation with the inspector had affected him deeply. Róbert could feel distant memories and the past's confused nightmares returning to haunt him.

Sunna eventually appeared with the psychologist at her side.

'Shall we go home, sweetheart?' he asked.

'Please,' she replied, apparently calmer than before, although it was evident from her expression, her body language – everything about her – that she was wracked with anxiety.

It was well into the evening and it was dark outside. Sunna sat wordlessly next to Róbert on the sofa. Róbert listened to the rain, his arms around her. Their little apartment had become a cold and unfamiliar place.

He avoided looking at the clock, preferring not to know just how long the little boy had been gone. All he could be certain of was that it had been too long.

Róbert had hardly been able to catch his breath all day, not least after his conversation with the Chief Inspector, and he had hardly given himself time to eat. Sunna had eaten nothing, as far as he knew. Now there was time for a meal, but he realised that he had no appetite, and assumed Sunna didn't have one either.

His world seemed to be falling apart before his eyes. He had started a new life, met a wonderful girl, set up home with her and become her little boy's stepfather.

He tried again to think of the boat in the Westfjords. It was less easy now – he could picture the sea, but it was no longer placid. Now, as he closed his eyes, he felt that he was at sea with a gale blowing; the little boat rode steadily lower and lower in the water.

26

The worst moment was when the last embers of hope had gone cold and Emil realised that he would never again hold her in his arms, that his dreams of a future with her were dead and that his life had irrevocably changed – for the worse.

He took care not to dwell too closely on what few people knew – that she had been carrying a child and was just a few months into her pregnancy. He hardly dared think about it, but underneath there was a barely controlled fury, a need for revenge.

Emil had done his best to live in hope ever since the assault had taken place, doubting the doctors, who seemed to want to dampen his optimism by telling him that he had no choice but to accept what had happened.

That could never happen. He would never give up. To begin with he sat with Bylgja day and night, her hand in his. Hope and anger kept him going, leaving no place for sorrow.

His regret that he had worked overtime that night was infinite. Every question he asked himself all began with the same two words: what if …?

Of course, he had no idea if he would have been able to save her. Maybe they would both have ended up in hospital, lying unconscious side by side, dying together. That might have been for the best. He simply couldn't imagine life without her. He could see – sometimes even in his dreams – that his presence could have changed things, could have averted the assault. He knew well enough that he was no musclebound character that people would think twice about taking on, but all the same, he could still be a proposition to be reckoned with when backed into a corner; and it would have been more of a challenge to take them both on than just her alone.

Shouldn't one be safe in one's own home? Neither of them had ever done anyone any harm. But it had happened all the same, on a cold winter evening. They had sat down to a spaghetti dinner together at around six, talking of the child that was on its way and the changes they would have to make. Bylgja had no intention of reducing her working hours over the next few months and was still aiming to continue her studies in the autumn.

'I'm absolutely fine,' she said. 'When morning sickness hits then I'll take a day off.'

Then he stood up, saying he had to go back to work to finish an urgent assignment. He had asked her if she wanted to come with him. Had he really said that? Maybe not. Had he wanted her to take it easy at home? His memories of that evening were badly fragmented, but he knew that she had said she preferred to stay at home and study. He had left her, not quite sure just how he had said goodbye to her; and that was the last time they'd been able to share words.

When he came home, the first thing he had seen was the blood in the hall. He must have seen Bylgja right away, but time stood still as he fought to believe what he was seeing. She lay on her back, dressed in the pyjamas she always wore when she was immersed in her studies. She was very still and the pool of blood by her head filled Emil with such deep dread that he was frozen to the spot. He couldn't tell how long he had stared at her before he snatched his phone from a pocket and called the police.

She hadn't been dead. That was the good part of it; the only good part.

She had lost the baby, of course. And she had been kept in a coma. But she was gradually dying and Emil had felt that his own desire to live was withering, as if it was keeping time with her weak heartbeat. He had made every effort to be strong to start with – even in interviews with newspaper and TV journalists as he fought to squeeze some justice out of the situation. He begged anyone who might have information to come forward. The case had remained open; there were some strong indications about who was responsible, but nothing that was strong enough to build a case on. Emil had no choice but to watch Bylgja's life trickle away in front of his eyes, without having anyone to pin the blame on.

When she finally died two years after the attack, getting the peace that she deserved, it was pure anger that kept Emil going. The fury overwhelmed him, ousting any sense of love or compassion. Deep inside he knew that anger was a dangerous companion for unresolved sorrow, but by then he didn't care.

There was never a convincing reason for the assault, although the police had their own suspicions, based on information from their underworld contacts. It was impossible to pin anything on the person whose name had been provided. The theory was that the assault on Bylgja had been an error.

An error.

That was the word the policeman had used. Emil had lost the person he loved the most – and his unborn baby – due to an error. Cold fate alone had destroyed his life.

Some petty criminal had lived further along the same street, only a few doors away, and the police theory was that this person's drug habit had left him deep in debt. Thugs determined to call in the debt, with violence if it wasn't paid, had knocked at the wrong door. Emil couldn't avoid imagining the scene. Bylgja had probably done her best to convince them they had called at the wrong door. She had never been one to let herself be trampled over and had undoubtedly been angry. There had only been one blow and that had been enough. The weapon was thought to be some kind of baseball bat.

Revenge was always part of his plan. He hadn't realised it until after Bylgja's death. An unexpected call put him on the trail. By now he wasn't thinking logically, and he knew it.

His parents were deeply worried about him. They were constantly trying to help, but he was a grown man and could look after himself. He had even fixed up a hiding place: an abandoned house not far from the city centre where he could sleep in peace, far from the overweening sympathy and the sorrow at his parents' house. The apartment he and Býlgja had bought now stood empty and he could not imagine ever setting foot in there again. He could see nothing but blood when he thought about the place.

His plan had worked out so far. He wasn't drinking much these days. He was pretty much in control. Bylgja deserved that much. He didn't know what would happen to him next. Maybe he'd give himself up. Or maybe he'd thrown himself in the sea. It didn't matter much either way.

He had been keeping tabs on Róbert's place for a while, and had stalked his wife and the child. An eye for an eye and a tooth for a tooth; wasn't that right? It occurred to him that the best punishment he could mete out would be to let Róbert experience the loss of his wife and child.

But now he was stuck with this screaming child in his arms; a boy who cried his eyes out and refused to sleep. It wasn't a perfect situation. He kept the baby in a shabby and dilapidated old house in the downtown area, a place which had maybe been filled with joy at one time, but now it was just a shell – just like Emil himself – and he had to admit to himself that he had no idea what to do next.

He had enjoyed following Róbert's wife, then he stole the keys and broke into their apartment one evening. First he had peered through the window and seen that they were occupied; then he had sneaked in and looked into the bedroom where the two of them were engrossed in their lovemaking. They hadn't noticed him, so he took care to leave behind a few signs of his presence, and had left without closing the back door behind him.

He kept lurking around the street, peeping through their windows from time to time, watching their every move. He was determined to scare the life out of Róbert before he went any further.

This morning he had followed the girl when she went for a walk, pushing the pram in front of her. When she left the little boy asleep in the pram outside a coffee house on Laugavegur, the opportunity was too good to let pass.

Now he was sitting here in the dark, in the middle of the night, listening to this endless crying as the boy called for his mother. He had no idea what to do next, but knowing how terrified Róbert must be at this very moment gave him a warm feeling inside.

27

An unexpected guest was waiting when Ísrún arrived at work the next morning.

This was her fifth working day in a row, four of them having been day shifts. She had also been offered an extra Saturday shift to relieve a colleague who had asked to swap so he could be at home for a children's birthday party. She had almost agreed, deciding that she could rest afterwards. Right now, though, she had two stories to chase that were at the top of her list of priorities: Snorri Ellertsson's murder and the abducted child.

The girl in the lobby got smartly to her feet as soon as Ísrún walked in.

'Hello. I was trying to reach you yesterday.'

Red hair fell over her shoulders and her eyes could just be seen under a long fringe. Her cheeks were flushed as she smiled at Ísrún. As she spoke she had the habit of speaking, not to the person in front of her, but upwards, as if in deep thought. Ísrún had often spoken to her before, though, and was used to this odd mannerism.

'Hallo, Lára,' Ísrún replied.

Lára had been Marteinn's assistant ever since he had become Prime Minister. Before that she had been active in the party's youth movement. There were stories of an affair between the two of them, before he took office, and that this was still going on. It had never been confirmed, but when Marteinn and his wife had split up, the rumours flew thicker and faster. By then he had been Prime Minister for six months; the official explanation was that the pressure of the

job had led to them going in separate directions. Still, Lára had been
the butt of much gossip, and this attractive redhead was thought by
many to be the marriage breaker, splitting Marteinn from his wife
and their two children.

'I'm sorry. I completely forgot to call you,' Ísrún said. 'It's been
so busy. I have to run for a meeting, but I have a few minutes. Shall
we sit down?'

Lára perched on the sofa again and Ísrún took a chair opposite
her. She had a good idea of what had brought the Prime Minister's
assistant there, but wanted to let her make the first move.

'This is just an informal call,' Lára said. 'Marteinn asked me to
come and see you.'

Ísrún smiled, and didn't believe a word.

'We can talk off the record, can't we?'

Ísrún nodded in agreement.

'That interview of yours with Marteinn was below the belt,' Lára
said. 'The poor man wasn't expecting a question about Snorri. They
were friends years ago, and that's all there is to it. After Snorri got
caught up in all kinds of nonsense, Marteinn didn't have anything
more to do with him. They hadn't seen each other for years. Then
he gets run over in a car accident – and the Prime Minister is being
asked questions about it.' Lára paused for effect. 'Not that I blame
you for that. It was quite a scoop.'

Ísrún waited for Lára to say that enough was enough, but knew
that the words hardly needed to be spoken out loud. Ísrún herself
still hadn't said a word, and reflected that these young politicians
were no slouches at the old art of having the last word, any more
than the old ones had been.

'I was thinking of you in connection with something else,' Lára
continued. 'Marteinn has been working on some ideas – a possible
merging of ministries. It's something that's close to his heart. I suggested that we could ask you to do an item about it; maybe in one
of your news reviews. You'd get an interview with Marteinn for him
to discuss it.'

Ísrún glanced at the clock.

'That sounds great, Lára,' she said, although she wasn't quite prepared to be bought off so easily. 'Let me think it over, will you?'

'Sure. But don't think too long. Marteinn wants to do this soon,' Lára said, apparently unaware that she had contradicted herself when she had said that Marteinn knew nothing about her visit. 'You have my mobile number, don't you? The new one?'

Ísrún nodded again.

'Wonderful. Give me a call; as soon as you like.' Lára stood up and placed a hand on Ísrún's shoulder. 'Always good to see you, Ísrún.'

'And you.'

Now Ísrún was convinced that Marteinn knew more about Snorri's murder than he would be prepared to admit. This could be something big.

28

They had finally fallen asleep on the sofa, exhausted with worry.

The piercing ring of the doorbell dragged Róbert from sleep. His head ached and he could feel that the effects of his cold had become more pronounced overnight. Róbert would certainly have liked to sleep for longer, although he had managed to sleep remarkably soundly, as if he had subconsciously retreated into sleep to protect himself from the trauma of the real world.

It was just after eight and it was Heida who had woken them.

'Were you asleep?' she asked awkwardly, shutting the door behind her and going into the living room where Sunna was stirring.

'Mum and Dad are on their way back from Spain,' Heida continued, filling the silence as Róbert said nothing. 'They are catching a flight today through London, I think.'

Sunna looked around in confusion, as if the previous day's events were suddenly returning to her. She stared at her sister, consumed with worry.

'Where's Kjartan? Have they found him?'

'I don't think so,' Heida replied with her usual bluntness and lack of consideration.

Róbert found his phone and saw that there had been no missed calls. So Kjartan had not been found during the night. He looked at Sunna and shook his head. She slumped down, head in hands.

He immediately dialled the number of the Chief Inspector running the investigation, but there was no reply.

'I'm sure they'll find him,' Heida said, planting herself on the sofa. 'Did Breki take him? You always did have lousy taste in men.'

Róbert pretended he hadn't heard, went into the kitchen and made tea. He needed something hot to start the day and wouldn't get far without it.

The sisters were still talking – or, rather, Heida was talking to Sunna – when he returned with a mug of tea for himself and another for Sunna.

'Róbert,' Heida said, turning to him. 'Maybe it's one of your old pals, from back when you were doing drugs.'

'Just stop it,' he snapped back at her.

'Anyway, you should be watching over your family, making sure this kind of stuff doesn't happen,' she said.

Her words stung. Róbert slammed his mug down on the table and was about to order her out of the apartment when his phone chimed.

They all fell silent. Róbert answered.

'Good morning, Róbert. I saw you were trying to get hold of me,' the voice of the Chief Inspector said, and there was a pause. 'We haven't located the boy yet, but we have a few strong leads. Would you and Sunna come to the station straightaway? This is best done face to face.'

Róbert felt his pulse quicken, beating at a rate that stole away the last shred of any peace of mind.

'We'll be right there,' he said.

Róbert flatly refused to allow Heida to come with them, so they left her behind in the apartment and swiftly made their way to the police station.

They were shown into the same interview room as before. There was a jug of water and some glasses on the table, in keeping with the old chairs with their shabby upholstery and the wooden table that had seen better days.

Róbert gestured to Sunna with the jug but she shook her head. He poured himself a glass of water.

'They must have found him,' Sunna said and smiled. 'I'm sure of it. I'm so looking forward to seeing him again.'

'Don't forget what he said on the phone, sweetheart. They hadn't found Kjartan then. Let's not get our hopes up. These things take time.'

'What the hell to you know about it?' she demanded, her sudden anger taking him off guard.

Then she looked away, as if determined to say nothing more.

The Chief Inspector came in after a while. He looked tired; his face was unshaven and he had black circles under his eyes. This was a man who had not slept much.

Róbert felt ashamed, now that he had managed to sleep. He should have spent the night doing what he could to help find the boy. There were plenty of old friends in the underworld he could have called on. These people were often resourceful, but deep inside Róbert knew that seeking their help would have meant taking a huge risk. He had left that part of his life behind and had no desire to re-acquaint himself with it, not even for something as important as this.

'We're making good progress,' the Chief Inspector said, trying unsuccessfully to manage a smile.

'Where is he?' Sunna demanded.

'He hasn't been found,' he replied. 'We have—'

'Where is Kjartan?' Sunna yelled, suddenly on her feet. With one violent movement she swept the water jug aside, sending it smashing to the floor.

The Chief Inspector showed no surprise. 'Let's stay calm, shall we?' he said in a tone that indicated he had seen plenty of angry passion before.

Sunna slumped back into her chair, shaking.

'We have a strong suspicion who has been at work here,' he said in a calm voice. 'Emil Teitsson. Twenty-seven years old; a business graduate who works – or worked – for a bank.'

'What? Who is this?' Sunna asked.

Róbert kept quiet. His cold was making it difficult for him to breathe properly through his nose. He felt that he was about to suffocate in the interview room's stuffy atmosphere, in this lumpy yellow chair.

'He seems to have gone badly off the rails two years ago, after his wife was the victim of a violent assault. She had been in a coma since the attack, but not long ago, she died.'

'So why do you think he took Kjartan?' Sunna gasped.

'As you'd expect, we've been looking into several suspects,' said the Chief Inspector, seeming to avoid Sunna's question, 'including the boy's father – who seems to have had nothing to do with it – and, now, this Emil. We've gone through CCTV footage from cameras on Laugavegur. Unfortunately two out of the three cameras weren't working, which seems to be a problem all over, now that these things are showing their age. However, on one of them we can make out a man who *could be* Emil. After that, we were able to get recordings from several privately owned cameras from shops along the street. From then on, it was clear. Emil was easily identified, and he was holding a small boy who fits your description of Kjartan.'

He paused to let them digest this new information.

'Where is this bastard?' Róbert demanded.

'He lives with his parents. They last saw him yesterday morning. He disappears sometimes, they say, but always reappears eventually. They're devastated, naturally. He hasn't been the same man since his wife was assaulted. Emil's parents tell us she'd recently become pregnant, and lost the baby in the attack. And now she's dead too.'

Nobody said anything. Sunna looked down at her palms.

'It seems he spent a lot of time with her at the hospital and it was a huge shock when she finally passed away,' continued the Chief Inspector. 'He had therapy with a psychologist for a long time, but a while ago he stopped turning up for his appointments. We're doing everything we can to find him. His parents can hardly believe that he could have abducted a child. They say he has been bitter and angry, but they can't believe he'd go so far as to kidnap an innocent baby; and they know him better than anyone, naturally. So now, it's just a matter of time before we find him and Kjartan.'

'Have you put out any announcements?' Róbert asked.

'We'll do that soon.'

'Why?' Sunna asked, her voice filled despair. 'Why Kjartan?'

'We have certain theories,' the Chief Inspector said slowly. 'I'm not prepared to go into that now, and it's not my main priority. Finding your baby comes first.'

'Why did he take Kjartan?' Sunna repeated.

Róbert moved his chair closer to hers. 'Let's not think about that, now, sweetheart.'

The Chief Inspector stood up. 'One of you is going to have to look at the CCTV footage to confirm that it really is Kjartan. Can you do that, Sunna?'

Róbert saw the expression on her face – or rather, he saw the blank look that said she would not be able to do it. She sat stock still, not saying a word.

'I'll do it,' he said.

'Good. I'll get someone to sit with Sunna in the meantime.'

Once the formal identification was dealt with, the Chief Inspector didn't take Róbert back to Sunna, but showed him into another interview room – even smaller, shabbier and more claustrophobic than the previous one.

Róbert had been in no doubt that the man in the pictures was holding Kjartan. He hoped that Sunna would never have to see those images. They were innocent enough at first glance, but in the context of everything Róbert knew, they became deeply sinister.

'I'm guessing you haven't discussed your past with Sunna,' said the Chief Inspector, sitting down. 'She doesn't know a thing, does she?'

'No,' Róbert said, closing his eyes and hoping that the headache that was starting to throb would not get worse. That was something he could do without, on top of everything else.

'You understand that we will have to explain your links to Emil to her, don't you?'

'I don't have any links to that blasted man,' Róbert snarled.

'Suspected links, then.' The Chief Inspector's brows knitted in a frown. 'We'll work on the assumption that you're innocent, although I have my doubts about that – serious ones. Just because there's no evidence, doesn't mean you're squeaky clean. And what's certain is that Emil doesn't seem to think so, either; and now a little boy has disappeared.' He paused, his frown even heavier. 'I have to say, if I thought telling your girlfriend the whole story would help resolve this case, I'd do it in a heartbeat. But, out of consideration for her – for *her*, you understand, not for you – I'll give you a chance to discuss it with her by yourselves. I'll talk to you again later today to go over the situation. And by then, you had better have come clean, otherwise I'll have to tell her, in my own words, just why her son was abducted by a stranger.'

Róbert didn't say a word as he stormed out of the room. The blank, cold walls of the corridor felt as if they were closing in on him.

He thought of Sunna – this wonderful woman who had breathed into him new life and new hope; hope for a better life and a brighter future.

Now he feared, and was almost certain, that his dreams were about to become a nightmare.

29

'The interview will be on TV tonight,' Ari Thór said.

He and Tómas were in the station's coffee corner. Tómas had taken the previous night's shift and had asked Ari Thór to be there for a morning meeting to discuss their next moves and the shift rota. They expected the town's quarantine restrictions to be lifted that evening; and the news had already spread in the way it always does in a small community. Life in general had begun to return to normal and some people had gone back to work, although most companies and shops remained closed. The news had swept around the town, however, that the baker had been back at work that morning and there was fresh bread available, even though the bakery had not formally opened. There was still a shadow over the town, though, its inhabitants still numbed by the death of the nurse, who had been a popular character and a Siglufjördur resident for many years.

'Interview?' Tómas asked, his gaze distant. 'Yes, of course. The journalist; Ísrún, wasn't it?'

'That's her.'

'That's fine, my boy,' Tómas said, his mind elsewhere. He ran a hand through his thinning hair.

It was obvious there were things on his mind.

'Are you concerned about the infection?' Ari Thór asked. 'Are you worried the quarantine is being lifted too early?'

'What? Worried? No, not at all. But that reminds me … I talked to the hospital last night to check the situation. Old Sandra's going downhill. You've been visiting her now and again these last few months, haven't you?'

Ari Thór nodded and felt his stomach turn over.

'Yes ...' he stammered.

'Won't you go and visit her? You might be seeing her for the last time if things don't go well. It's an exceptionally heavy flu, but there's no special infection hazard.'

'Of course,' Ari Thór said, avoiding Tómas's eye.

They sat in silence for a while.

'I put ...' Tómas began, but left the sentence unfinished. He paused and tried again. 'Listen, my boy. I put the house on the market.'

'House? Your house? You're moving?' Ari Thór asked in astonishment.

'That's right, our house. But don't worry. I won't be going any-where for a while. I had a talk with my wife and she wants me down south, to try and keep things together. So I told her I'd put the house on the market and see what happens. But I'm not sure anyone's going to snap it up. People think you can buy a house up north for prac-tically nothing, my boy. Maybe someone will rent it from us, you never know. But it's advertised for sale. I just thought I'd tell you, in case you see it in the paper or on the net. Nothing's been decided. Don't you worry,' he added, almost as an afterthought, and looked curiously at Ari Thór.

But now Ari Thór really did have something to worry about.

If Tómas were to move back south, then he would have to decide whether or not to apply for the inspector's post at the Siglufjördur station, and he would have preferred not to have had to think about it yet. To begin with, he wanted to get his own personal life in order, to figure out where his relationship with Kristín was heading. Should he move to Akureyri to be with her, or even go with her when the time came for her to continue her studies abroad?

He tried not to let his concerns show.

'We'll see,' he said with a smile.

*

Tómas had gone home. Ari Thór was alone on duty and walked down
to the small-boat harbour. It was a bright day and the waters of the
fjord sparkled. He even met two people out walking, and nodded to
them. They nodded back, but there was a gloom about them.

Maybe he should visit Sandra, sit with her and listen to her tales
of the town as it used to be. They had become close friends, able
to discuss virtually any subject. She always told him to take it easy,
to not let himself get irritated by the little things in life that don't
matter, and, even though she had never met Kristín, she urged Ari
Thór to hold on to her tight.

Thinking about Sandra reminded him that he had meant to get
in touch with Hédinn before the interview was aired; it would be as
well to do that right away.

He strolled along the wooden dock with his phone to his ear,
waiting for Hédinn to answer, watching the colourful boats rocking
peacefully at the quayside. It almost felt as if there might be a touch
of spring in the air, but Ari Thór knew that this still air could be
treacherous and that the weather might well take a turn for the worse
before spring reached Siglufjördur.

The phone was at last answered. 'Hello,' Hédinn said.

'Hello, Hédinn. Ari Thór from the police. Am I interrupting you?'

'Not a thing. I'm just at home. There's no school these days so
there isn't a lot for us teachers to do. Have you made any progress?'

'I'm getting there. There are a few things I need to go over with
you. Could we meet at the weekend, if that suits you?'

'That's fine,' Hédinn said, the anticipation clear in his voice.
'What have you found?'

'I'm still working on it, but I can tell you that you have a cousin
out there somewhere you didn't know about.'

'What did you say? A cousin?'

'That's right. Jórunn and Maríus had a boy in 1950, but I don't
know what became of him. He seems to have been adopted; I guess
things were tough for Jórunn.'

'You think he might be ... alive?' Hédinn gulped.

Ari Thór sensed there might be something more than curiosity behind the question.

'To tell you the truth, I have no idea. Why do you ask?'

'I was thinking of something my father said shortly before he died,' Hédinn said after a pause. 'He was pretty much in a world of his own by then, the old man, but now and again we got some sense out of him.'

'Did he say something relevant?'

'No, I'm not sure it is, otherwise I'd have mentioned it before. But I guess it could have something to do with Jórunn's son. Maybe ... it's not a pleasant thing to say ... but maybe she didn't give him up when it came down to it.'

'What do you mean?'

'The old man was saying something about how well I'd done for myself, and said that the bad genes had not been passed down to me, only the good ones. At the time I didn't know what he was talking about, and then he said – and I've never forgotten his words – "I was just thinking that you had an aunt who took a life ..." I did my best to ask him what he meant, but couldn't get anything more out of him. Maybe he'd said too much, or he might have just been confused.'

'Do you think he meant Jórunn?'

'It's possible. I never heard that she was involved in any kind of murder case, or he may have meant that she took her *own* life. I had two aunts on father's side as well, and never heard anything untoward about either of them. I've only just remembered all this, when you said she'd had a child and nobody knew what became of it. Maybe, you know, she took the child's life, for some reason?'

'It's a shocking thought. That's all I can say ...' Ari Thór shuddered. 'We ought to talk at more length tomorrow if we can find time to meet. And, by the way, there'll be a picture of you on the TV tonight.'

'What?' Hédinn asked in surprise.

'Don't worry,' Ari Thór said and realised that he was starting to sound like Tómas. 'Nobody will recognise you. It's the picture of you and the lad that was taken in Hédinsfjördur. I'm being interviewed in a news roundup about the infection and the horrible situation here; and the journalist and I have decided to sneak in a mention of the photograph. We'll see if anyone can identify the young guy.'

Hédinn was silent for a moment. 'Well,' he hesitated. 'I suppose it'll be alright.'

'It'll be fine,' Ari Thór assured him, suspecting that he had more enthusiasm than Hédinn to find a solution to the mystery. 'I also have testimony from someone else that this young lad lived there with your parents and Jórunn and Marías.'

'Really?' Hédinn asked, clearly intrigued. 'He lived there? In our house in Hédinsfjördur?'

'That's what it looks like. There's a movie from Hédinsfjördur and he can be seen in it.'

'Well!' Hédinn said. 'Where did you find that?'

'Delía. You know her?'

'Yes, of course. Can I see this movie?'

'Yes, why not. In fact, should we meet at Delía's house tomorrow evening, assuming she doesn't have any objections?' Ari Thór suggested and didn't wait for a reply. 'I'll speak to her and let you know,' he said, and ended the call.

He spent a moment taking in the mild weather, but still sensed a chill in the air. The cold northerly winds of winter were never far away in Siglufjördur, but Ari was used to this by now. Days of snow in May, even in June, did not surprise him any more.

Ari Thór had plenty to tell Hédinn, but nothing concrete. What had happened to his aunt remained a mystery and he was afraid that it would stay that way. This story belonged to an earlier generation; maybe it was not his place to make sense of it all.

Now his thoughts went back to Sandra – on her deathbed at the hospital. Was it time to steel himself to pay her a visit? He wanted to see her, and she deserved a visit from him, but he knew that deep inside he lacked the strength to watch her die.

He took out his phone again and, to give himself something else to think about, he called Kristín.

'I'll be on TV tonight,' he said, rather proudly.

'On TV, really?'

'Well, only my voice and a still image, but that's still something.'

'That's very nice, Ari,' Kristín said in her matter-of-fact manner. She was always so calm, never really getting overly excited about anything.

'Maybe we can watch it together …?'

'What? You mean …?' And now there was some colour in her voice, finally.

'Yes, the danger has passed, so you can come over, if you're up for it.'

'Of course, Ari, of course, absolutely.'

30

'Ísrún,' Ívar called as she opened the newsroom door.

She sighed, walked over to him and forced a smile. She didn't like the smug look on his face, not that there was anything unusual about it.

'There's a message for you,' he snapped. 'I hadn't realised I'd been promoted to being your secretary.'

'Message?' she asked impatiently. 'What was it?'

'A call from an old people's home.' And then, in a voice that was unnecessarily loud: 'They wanted to let you know that your room's ready.' He was clearly hoping to raise a laugh among the staff, but his joke fell flat.

'What do you mean?'

'A woman from an old people's home in Breidholt called,' he said with a grin. 'Someone called Nikulás wants to meet you.'

'Ah. Thanks,' she said, about to hurry away.

'Not so fast, Ísrún,' he said awkwardly. He didn't have the same smooth way that Marteinn had of addressing people by name. 'Who's this guy? Is this something you're keeping quiet about?'

She rolled her eyes. 'I'm working on all sorts of things. This is linked to the Siglufjördur story that María asked me to do for the supplement,' she said, placing emphasis on the news editor's name. 'I'd better call the old guy right away,' she said, taking out her phone and walking away with it to her ear before Ívar could complain.

*

'That's right, Nikulás asked me to give you a call,' the girl at the rest home said. 'He's been going through some old stuff and he has a box of things he said you can take a look at. There's no point trying to talk to him on the phone.'

'Could you send me the box?' Ísrún asked, with little enthusiasm for another trip up to Breidholt.

'Well, I suppose I could put it in a taxi if you'll cover the fare. But I think Nikulás would really like to see you, if you could come and get it yourself. You wouldn't have to stop long. The old fellow doesn't get many visitors, you see.'

Ísrún checked her watch. The morning conference was about to begin. She might be able to go right after the meeting, as long as there were no developments in the child abduction case.

'I'll do my best,' she said and ended the call, before scrolling down to her police contact's number. It rang a couple of times, was answered and the call immediately terminated. This was the second time that day that he had abruptly declined to take her call.

She had hardly sat down when Ívar made his announcement.

'There's a press release from the police,' he said, and waited as he savoured the moment. 'They've released details of someone they want to interview in connection with the abduction case.'

Ísrún's eyes widened.

'Who?' she asked after an unnecessarily long silence.

'His name's Emil Teitsson,' Ívar said with a quizzical look on his face. 'They must have some solid evidence if they've released the man's name. They even supplied a picture of him.'

He placed the press release and the printout of the photo on the desk, before turning to Ísrún.

'What do your copper friends have to say?' he demanded harshly.

She examined the picture and saw that the man wasn't someone she recognised straightaway. She may have seen him before, but couldn't be sure. He looked an amiable young man, wearing a striped shirt, a smile and a neat haircut.

'They're not telling us a lot,' she said. 'I'll have something more for you by the end of the day.'

She swept up the press release and read through it quickly.

'Is this guy a known criminal?' one of the other journalists asked doubtfully; the man in the picture clearly didn't have a criminal look about him.

'Quite the opposite,' Ívar said. 'He's a business graduate. The police aren't saying a lot, but I've just done a quick background check on him.'

Ísrún smiled to herself, certain that Ívar's background check had gone no further than typing the man's name into a search engine.

'He was in the news a couple of years ago when his girlfriend was assaulted,' Ívar continued, bursting with self-importance. 'You must remember it. He was interviewed a few times and criticised the police for the slow investigation.'

Ísrún remembered the disturbing case well. 'The woman died not long ago,' she said.

Ívar nodded. 'Was that case ever resolved?' he asked, the question directed at Ísrún.

Now she was on home turf. 'No,' she replied. 'There was never a conclusion. I gather there was a man who was strongly suspected, but I don't recall his name, although I can probably find it if I go through my old notes. He was never mentioned in the media and there was no evidence against him.'

'Check it out, would you?' Ívar said with unexpected courtesy. 'Was the man's name Róbert, by any chance?' he added.

Ísrún searched her memory, without success.

'I don't recall,' she said. 'Why do you ask?'

'I heard this morning who the abducted child is,' Ívar said, purring with pride. 'Maybe you'd heard as well?'

Ísrún shook her head, cursing inwardly.

'The child's mother is a girl called Sunna. She's a dancer, living on Ljósvallagata with a man called Róbert. We need to find out if he has a connection with this Emil, and we need to find out right away.'

Once the meeting was over, Ísrún went gloomily to her computer and searched through her notes. She quickly found the name of the man who was at the top of the list of suspects – in reality, the only one – linked to the assault two years ago: a drug user and known debt collector.

She closed her eyes and made an effort to control her rage.

Hell.

The man's name was Róbert.

A brief search gave her his full name, and the national registry told her that he lived on Ljósvallagata with his partner, Sunna, and a one-and-a-half-year-old boy, Kjartan.

It had been a lousy way to start the day.

31

The winter sun fought to break through the clouds. Emil screwed up his eyes and peered down at the pavement below. He savoured the warmth the occasional beam of sunlight brought. In between, he was cold but had more important things to concern himself with. He was on his way to his parents' house, on foot. He was also alone, free of the whining child.

The endless crying had been too much for him but he had found no way to calm the baby.

All the same, it hadn't been a mistake. Róbert had taken his and Bylgja's unborn child from them, so there was a certain justice in what he had done. For a moment, Emil had imagined that the child had been his. It had even occurred to him to take the boy and disappear.

He walked briskly through the streets of downtown Reykjavík. He instinctively kept away from the edges of the pavements, seemingly drawn as close as possible to the trees and shrubs around the gardens – the boundaries of the places where people should be safe in the security of their own homes. Bylgja had been so certain she was safe at home – free to spend her evenings wearing pyjamas, engrossed in her studies.

There were no other people about, or if there were, Emil didn't notice their presence. He had enough on his mind and, in spite of everything, his work was only half done. He couldn't be sure how long his endurance would last, but his hatred seemed to keep him going. He was certain that Róbert was to blame for his wife's death and was determined he would pay for it. Emil had no fear of any repercussions. He had made no real efforts to cover his tracks, apart from staying in the shadows to give himself the space he needed to finish what he had started.

He rubbed a cheek and felt the bristles. Maybe he'd take the time to shave once he was home, if he had the energy. He smiled to himself at the recollection of how Bylgja had always complained if had gone a few days without shaving. He admitted to himself that now there was no reason left to shave or look after his appearance. He only had his parents left. They'd still love him unconditionally even when he told them what he had done. They'd understand. His mother would wrap her arms around him, her embrace warm and reassuring, and tell him that everything would work out for the best, that nobody would blame him for it.

The sun appeared again. He stopped for a moment, faced the sun and closed his eyes. Most of the chill left him.

Maybe taking a small child from its mother had been going too far. Then he thought of Bylgja, as he did every day. The only thing he avoided thinking about was the feeling that maybe his revenge was not quite as sweet as he had hoped. He had done his very best to avenge her, but he didn't feel any better for it. Perhaps he hadn't expected to.

32

Heida was there to meet them at the apartment on Ljósvallagata. She had made coffee and laid the kitchen table. She had found cinnamon rolls in the freezer, had heated them up and put them on a plate in the middle of the checked tablecloth.

Róbert had not expected this. Maybe she was trying, in her own way, to make up for her previous rudeness. She asked no questions and they said nothing. Their silence told the whole story; the boy had still not been found.

There was an unaccustomed warmth to the apartment. Róbert found the feeling coming over him that nothing was wrong, that Kjartan was asleep in his bed and the events of the last few days had been long forgotten. It didn't take him long to get over such a ridiculously false impression.

It was public knowledge that the police wanted to speak to Emil urgently and it was only a matter of time before his name and Sunna's would also become widely known. He hoped it wouldn't happen, but knew better than to hope for too much. The question was how deep the media would dig. Would he and Sunna be granted a level of consideration when the time came for questions about their past – his past?

The three of them sat at the kitchen table.

'Do you want me to stay here in case anyone comes?' Heida asked, and Róbert wondered if he had misjudged her now that she had been considerate and courteous for so unusually long. It didn't last, however. 'You know I have a flight home booked for next week and I can't change it, so I won't be able to help after that if the boy isn't found.'

Sunna burst into tears and left the table.

Róbert followed her into the bedroom, leaving Heida at the table, her words echoing around the kitchen.

He shut the door and did his best to comfort Sunna. She was weeping inconsolably; a flood of tears that seemed to have no end. This wasn't the time to tell her why Emil had taken the boy, but how long would he be able to put it off?

After a while, Sunna regained some composure and they went back to the kitchen where Heida was finishing the last of the cinnamon rolls.

Maybe it was as well that Heida was there. It excused him from having to sit down with Sunna and calmly explain his past. Heida was granting him a stay of execution by being there.

He was almost hoping for a miracle; not just that the boy would be found, but that there would be a way for him to save his own skin.

When the phone rang, he was certain of two things: that it was the police and that Kjartan had been found safe and well.

The Chief Inspector got straight to the point.

'We've found him,' he said, with gloom in his voice. 'We've found Emil, I mean,' he added awkwardly.

'What the hell do you mean?' Róbert asked, immediately regretting the tone of voice that made Sunna start in alarm.

'He didn't have the boy with him. We caught up with him not far from his parents' home. He didn't seem to have any idea that we were looking for him. He didn't resist. You can be sure that every available officer is searching for Kjartan.'

There was a painful silence that followed his words.

'Did he say anything?'

There was another long silence.

'He just grinned at us. Said he'd left the boy by the Tjörnin lake.'

'By the lake?' Róbert yelled. Sunna burst into tears again and stretched to snatch the phone from him. 'Do you ... do you think ...?' He was unable to finish his sentence.

Heida hugged her sister.

'You'll just have to trust us. We're organising a search of ... of the area.' The Chief Inspector was clearly avoiding voicing what they all feared.

'Can I help?' Róbert asked.

'No. You just stay with your girlfriend. We'll be in touch as soon as we find the boy.'

Róbert could feel his heart beating faster, and he could again feel the throbbing headache and the cold that refused to leave him alone. A day and a night of stress had worn him out. He rubbed his eyes in an effort to relieve the pain.

Right now he would have given anything to be alone with Emil, man to man; only one of them would walk away alive. But his anger was mixed with fright. He feared the worst for Kjartan.

And he was also terrified of Sunna. Time was running out for him now; soon she would hear about the assault that had taken place two years before. He was sure he wouldn't be convincing enough when he denied any involvement. It seemed there was only one way this could all end.

33

Ari Thór searched without success through online newspaper archives from March 1957 for Jórunn's obituary. All he was able to find was a bland death notice; it wasn't even accompanied by a picture. Jórunn had lived and died privately.

He called Kristín again.

'I thought you might like to bring something good to eat with you tonight – a curry or a pizza. It would really make a welcome change.'

She thought for a moment, just long enough to make a point, and agreed.

'OK. You've got yourself a deal. I'll be there around seven thirty with some take-away. Shall I bring a bottle of wine as well? I don't suppose the liquor store is open?'

'Siglufjördur has never been as dry as it is right now.'

'How are you holding up, Ari?' she asked with warmth.

'It's tough, you know, it's been hellish, I can tell you. I wish you were here, Kristín.' Then he added, before she could reply: 'Sandra, you remember her?'

'Yes, of course – the old girl you keep visiting behind my back,' Kristín said teasingly.

'She isn't doing too well.'

'Oh, really? I'm sorry, Ari, is it this virus?'

'Apparently not, but she's getting on in age, and I'm worried. And this, on top of everything else.'

'I'm sure it will be OK. See you tonight, I have to run,' she said.

'There's a storm forecast for tonight,' Ari Thór said. 'You might get snowed in with me.'

'I can think of worse things,' Kristín replied.

At midday Ari Thór had an appointment to meet Helga, the senior doctor at the hospital. Representatives of the Civil Defence Authority had already travelled to Siglufjördur and had a meeting with her that morning. Helga said their discussion had been quick and the result was that the quarantine would be officially lifted at six that evening.

Helga looked as if a weight had been lifted from her shoulders and she had the look of someone who had not slept well for days.

For his part, Ari Thór was thankful that he had come out of this crisis unscathed. He had escaped any infection, despite being one of the few people in the town who was required to be out and about, and had managed to rest fairly well between shifts. He had even found time to dig into a forgotten case that had turned out to be much more interesting than most – in fact, all – of the cases that the Siglufjördur police force had dealt with so far that year.

Ari Thór was on his way out of the hospital when he noticed a door marked 'Midwifery'. He stopped, a thought surfacing in his mind. He was reminded of the boy in Blönduós – the baby who might well have a father in the Siglufjördur police. There was a possibility that Ari Thór might have missed out on the birth of his own son; he felt a stab of regret.

But before any further doubts could assail him, another idea crystallised in his mind. Hédinn had been born in Hédinsfjördur, so the midwife from Siglufjördur must have gone over there to attend to the birth – undoubtedly one of the few people who would have had reason to visit the inhabitants of Hédinsfjördur. Could she be still alive? He rapidly worked out the dates. It might just be possible. If she had been in her twenties then, she would now be into her eighties.

He knocked at the midwife's door and a middle-aged woman opened it.

'Well,' she said. 'A visit from the police?'

'Could I come in for a moment?' Ari Thór asked with a smile.

'Be my guest,' she replied, and took a seat behind a desk piled high with paperwork. 'Normally you'd have to make an appointment, but things are quiet at the moment. When are you due?' she asked, her face straight.

The joke took Ari Thór by surprise; he reacted by retreating deeper into formality than usual.

'I'd like to find out about midwives working here in the town around the middle of the last century.'

'Listen, I'm not that old, even though I'm coming up for retirement,' she replied with a warm smile.

'Is it possible to look up midwives from that time? Specifically, in 1956?'

'I don't need to look that up. That would have been Sigurlaug.'

Ari Thór instantly felt buoyed up again. 'Where can I find her?'

'You can't find her anywhere. She died years ago.'

So that avenue was closed, he decided, and stood up.

'Alright. Thanks. I'll leave you to deal with the next baby.'

'Hmm. Babies aren't born here anymore. Some of them go to Akureyri and others go all the way to Reykjavík. I just look after ante-natal stuff and then post-natal assistance. Endless paperwork, as you can see,' she said, resting a hand on one of the stacks of documents.

Ari Thór sat down again. 'Do you have reports from that time? I'm looking for information about a birth in Hédinsfjördur, in May 1956.'

'That would be Hédinn, wouldn't it?' she said thoughtfully. 'He was the only one born in Hédinsfjördur, as far as I know.'

'That's right.'

'Well, we have reports on all kinds of things. You just need time to search through them.' She peered at him and her eyes narrowed, twinkling with humour. 'Would you like me to see what I can find?'

'I'd very much appreciate it,' he said bashfully, and saw from the look on her face that she was waiting for an explanation. But he decided to wait for her to ask him directly.

'It's an unusual request, you know,' she said, hesitatingly. 'Can I ask why you're interested in these documents?'

Ari Thór grinned, pleased that he had figured her out correctly. 'If you can find the report, then I'll tell you the whole story. I'll drop by again later,' he said, getting to his feet.

'My pleasure. I'll do my best. I should be able to look into it first thing on Monday. Is that all right with you?'

'That would be perfect.'

It wasn't as if this was a priority, but it would be interesting to have any impressions from someone else who had been in Hédinsfjördur at that time.

Outside, in the car park in front of the hospital, Ari Thór turned back. He had meant to ask after Sandra. Back inside the building, he asked for Helga and she appeared after a few minutes.

'Hello again,' Ari Thór said. 'I completely forgot. I wanted to ask how old Sandra's getting on.'

'She talks a lot about you,' Helga said, without answering the question.

'Is she recovering?'

'I shouldn't really discuss her condition with someone who isn't a relative,' she said. 'But I suppose I can make an exception. The police ought to be aware of how the hospital is coping with other illnesses during this unusual time.'

Ari Thór waited anxiously.

'She doesn't look good and the flu has weakened her. She's worn out and I don't think she has long left. Won't you go and see her? She's probably awake now and I know she would appreciate it.'

Ari Thór looked at his watch as if he were already late for another meeting.

'I'm tied up for the next hour or so,' he lied, feeling like a coward. 'I'll drop by this evening or tomorrow. Would you say hello to her for me?'

34

'They are searching for Kjartan, we just need to wait,' Róbert said when Sunna had calmed down a bit.

'Why did you mention the lake?' she yelled.

'They got the guy who took him, Sunna, he says the boy's alright. That he left him by the lake.'

'Not *in* the lake? Are you sure? Tell me, Róbert, tell me … I need to know!'

'*By* the lake, darling, he said by the lake. It's just a matter of waiting now.'

She sat on the floor and cried.

He watched her helplessly. It was like waiting for a countdown to end – a ticking time bomb. There was an explosion due and it was anyone's guess who the survivors would be.

'I have to leave,' Heida said after a brief silence.

Normally Róbert would have been delighted, but now he would have given anything for her to stay. He had no desire to be alone with Sunna. It was too difficult; he would have no excuse then not to tell her the truth.

'No, please, Heida, stay with us. You're part of the family.'

'Sorry, I really have to go, Róbert. I'll be in touch, let me know if anything happens, OK?'

He sighed and nodded. Sunna didn't say a word; she simply moaned a little.

Emil had grinned when the police asked where the little boy was. What the hell did that mean?

*

Róbert had lost track of time when the phone finally rang. It was
the Chief Inspector. Róbert answered with his heart in his mouth.
Sunna, still on the floor, looked up at him, her eyes wide.

'We've found Kjartan. Safe and well.'

Róbert gasped with relief and the phone dropped from his hand.

'They've found him,' he gasped, crouching down and wrapping
his arms around Sunna. 'They found him. They've found Kjartan.
He's OK. He's safe now.'

But it was like holding a mannequin. She was stiff and still in his
arms; she didn't speak, didn't make a noise. Showed no reaction at all.

He grabbed the phone from the floor. 'I can't tell you how relieved
I am,' he said, choking back his tears. 'Where did you find him?'

'Believe it or not, in the playground of a kindergarten near the
lake. The little fellow is exhausted and hungry; he was probably too
weak to cry loud enough for someone to notice him. It wasn't until
the kindergarten kids were let out to play that the teachers noticed
there was a distressed child out there.'

Róbert looked over at Sunna and saw that some life had now
returned to her. Something like a smile spread across her face, but it
was twisted up with a grimace, almost of pain. And then her relief
broke through in a flood of tears and sobs.

'Are you on the way over here?' he asked the Chief Inspector.

'We'll be there soon. We're just getting the doctor to check the
boy first.'

'That's wonderful. Thank you,' Róbert said.

He held Sunna again, feeling her shaking body against his. Could
he allow himself to hope that there was no longer any need to discuss
his connection to Emil with her? Had his prayers been answered?

By the time the Chief Inspector and his team arrived shortly afterwards, Róbert had worked himself up into such a new panic he
hardly noticed the little boy who had been missing for a day and
a night. Instead all his attention was on trying to read what was

behind the smile on the policeman's face. Was he simply satisfied with the happy outcome to the case? Was he going to give away the secrets of Róbert's past? Perhaps he was even looking forward to it. Or maybe he wouldn't say anything unless Sunna asked. The waiting was torture; Róbert realised he was longing for a drink. No, not a drink. Something stronger than that. For the first time in months, he could hardly bear to face reality sober.

'It worked out in the best way it could,' the Chief Inspector said, once Sunna had held Kjartan tightly in her arms for a long time. 'The boy seems fine now. He just needs a bit of mother's love.'

'As I told you before, Emil is in custody.' He paused and then went on. 'We searched his place – or, rather, his parents' home, and there were several interesting things we found there. The media are going to latch on to this, so it's best that you're forewarned. You'll get plenty of attention.'

He seemed ready to go, and Róbert thought he might be able to relax.

But Sunna looked up, dragging her eyes away from Kjartan's face for a moment and stopping the Chief Inspector by the door. 'Did he say why he did it?' she asked quietly.

Róbert felt the world going dark in front of him. The Chief Inspector was staring at him. The question remained unasked; *didn't you talk to her?*

Róbert sat down on the sofa, looking at the floor and hoping his face didn't betray his emotions. Sunna stood in the middle of the room with Kjartan clasped in her arms.

'He had staked you out, and he had followed you,' the Chief Inspector said, directing his words to Sunna.

She said nothing but the shock was clear in her eyes. Her eyebrows creased up and he mouth fell open.

'He had meant to seek revenge, as we had suspected.'

'Revenge?' Sunna asked in astonishment.

'He felt he had unfinished business with Róbert.'

Sunna stood silent, her mouth still hanging open, looking from the Chief Inspector, to Róbert and then back again, seemingly unable to speak.

'It's connected to an assault that took place in January two years ago. There was a break-in at a private house one evening, almost certainly in error; we think whoever broken in chose the wrong house. A young woman was at home alone, her husband was at work. She suffered a brutal assault and we think a baseball bat was used.'

'I remember the case...' Sunna said. 'But ...' she began, her face a picture of confusion.

'She never recovered from her injuries and passed away earlier this year. Her husband – Emil – has suffered from significant mental problems since then. He hasn't been able to work and has lived with his parents. He appears to have been determined to seek revenge.'

'But what does all that have to do with Róbert?' she demanded, her voice sharp now. Kjartan gave out a scream and began crying.

The Chief Inspector hesitated before continuing.

'He was a suspect at the time. Emil was aware of that. In fact, Róbert was our only suspect in the case, but there was no evidence against him. So, I'm afraid, it's not exactly a surprise that Emil focused his anger and sorrow in your direction. It's a tragedy from start to finish.'

Sunna said nothing. She turned to the window, trying to calm Kjartan down.

The Chief Inspector made for the door. Róbert got to his feet and followed him out of the room. On the doorstep, he murmured his thanks for all his efforts.

The Chief Inspector turned, gave him a steely glare, and walked to his car without another word.

The steps back to the living room felt long and arduous. He was met with Sunna's unwavering gaze.

'I'm not going to get myself worked up,' she said slowly and quietly. 'Not while Kjartan is here. But I can't believe that you kept this from me. I can understand why you did, but that doesn't mean to say I forgive you for it.' She paused and took a deep breath, closing her eyes as she did so. 'But I have to ask you, Róbert. Did you assault that woman?'

The silence that followed crackled with tension.

Róbert stood still; sweat broke out once more over his entire body.

'No ... no ... Of course I didn't, sweetheart...' he stammered at last and knew instantly that she could see through the lie.

Hell.

It was so unfair. He was sick and tired, and drained. Just one drink would have got him through all this so easily. He didn't dare look into her eyes, conscious of the anger radiating from her face.

'Get out,' she snapped, the tears about to choke her. And keeping her voice low, she repeated it several times: 'Get out, get out, get out.'

He didn't say goodbye, just put on his coat and shoes and walked out into the bright day outside.

All he could think of now was walking downtown and finding somewhere he could sit down and get himself a drink.

He had known it would end this way. He'd been kidding himself if he thought it wouldn't. Sunna was too good for him. It was always going to be difficult for a small-time villain to turn over a new leaf – more than likely it couldn't be done.

Small-time villain. He smiled to himself. That assault was no minor offence, but he had an excuse. The drugs had taken hold and he had been in a bad way when he took the job on. It should have been so simple – just collecting money and using threats. Nothing properly serious. No real violence.

He remembered that night well, even though he'd been in a doped-up fog. He was sure the girl was lying when she said she didn't know the man he was collecting for. He had been so angry at her. He'd lost his temper and let fly with the bat. He could still see the look on the woman's face as he swung; pure surprise. It was as if she didn't believe he'd go that far. He hadn't believed he could go that far ...

It was when his head cleared and he realised what he had done that he knew he had to get a grip – seek treatment and say goodbye to the drugs.

All the same, the memory of that night stayed with him, keeping him awake and coming to him in his dreams. There had been all that blood, not to mention the sickening crack of the bat on the girl's head as he'd put all the power he could behind it.

He had been interrogated again and again, but there was never enough evidence to pin anything on him. Of course he didn't admit to anything. It was as if some higher power had protected him. Maybe it wasn't right to punish him for something that the drugs were responsible for. By turning over a new leaf, he felt that he had made a kind of penance and ensured that it would never happen again. But the nightmares had never gone away.

He continued on his way downtown and knew there was no doubt that he and Sunna were finished. Maybe Emil had managed to extract some kind of vengeance after all.

35

Persistence finally paid off; after endless attempts Ísrún was able to speak to her police contact. By then she had already heard that the little boy had been found and the suspect arrested. She wouldn't be the first one with this piece of news that evening.

'At last,' she said cheerfully. You've been busy?'

'You have no idea.'

'Congratulations. It's great that you found the boy and caught the kidnapper,' she said. 'Case closed?'

There was silence on the phone.

'Not quite,' he said eventually.

'What does that mean?' she asked, feeling her pulse quicken.

'If I tell you, then you promise not to use it until tomorrow; you can't breathe a word about it before then. There'll be a statement tonight.'

Ísrún swore under her breath; she had no choice but to agree to his conditions.

'This guy, Emil, lives with his parents and we searched the house. The real surprise was in the garage,' he said and waited, clearly in no mood to tell all without encouragement.

'Right. Was there anything more than a car in there?' Ísrún asked.

'No. It was the car that was interesting, especially the blood on the bonnet.'

'Meaning what?'

'The car appears to have been involved in a collision; or rather, it seems it was in a hit-and-run. Don't forget. Not a word to anyone.'

Ísrún rapidly joined the dots but was hardly able to believe her own theory.

'A hit-and-run – you mean Snorri Ellertsson?'

There was a long silence. 'We have been questioning Emil about it,' he said at last. 'He's admitted that it was him. He ran Snorri over.'

'But why?'

'He's seeking revenge for the death of his wife. I gather he believes that Snorri was involved, along with the boyfriend of the girl whose child was abducted. He was determined to pay both of them back.'

With so little information to work on, Ísrún was finding it hard to pull the pieces of this story together. The same man – Emil – seemed to have murdered Snorri and abducted the baby boy, clearly working on the premise that both Snorri and this man Róbert had been involved in the assault that had led to his wife's death.

It was unbelievable.

Had the son of national treasure Ellert Snorrason murdered a young woman in cold blood? There was no doubt in her mind that this would be the news story of the year.

It was common knowledge that Snorri had at one time struggled with an alcohol problem, and probably drugs as well, and had been close to some dubious underworld figures. This had cast a definite shadow over his father's work, but Ellert had seemed to weather the potential storm around his son's affairs.

Or had he?

She recalled that the old man had abruptly retired from politics not long before the formation of a government of national unity that he would most likely have headed as Prime Minister.

She hurried over to her computer and searched for the exact dates of the assault, comparing them to the dates of Ellert's retirement from public life. Her search told her that Ellert's announcement that he was about to stand down as party leader for personal reasons had come only a few days after the assault had taken place. A curious coupling of events, Ísrún decided.

She picked up her mobile and called Lára, Marteinn's private secretary, hoping that she hadn't yet heard the news about Emil.

'Ísrún,' Lára said, smoothly greeting her like an old friend. 'Good to hear from you.'

'Likewise,' Ísrún said, faking a similar level of sincerity. 'I've been thinking things over and I'd like to interview Marteinn about these cabinet changes he has in mind.'

'That's brilliant!' Lára said. Ísrún wondered if she looked up at the ceiling while she was on the phone, or if it was a habit that only took hold when she met people face to face, if that expression could be applied to someone who never looked you in the eye. 'Let's make an appointment for next week, shall we?'

'I'll be mostly off duty then,' Ísrún said. 'We ought to do it as soon as possible; today would be ideal. Things are quiet now that the kidnapped child has been found, so there isn't much happening. This could be a lead item.'

'There's no chance of doing it today. The earliest he'll be available is tomorrow.'

'Fine, let's fix a time,' Ísrún replied, hiding her disappointment. 'When's he free?'

'Just a moment,' Lára said, 'I'll check his diary.' She was back a moment later. 'How about three tomorrow? At the Ministry?'

He prefers to be on home ground, Ísrún thought, and accepted the offer.

It was barely an hour later that the red-haired private secretary called back. Ísrún watched the phone flashing in her hand before deciding to answer it, certain that she knew what the call would be about. Lára had undoubtedly got wind of the police investigation linking Snorri to the assault.

'Hello again, Ísrún,' Lára said, her voice tense, as she clearly did her best to hide the fact that she was under pressure.

'Hi, Lára,' Ísrún replied, leaning back in the creaking danger zone that, in a poor light, could pass for an office chair. She was determined to take no prisoners and make the most of the conversation.

'I'm afraid we'll have to postpone the interview.'

'That's no problem. I'm free at two, and could be available at four. Anything later is going to be awkward as I'll need time to edit the footage.'

'No, please don't get me wrong. It'll have to be next week, or the week after that.'

'Hold on a moment. Hadn't we made an appointment just now? Why are you so keen to back out of this all of a sudden?'

Lára took her time answering, so Ísrún took the opportunity to increase the pressure.

'Does Marteinn have something to hide? Something to do with Snorri Ellertsson, maybe? I didn't think he had anything to do with that, but now you're making me suspect otherwise, Lára.'

'No, he has nothing to hide. Nothing at all,' Lára said. 'Sorry for the confusion. I'll make sure it'll work out tomorrow. Three o'clock.'

Ísrún was surprised at how easy it had been. It was obvious that Lára was far from being on top form right now.

'Excellent. I'll see you then.'

36

The evening news bulletin was about to start when Ísrún remembered the package she was meant to fetch from Nikulás. She hadn't promised anything, but, all the same, she was reluctant to disappoint the old man.

She had also promised to be at her father's place for dinner right after work, although describing it as dinner was stretching the description of what she knew was likely to be on offer. Her father was no chef and he would either order them a pizza or buy a grilled chicken from the shop on the corner. The chicken would be served whole, probably with nothing more than chips and ketchup to accompany it. She'd be happy with that and the comfortable atmosphere that reminded her of how things used to be. They would undoubtedly eat in front of the television and, with luck, she would be able to relax after a tough week.

The only way to avoid disappointing both her father and Nikulás was to disappoint Ívar, and she had no qualms about letting him down. She went briskly over to where he sat in the desk editor's enveloping chair, absorbed in the news bulletin.

'I have to go,' Ísrún said.

'And miss the meeting?'

She nodded. It was hardly likely that anything important would be discussed at the end-of-day meeting, but being present for it was practically mandatory.

'I'll be here in the morning, so if there's anything, I'll see you then.'

Ívar snorted. 'I'm off for the weekend. María's the weekend desk editor, so you can talk things over with your pal in the morning.' He made no effort to hide his scorn. 'You'd better be off if you have to go.' And with that, he turned back to the news.

The conversation had been over quickly and Ísrún hadn't even had to use the lie she had prepared. She grinned to herself and hurried out before he could change his mind.

Nikulás was also watching the news when Ísrún arrived. He smiled broadly when he saw her and, with some difficulty, got up from the sofa.

'Hello. I saw you on the news just now,' he said. 'I couldn't hear it properly, but I'm sure it was full of insight,' he said with a laugh and motioned her towards his room. Leaning on a stick, he followed her, slowly but surely.

The box was next to his bed, where he took a seat and sighed.

'I'm sorry. It's quite a walk, even though it isn't far,' he said and lapsed into silence for a moment. 'These are Maríus's papers. So that's something for you to dig through. He wasn't much for the written word and didn't collect too much unnecessary junk. He just kept things that might be important – old bankbooks and letters, that sort of thing.'

'Have you been through it yourself?' she asked, leaning close to him and speaking clearly. 'Is there anything there that I should take a careful look at?'

'I read through all this for the first time last night. I never saw a reason to before. These were his documents, and none of my business. My hearing's going, but I can still see well enough,' he said.

'Just as well,' Ísrún said, to contribute something to the conversation.

'I don't know about that. I reckon I'd have been happy to have been able to strike a deal with God on that score,' he said and Ísrún stared at him in amazement. 'I'd still be able to enjoy music, you see. I've seen everything I'll ever need to see, but it's a tragedy not being able to enjoy a symphony any more,' he said, shaking his head in frustration. 'But that's another matter. I did find a letter in there that you'll find interesting. But take the whole box with you, anyhow. You can have it for a few days, but I'd appreciate it if you could bring it back soon.'

Ísrún nodded. Nikulás took the document that lay at the top of the pile in the box and handed it to her. She saw that it was a letter dated 1950, addressed to Marías Knutsson, from his brother-in-law, Gudmundur. The script was clear and neat.

As she started to read, Nikulás continued with his tale.

'This was sent when the boy – Jórunn and Maríus's son – was a newborn. Gudmundur and Gudfinna must have found out that there was talk of putting the child up for adoption. I imagine the sisters were in touch and Jórunn told Gudfinna about it. You'll see in the letter that Gudmundur offered to adopt the boy. It's typical of the time that this was something that the husbands discussed, with Gudmundur writing to Maríus. There's not much else of interest there, just news from Siglufjördur – about the weather and the fishing. He mentions the adoption right at the end. It didn't come to anything, as I told you before. Strangers adopted the boy. But I hadn't known that Gudmundur and Gudfinna had offered to take him.' He cleared his throat. 'It confirms what I had always felt – that deep inside Gudmundur could be a generous man. He was always ready to do someone worse off than himself a favour, just as he did when he found work for Maríus up north.' The old man smiled.

'What was Gudfinna like – as a person, I mean?' Ísrún asked.

'They had much the same temperament, those two. There was a determination about her; she liked to have her own way. On the bossy side, I think you could say, and easily jealous. That was my impression of her. I reckon she'd have preferred to live in Reykjavík than up there on the coast, but apart from that she never wanted for anything.'

'Tell me one last thing,' Ísrún said. 'Do you think it's possible that Jórunn's death was neither suicide nor an accident?'

Nikulás thought. 'It's hard to say,' he said. 'I don't think it's likely.'

'In such cases the spouse is generally the suspect. You knew your brother well. I apologise in advance if it's an insensitive thing to suggest, but do you think he could have been capable of doing such a thing?'

He shook his head. 'I'm not easily shocked these days, so don't worry. And, anyway, it's a good question. But the answer is no. Maybe I'm not impartial enough to give you an honest answer, so you can take or leave my opinion. It's true, Maríus didn't cope well under pressure. He'd get agitated if he was stressed. Those were tough years for them: he struggled to keep a job and they didn't find it easy to make ends meet. And things only got worse. Then Gudmundur invited them up north and helped him find work; as I say, he probably did it out of the goodness of his heart – and to please his wife, of course, who must have been worried about her sister. After that, I don't imagine Maríus had much to complain about up there, really. And even though there could be an anger in him in the heat of an argument – he got into a few fights in the old days – I know he didn't have it in him to commit murder.' He paused, looking at her. 'That's what I believe, anyway,' he added quietly.

The house owned by Ísrún's parents, Anna and Orri, stood in a quiet, tree-lined street in Grafarvogur. The skinny saplings that had been in the garden when the family had moved there all those years before were now established trees, reminding Ísrún of how fast time passes. Now Orri had the whole two hundred square metres of the house to himself and the longer his separation from Anna lasted, the more lost he seemed in its great expanse.

Ísrún still had a key. She opened the door and went straight into the living room where she found her father watching the news from a leather armchair sat beneath a giant painting. It was a painting that Ísrún had always had a fondness for. Her mother had bought it during a business trip to Russia at a time when her publishing business was thriving. Two metres square, the painting immediately attracted the gaze of anyone who came into the room; it showed a group of foot-ballers standing in the middle of the pitch at the end of a game, some of them already with their shirts stripped off. The men were so realistic, their presence so immediate, that it was as if they were part of the family. Orri had never liked the painting, while Anna said that she had bought it for what she called a 'good price'. Ísrún was sure that it must have come with a respectable price tag, because, shortly afterwards, Orri brought home a beautiful watercolour by Ásgrímur Jónsson that he had picked up at an auction and which he hung next to the television, opposite the footballers. Ever since there had been a cold war between Soviet realism and Icelandic romanticism.

'Good to see you, darling' Orri said, getting up from the sofa to hug her. 'I bought us a grilled chicken. You are hungry, aren't you?'

'Starving,' she assured him and smiled, noticing the tomato sauce bottle was in its place on the table next to the chicken and chips.

They watched the rest of the news bulletin in silence. The last item was the interview with Ari Thór in Siglufjördur, which ended with the passing mention of the photograph of the unknown young man.

Not bad, Ísrún thought to herself.

'How's your mother?' Orri asked.

'I haven't heard much from her since I came back from the Faroes. Wouldn't it be best for you to call her at the weekend?' she asked, interested to see what the response might be.

Orri looked awkward. 'I don't think so … I'm expecting her to call sooner or later. She must want to come home soon.'

'I think she's very happy in the Faroes at the moment. Maybe she just needed a break,' she said. Then she attempted to change the subject. 'How's business?'

'Pretty good,' her father replied, which she took to mean that he wasn't as busy as he would like to be. 'Maybe I shouldn't have been quite so enthusiastic. Your mother's normally right, you know.'

'How are you getting on, though? Still going to the gym?' she asked, her conscience nagging at her for having not yet mentioned to him the genetic illness she had inherited from his mother.

'Don't you worry about me, darling. The doc says I have the heart of a man of twenty,' he said, but Ísrún could see from his face he was, to some extent, embroidering what the doctor had told him.

Should she tell him the whole story?

She could – as long as she could extract a promise that he would not tell her mother about the illness. Anna didn't need to know. She would never get over news like that. In this respect Ísrún knew that her father was the more robust character.

It would certainly be a relief to be able to talk things over with someone other than the doctor, she thought. He was pleasant enough, but that only went so far, and anyway, she would hardly be anything other than a case as far as he was concerned: a number and a patient who would survive – or not.

'And how are you keeping? Aren't you working far too many hours?' her father enquired.

This was her opportunity. A choice between; 'Not doing as well as I'd like,' or else; 'Fine, thanks, but I was diagnosed the other day with this condition.'

It was a struggle to get the words out. She hesitated, needing a few minutes to plan her words.

'Busy at work and I don't dare turn down any shifts, not at the moment,' she said and smiled at him.

'You're doing well keeping on top of that crime story. But can't you do something different, maybe assignments that are a little less brutal?'

'Things are fine as they are. When I'm the news editor then I'll be able to pick and choose for myself.'

'Ambition,' he said with clear approval. 'That's what I like to hear.'

The chicken had been reduced to its bones and her father had fetched a film he had rented – a fairly recent thriller that Ísrún had not seen. She rarely went to the cinema and didn't follow the world of movies closely. So she was happy to let him decide what they watched. This had been a family tradition for years; Ísrún would come over for dinner once a week and they would watch a film together after a meal – which would be something more appetising than the standard chicken or pizza when her mother had been in the kitchen.

She made herself comfortable on the sofa, the perfect place to relax. She might even get to doze off during the film if she were lucky.

A few minutes into the film, and her eyelids were drooping already. She felt secure there, although her thoughts drifted to the illness and the results of the MRI scan that she was still waiting for. If things turned out for the worst, she would have no choice but to tell her family and her employers the whole story. Maybe it would be as well to do it right now, on a relaxed Friday night, under the noses of the Russian footballers?

The jangling of her phone brought her back to reality. She wasn't sure she had fallen asleep or not; but she was now fully alert – the newsroom's phone number was there on the screen.

'Yes?' she replied in a tired voice.

'Hi, Ísrún. Not interrupting anything, am I?' her colleague on the evening shift asked.

'No, that's all right,' she muttered.

'Someone called the news hotline just now, wanting to talk to you. I didn't want to give him your number, so I took a message.'

'And?'

'He saw the item with the policeman – about the infection in Siglufjördur. He said he knows who the boy in the picture is.'

37

Siglufjördur's quarantine was formally lifted at six that evening. People had already been appearing on the streets for a while, prepared to stop and pass the time of day. The town's usual atmosphere was gradually returning. The place had become brighter, in spite of the rainclouds that were forming overhead. The sign in the Co-op window announced in big letters that the shop would be open that evening. Ari Thór was there as well, turning up at six thirty to buy some weekend essentials. The choice was limited, but nobody seemed to be concerned.

Kristín knocked at his door an hour later. Ari Thór had been eagerly anticipating seeing her again, but was also nervous at the prospect, aware that this time he couldn't afford to mess things up.

She had kept her side of the bargain, bringing with her a fine pizza as well as a bottle of red wine.

They sat in front of the television and watched the news while sharing the pizza. They sat close together on the sofa, just as they had always done before. It was as if nothing had changed between them – as if she had simply moved with him to Siglufjördur and never left his side. All the same, there was a tension between them; each seemed unsure of what to say to the other. Fortunately, the television rescued them from too many awkward silences.

Like the other evenings they had spent together recently, it felt like a first date, but with a warm, familiar feel to it. Ari Thór knew that he was being given a second chance, for which he was deeply thankful. But he also knew that this was a last chance. He had matured since their split and felt that she had done the same. In recent meetings, they had treated each other with more respect than before, but maybe also with less passion. He was still deeply in love with her, but there was perhaps a bit less emotion in their exchanges. He wasn't sure whether that was a good or a bad thing.

Ari Thór was off duty for the evening and for the whole of Saturday. He took care to mute his phone so they could enjoy the evening with no interruptions.

'Not a bad interview,' she said as the item about Siglufjördur came to an end. She rested her hand on his knee. 'A shame it was just a phone interview. What's all that about the old photograph?'

'Good question,' Ari Thór said, and told her the whole story, starting with Hédinn's visit, the death in Hédinsfjördur and the things that he and Ísrún had managed to uncover between them. Being a storyteller helped him relax and as he had the facts at his fingertips, the narrative flowed easily. The wine helped as well.

'I was wondering if you'd come with me to meet Hédinn tomorrow evening,' he said, hoping for a positive response. He had already spoken to Delía and she was happy to show Hédinn the film, adding that she regretted never having told him about it. 'He'll get to see the film from Hédinsfjördur for the first time,' he told Kristín.

'You're inviting me to come and watch a movie with you?' she asked.

'Sort of.'

'Sounds good. We can go out and have some fun tomorrow night,' she said and leaned close to whisper. 'But tonight we'll have our fun at home.'

38

Ísrún tried repeatedly to call Ari Thór. Becoming impatient, she followed the third unanswered call with a text message: CALL ME.

The man who claimed to know the identity of the youngster in
the photograph was called Thorvaldur. She had his number, and des-
perately wanted to call him and satisfy her curiosity, but she held
back. This was Ari Thór's affair and it would be better to talk to him
first to decide which of them should speak to him. But it hardly
mattered if they spoke to him now or in the morning, she supposed.

Her father had paused the film when she stood up to answer the
phone. Habit had taken her into her old room to take the call. By
the time she returned to the living room with her phone in her hand,
he had moved from the sofa to his favourite armchair where he was
snoring peacefully. There was no reason to wake him, she smiled to
herself. The movie could wait. She was deeply fond of the old man
and he had always been good to her – had always had time for her.

She thought of Emil, who had lost the love of his life without
a moment's warning in that brutal assault. How would she have
reacted in his position? What would she do if someone were to knock
one evening and beat her father to death with a baseball bat? She
shuddered, feeling the rage welling up inside her even at the thought
of it. She would want revenge, no doubt about it; but how far would
she be prepared to go? Not as far as Emil, surely?

But then again, was it even possible to imagine herself in the
position of a man whose world had crumbled to nothing in a single

evening? Emil's crimes had been unforgivable, and she had congratu-
lated the police for catching him. But maybe it was all too easy to
stand aloof and condemn him. Maybe she had been too harsh in
her judgement of the man, as she knew she was inclined to be. At
the very least, she had to admit to herself that she could sympathise
with the fury that had overwhelmed him. And there was no doubt
that he had evened out the score with Snorri Ellertsson, and that the
abduction would have lasting effects on Róbert.

A police press release had come in half an hour before the evening
news bulletin was due to air, announcing that there had been a search
of Emil's parents' house, and mentioning his alleged connection with
Snorri's murder. Ísrún had boiled the press release down into a short
item that went out as part of the bulletin.

It had been painful to have to sit on the bombshell that Emil
was convinced of Snorri's involvement in Bylgja's death, but she had
promised her contact that she'd keep it to herself until the morning
and dared not go against his instructions. That would be something
she'd only get to do once, and even for a piece of news like this, it
wasn't worth it. But, just for a moment, it had occurred to her to do
it all the same.

She had a one-to-one interview with the Prime Minister lined
up for the next day, just as the Emil–Snorri story would become
public knowledge. Admittedly, the interview was supposed to be
about changes to the cabinet, but there was always a chance she
could extract a reaction from Marteinn.

Ísrún padded to the door and out to her car to collect Nikulás's
box. Looking through the old papers would give her something to
occupy herself with while she waited for Ari Thór to reply.

Back in her old room, she shut the door behind her. Her bed was
where it had always been, but this had become a guest bedroom and
a storage space for the books there was no longer room for in the
living room.

Leafing through a dead stranger's documents gave her a chill of
discomfort; it was as if she were taking a look at something that was

no business of hers, or peering through someone's window. She put the savings books aside, as there was nothing to be learned from them. The letters were more interesting, though. Only the letter Nikulás had told her about had come from Gudmundur. Otherwise the letters appeared to be mainly from a friend who lived somewhere in the Westfjords and rarely came to Reykjavík. There was a warmth to his correspondence with Maríus – a genuine concern for him and frequent questions about the state of his and Jórunn's finances.

'I've enclosed a little something,' one letter ended. 'To help see you through the winter. You can pay me back when you can.'

There was nothing in the box that Maríus had written himself. There were lots of cuttings, every one of them about cars: advertisements for cars and pictures of limousines. Ísrún drew the conclusion that Maríus must have had a special interest, but one that he must have had to indulge from a distance. It was unlikely that he could have been able to afford any of them.

She lay back on her old bed and closed her eyes.

In this place all the problems of the world retreated into the distance. Her illness not only vanished, it seemed as if it had never even existed. The future became an unwritten book with a wealth of options open to her. She felt warm and secure as she fell into a deep sleep.

39

Ari Thór eased himself gently out of bed, leaving Kristín asleep.

It was almost midnight and he had remembered that he had left his phone on a shelf downstairs. Although he wasn't expecting any calls, he was reluctant to go to sleep without it nearby.

He went downstairs, taking care on the step that always creaked and hoping he hadn't woken Kristín. Picking the phone up, he was surprised to see three missed calls from Ísrún and a text message clearly stating that he should call right away.

He called her back, even though it was late; this had to be important.

Ísrún woke from a peaceful sleep to the sound of the phone buzzing. She shook herself awake and hoped Ari Thór would not realise that she had been asleep.

'Hello, thanks for calling back,' she said, unable to disguise the fatigue in her voice.

'No problem,' he replied. 'Anything new?'

'We're on the trail,' Ísrún said with satisfaction.

'Really? After the news? Any response?'

'You could say that. Someone called the news desk saying he knew who the young guy in the picture is.'

'What? Really?' Ari Thór asked in astonishment. 'Is the teenager in the picture still alive, then? What's his name?'

'I don't know, I'm afraid, I didn't take the call. I was just given a message. The man who phoned in is called Thorvaldur. I thought it might be best if you speak to him yourself. Do you have a pen and paper handy?'

'Just a moment,' he said and was back with the phone to his ear as Ísrún read out the number for him. 'Thank you. I'll call him in the morning. It's probably too late now, isn't it?'

'I reckon so,' Ísrún said, unable to keep the sarcasm out of her tone. 'Let me know what happens, you've no idea how curious I am about this.'

'Don't worry. We're a team now; it was fantastic that you could get the photo onto the news tonight, and it really made a difference that you could go and see old Nikulás.'

'Which reminds me …' she said, looking down at the box on the floor. 'Nikulás lent me a box of Maríus's papers: cuttings, bankbooks and the like. There's a letter from Gudmundur suggesting that he and Gudfinna should adopt the boy that Maríus and Jórunn had in 1950. That never happened, but Nikulás seems to think that it shows Gudmundur's goodwill towards the young couple.'

'That's interesting,' Ari Thór said. 'I have to admit that I'm wondering about Gudmundur. He's described as being either good-natured and helpful, or else arrogant and awkward. I'm finding it difficult to figure him out. He seems to have been a complex character. Or am I just reading the evidence wrongly?'

'They must have been an interesting group in Hédinsfjördur,' she said, not answering the question. 'Nikulás said that Gudfinna liked to get her own way and had been bossy by nature, even envious; the kind of woman who got what she wanted. Maríus appears to have been a simple soul, easily led and pushed around.'

'Jórunn must have had a hard time of it,' Ari Thór said. 'She had to give up her baby and then move north to such an isolated place. Then she got lost in the winter's darkness and died. Hédinn told me about something his father had said, which could concern Jórunn and her son.' And Ari Thór recounted Hédinn's father's disturbing tale.

'That's very interesting,' Ísrún said when he'd finished. 'But I find it hard to believe that Jórunn could have murdered her own child. However you look at it, though, Jórunn must have found it hard to bear seeing her sister having a child of her own. That may have added to her depression.'

'More than likely.'

'So there's a question,' Ísrún said, enjoying the speculation. 'What sort of person was this young lad, and what effect did his presence have on such an isolated group of people?'

'Let's hope we find out tomorrow,' Ari Thór said and Ísrún could sense his excitement.

She wondered for a moment if they were both just seeing this as a fascinating game; a mystery with a solution that would affect neither of them, just a pleasant diversion during the depths of winter. Had they forgotten that the people they were discussing had been real men and women who experienced joy and sorrow? Now, half a century later, free of any responsibility, she and Ari Thór were digging through these people's lives – and even their personal papers – to work out if one of them had committed a murder. The thought made her squirm a little.

'I'm waiting for some information from the local midwife as well,' Ari Thór added. 'She may be able to shed some light on the conditions over there.'

'She's still alive?' Ísrún asked in surprise. 'The midwife who delivered Hédinn?'

'No, nothing as good as that. The woman who is the current Siglufjördur midwife is going to go through the old paperwork; we'll see what she comes up with.'

'You're sure the midwife came from Siglufjördur?'

'Why do you ask?'

'Why do you think that the midwife would have come from Siglufjördur and not from Ólafsfjördur?'

'They were from Siglufjördur themselves, so I reckon that's more likely, and it's a longer journey from Ólafsfjördur. But you have a point, I suppose. I'll check tomorrow.'

'We're both going to be busy, and I need to get some sleep,' she said, stealing a glance at the clock. 'I have a shift tomorrow, yet again.'

'At least you get some variety,' Ari Thór replied, with a touch of bitterness. 'No two days are the same.'

'That's true enough,' she said thoughtfully, wondering if the young man was bored in his north-coast town. 'But people burn out quickly in this job,' she added, as if trying to give him some encouragement. 'And a journalist's job security is as good as zero. I envy you having that. You'll be able to stay on the force until you retire,' she said with a laugh, expecting to get a similar response from him. Instead there was silence.

'Anyway,' she said. 'I have to go. There's another murder to deal with tomorrow. Snorri Ellertsson's.'

'I saw it on the news. Hasn't that been resolved, now?' Ari Thór asked. 'Wasn't it the child abductor who murdered him – for the same reasons he took the child? My guess is that it was some kind of revenge; perhaps Snorri was involved in the assault on the man's wife, too.'

Ísrún had mentioned the resolution of the kidnapping during the news bulletin, which had included the theory that Emil had been seeking revenge for the death of his wife. No reason for Snorri's murder had yet been made public, but Ari Thór had clearly put two and two together. Ísrún thought carefully before replying. She took the decision to trust him.

'That's the way it looks, but please, not a word to anyone. Can we keep this between ourselves? I'm running a story on it in the morning. You can imagine the shock waves if it turns out that Ellert Snorrason's son beat a young woman to death.'

There was a moment's silence.

'I was imagining what happens if it turns out he *didn't* do it,' Ari Thór said, 'if he actually had nothing to do with the murder…'

40

As Ari Thór's conversation with Ísrún ended, he noticed that there were also messages from Tómas on his phone. They were more courteous that Ísrún's message, but the gist was the same.

Tómas was on duty so Ari Thór called him right away.

'Ah, dear boy. I hope I'm not disturbing you. You weren't asleep, were you?'

'No, not at all. Is anything wrong?'

He could hear Tómas hesitating, before his voice dropped to a grave bass.

'News from the hospital that I need to pass on to you dear boy,' he said.

Ari Thór sensed instantly what this was likely to be.

'Old Sandra passed away this evening. Poor old girl. Her time had come.'

Ari Thór didn't reply. He stood still and felt the energy seep out of him. The sight of the police car in the driveway that rainy afternoon fourteen years before came flashing back to him. The police were there to give the youngster the bad news that his mother had died in a car crash.

'I hope you're not too upset. She had a good, long life.'

'Thanks for letting me know,' Ari Thór said shortly. 'I'll come in and see you tomorrow.'

'You just take it easy tomorrow, and I'll see you on Sunday,' Tómas told him. 'Good night.'

Ari Thór was frozen to the spot.

He had wept when his mother died and had been unable to control the flood of tears. Now he had the urge to weep, but refused to give way to it.

His sorrow was mixed with deep regret. Why hadn't he made the effort to pay the old lady a visit?

As he padded up the stairs, his thoughts took him back to the cold autumn day of his mother's funeral.

He lay down next to Kristín, but he struggled to fall to sleep.

What a weakling he had been – wanting to avoid a difficult farewell. He was ashamed of himself and knew that this was something he would regret for the rest of his life.

41

At home in her little apartment, Ari Thór's words stayed in Ísrún's mind as she tried to get to sleep.

She turned over and over in bed, and was finally able to find some peace.

When she woke the following morning, however, she found that a new idea had formed in her mind.

What if Snorri had *not* been involved in the assault on that unfortunate woman? What if he had been innocent? If this was the case, why had Emil been convinced he was involved in some way in the assault?

Could this have been some kind of vicious political double-dealing, courtesy of Snorri's father's opponents? Her mind buzzed with ideas.

She was the first one into the newsroom, and as soon as she arrived, she tried to get through to her police contact, although she knew that she was pushing hard at the boundaries of their relationship. It was a shame really; now she only used him as a source of information, but at one time, briefly, they had been a couple.

They had met a few times and he hadn't hidden his interest in her. Then, one evening, she decided to take things a step further – to sleep with him once and see where that would take them. He was a good man: warm and trustworthy – not to mention good-looking. She had invited him to her place, but when it came to the crunch, she couldn't go through with it. She made a poor excuse and asked him to be on his way. She felt uncomfortable alone with him and didn't want to allow him to come too close. She knew very well why this was: she still hadn't recovered from being assaulted and raped a few years earlier. She would probably never fully get over that experience.

Now she needed him one more time, she told his answering service – to answer a single question: where had Emil's information that Snorri had been behind the assault come from?

Her police contact called her back a few minutes later. Ísrún had been right in her suspicion that he was becoming tired of her demands, but he said that of course he could 'understand her ambition'. She smiled to herself, conscious of why he was being so co-operative.

'There were rumours along those lines going around the party a while ago,' he said.

The answer she got when she asked which party he meant took her by surprise; it was Ellert Snorrason's party.

'Emil had a call from a guy who was active in party politics at that time, a man called Nói. He seems a normal guy, with a day job at an engineering firm. He said he'd heard about Snorri's involvement in the assault a couple of years before and was uncomfortable keeping that kind of secret. When the girl, Bylgja, finally died of her injuries, he wanted to pass the information on to her partner, just to be a Good Samaritan really. In fact, he didn't give his name, but he made the call from his mobile to the landline at Emil's parents' house, so it wasn't difficult to track him down. I spoke to him myself; he's the most innocent character you can imagine, but he managed to start all this rolling with one phone call. Emil admitted when we questioned him that this was the straw that broke the camel's back. Remember, this is all strictly between ourselves, Ísrún, but he said he had always known that Róbert was a suspect, and the call had given him the vital information that a second man had also been involved. He was determined to get revenge, and started stalking Róbert and his family; and he also got in touch with Snorri and laid a trail that would lead him somewhere quiet. And that's where he ran him down.'

Ísrún felt sick at what her contact described, but she tried to put herself in Emil's position – being forced to watch his partner gradually lose the battle for life following that terrible attack.

'Are you re-opening the case of the assault on Bylgja?'

'Certainly. Snorri has got away with it, if I can put it that way. But we'll be interviewing Róbert again. All the same, I don't imagine we'll be able to pin anything on him after all this time. I gather he's as slippery as an eel.'

Ísrún thanked him for taking the time to talk to her, and promised to buy him a drink when they both had time to meet. She immediately wished she hadn't, regretting having given him something to hope for, but it was still worthwhile to keep him warm.

So, it seemed the police were working on the assumption that Snorri was guilty, she thought, and that the rumours had some basis in fact.

Her own theory was quite the opposite, however.

Could this Nói, or someone he knew, have spun the rumour about Snorri? Could someone in his father's own party be behind this?

Now that she knew about Nói's political involvement, it was the work of a few minutes to find his full name. He was thirty-four and did, indeed, work for an engineering company. Other information about him on the internet was of no special interest, not until she started searching through the online images.

He was there in an old picture on the party website, standing next to someone Ísrún knew well. Standing side by side were the youth wing's chairman, Nói, and the vice-chair, now the Prime Minister's adviser, Lára.

42

Ari Thór was awake first thing.

He felt it was too early to call the man Ísrún had told him could identify the young man in the photograph, so, taking care not to wake Kristín, he pulled on jeans and a thick sweater and sat outside on the veranda off the bedroom. This was the first time he had slept in the house's main bedroom; up until now he had made do with a smaller room with a narrow single bed, as if he was unwilling to confirm his loneliness by sleeping by himself in a large bed.

It was a two-storey house, painted red but slightly dilapidated, with the upper level built into the eaves. That's where the bedrooms were: the small one and the large one, as well as an extra room, plus a landing with a nice window seat. The ceiling was low and the rooms were old and cosy. Downstairs was a living room, a kitchen, a TV room and an old-fashioned pantry – far too big for one man, but perfect for the two of them, and perhaps a larger family later on.

He savoured the fresh morning air out on the balcony, perching on a stool he had taken out there with him. His date with Kristín, if that's what it could be described as, had been better than anything he could have hoped for. Maybe there was still hope for them as a couple? There was a warm feeling about this house in Siglufjördur; maybe it wasn't such a bad idea to settle down here – as long as Kristín would be happy here too. In his imagination he saw small children scampering up and down the stairs.

When the chill outdoors began to worm its way through his

sweater, Ari Thór tiptoed back through the house, past Kristín, who slept peacefully in his bed, and down to the kitchen, where he made tea for himself, brewed coffee for her and made toast. He went back upstairs with a full tray.

They followed breakfast in bed with a walk around the town just as it was coming to life. They talked of everyday things, confirmation that their relationship was once again on an even keel.

It was almost eleven o'clock when Ari Thór finally made the call to Thorvaldur – while Kristín was in the Co-op, buying something for dinner.

He was hopeful as he punched in the numbers, wondering if he might be closer to meeting the young man from the photograph face to face.

'Hello?' a grave voice answered.

'Good morning,' Ari Thór said. 'Is that Thorvaldur?'

'And who might you be?'

'My name's Ari Thór. I understand you called the news desk last night, after the interview with me was aired, when there was a picture shown of a young man with a small child in his arms.'

'That's right. You're the policeman from Siglufjördur?' Thorvaldur asked. Ari Thór noticed he spoke with an accent, and that this was the voice of an older man.

'Yes, that's me.'

'Pleased to hear from you,' Thorvaldur said. 'Call me Thor. Nobody has called me Thorvaldur for years. The Norwegians always called me Thor when they couldn't cope with my name.'

Ari Thór realised then that it was a Norwegian accent he could hear. 'You lived in Norway for a long time?' he asked.

'Yes, I went to Norway when I was twenty, back in 1960. I only moved back here a couple of years ago. Everyone always comes back home eventually, don't they? I got to know Anton in Norway. I recognised him from the photo right away. It was taken in Hédins-fjördur, wasn't it?'

'Exactly,' Ari Thór confirmed.

'Well, I knew Anton well. He was working for an oil company when our paths crossed. I'd finished my exams over there and we both worked for the same firm for a long time. He never went to university. He hadn't finished college in Iceland, you see. But he had a scholarship to some agricultural college in Norway. He was there for a year, I think, and then he came to work at the oil company. He did all kinds of work jobs there – a real grafter, you know. It didn't seem to make any difference that he didn't have a degree; I think he could have gone higher than he did, really. We were the only Icelanders at the company for a long time, which is why we got to know each other so well, I suppose.'

'Is he still in Norway?'

'No, no. Anton's dead,' Thorvaldur answered after a short pause. 'He had a stroke a few years ago. He didn't even get to retire.'

Hell, Ari Thór thought to himself.

'I'm sorry to hear that. Does he have family in Norway?'

'No. He was married for a while to a Norwegian woman, but they split up. That family ends with Anton. He had been an only child, you see.'

'Was he from Siglufjördur?' Ari Thór asked, sure that he knew the answer already.

'No, he was from a poor family in Húsavík. I met his parents once when he and I travelled to Iceland together. We hiked over the highlands. His parents were quite elderly by then, but it was interesting to meet them. They followed his progress in Norway; I think they were very proud of their boy.'

'You mentioned a scholarship? So it wasn't his parents who paid for him to study?'

'Good heavens, no. I can't imagine they could have afforded that. They couldn't even make sure he got a decent education in Iceland. He had to go to work and earn his keep from a very young age; there were no luxuries back then. But why are you asking about Anton? Is this a police matter?' Thorvaldur asked, suspicion now entering his voice.

'No, not exactly,' Ari Thór said, choosing his words with care. 'In fact, it was the small child in his arms in the photograph who asked me if I could find out who the young man was. His name is Hédinn; he wasn't aware that anyone other than his own family – that's his parents and an aunt and uncle – had lived in Hédinsfjördur at the time.'

'I understand,' Thorvaldur said. 'Wasn't it the aunt who drank poison and died?'

'Did he tell you about that?'

'He did. He said it wasn't a good place. He told me that, by the time she died, he had already gone back to Húsavík; I gather his father gave him the news. We shared many confidences, you see. He spoke about that time of his life with horror. He told me that he'd been in Hédinsfjördur as a workman for a few months, but he never went back. Of course, it wasn't the easiest place to get to, even if you wanted to.'

'It isn't difficult now,' Ari Thór commented.

'That's true. These days I live in the western end of Reykjavík, but it has occurred to me to take a trip north to take a look at these new Hédinsfjördur tunnels and the place where Anton stayed. Is the farm still there?'

'An avalanche fell on it, unfortunately, but the ruins are still there.'

'I don't think it was a good idea for a young man to stay there, not in a place that's so completely isolated. The endless darkness affects people's state of mind; it did the lady of the house, I believe. According to Anton, she became increasingly peculiar by the day. I can hardly imagine how it must be to live in such a remote place.'

This supported the theory that Jórunn had taken her own life, Ari Thór thought. The same details of how badly she had coped with conditions there kept coming up. He realised that Thorvaldur still had not said who had supported Anton's studies, so he asked again.

'It was the man who took him on to work in Hédinsfjördur,' replied Thorvaldur. 'I don't recall his name. He was the little boy's father. He was an acquaintance of Anton's father's. I gather he was pretty well off.'

'Gudmundur,' Ari Thór muttered, surprised once again at the man's generosity. 'Do you know when Anton went to Hédinsfjördur?'

'Let's see,' Thorvaldur said. 'I'm not sure of the year, but he was fifteen or sixteen at the time.'

'When was he born?'

'1940.'

'So could he have arrived there shortly after Hédinn was born?'

'That sounds right to me. They needed the help as the baby took up so much of their time. I think it was autumn when Anton went there.'

'So that was probably 1956,' Ari Thór said. 'Hédinn was born that spring. Was Anton there the whole winter?'

'Yes, through the worst time of year. We used to talk about it when we met at Christmas; he often said what a miserable Christmas it had been there. I have a feeling that the time he was there left him with a terrible fear of the dark that stayed with him for many years.'

'And he went back home in the spring?'

'He was gone by the time the woman died, as I said,' Thorvaldur replied. 'I think he left not long after Christmas – in January or February. He was asked to leave, as far as I remember, but his wages until the spring were paid.'

'Do you know who asked him to leave?'

'The one who paid for his studies. I understand that he set it all up.'

'And this scholarship was part of the package?' Ari Thór asked, thinking that Gudmundur's behaviour towards Anton was certainly very peculiar.

'Good grief, no,' Thorvaldur replied. 'That came later, not long after the woman's death. The man came to see Anton's family. Anton remembered it well, because he was afraid he'd have to go back to work in Hédinsfjördur, which was the last thing he wanted to do. But it turned out that the man just wanted to thank him for his work by paying his passage to Norway and giving him enough money to study for one winter once he was there. But, in the end, things worked out in such a way that Anton only ever returned to Iceland as a visitor. The same's true of me, I suppose. Although I've moved back now, I still feel like a tourist every single day.'

Another surprise from Gudmundur. Ari Thór wondered if something other than altruism lay behind his generosity. Thorvaldur was hardly likely to answer that question for him, though, so he steered the conversation elsewhere, towards Delía's opinion that the place in Hédinsfjördur had been haunted.

'Did Anton ever mention that the place might have ghosts?'

'Ghosts?' The surprise was evident in Thorvaldur's voice. 'Not that I recall. He didn't have much to say about Hédinsfjördur that was pleasant, though. He said that it had been a terrible place to live, but I don't remember him saying he had seen ghosts there.'

Ari Thór then repeated Delía words to Thorvaldur; 'He said that he had seen something supernatural … or, yes, something abnormal.'

Thorvaldur was silent for a moment.

'Well, now that you mention it, I recall something along those lines,' he said finally.

'Do you remember what he meant?' Ari Thór asked eagerly.

'I vaguely remember … that's right. It was something to do with breastfeeding. It's hard to believe, but it's true. He mentioned something once, when my wife was breastfeeding our son; but I can't recall the details,' he chuckled.

There was something sinister about this whole affair, Ari Thór thought, some inexplicable incident that had been kept secret. He was certain that he was coming closer to a solution, but he would need to dig deeper.

'That's all he said?'

'As far as I recall. He just said that my wife breastfeeding our boy reminded him of something that had given him sleepless nights. He said it was something abnormal; yes, I think that was exactly the word he used. Odd expressions like that stick in your mind.'

'That's been a great help,' Ari Thór said. 'Do you mind if I get in touch with you again if I have more questions?'

'Be my guest. It's not often there's a chance to talk about such a fine man. He had few friends in Norway and he didn't know his relatives in Iceland well, having left the country at such a young age. Any memories of Anton will die with me.'

'There's one thing I must ask,' Ari Thór added. 'It certainly looks as if Anton was in Húsavík when the woman died, but can you imagine that he might have had anything to do with her death?'

'You mean, could he have poisoned her?' Thorvaldur asked in amazement.

'Yes; is there any possibility?'

'Are you off your head, young man?' Thorvaldur rumbled, his voice rising.

Ari Thór did not answer right away, leaving Thorvaldur to continue.

'He was a fine man. The idea is ridiculous. Out of the question,' Thorvaldur said, calming down. 'Anton was certainly no killer.'

43

It was Saturday afternoon when Ísrún tracked Nói down. When she introduced herself, he was suspicious.

'What? Why are you calling me? You're not taping this, are you?'

She assured him that she had no intention of recording the conversation.

'Is this something to do with the power station we're working on?' he asked, but Ísrún could hear in his voice that he didn't think this was likely. He clearly suspected the reason for the call, but didn't hang up, maybe because he wanted to be sure of what was happening.

'It's not something I can comment on; it's not my responsibility. All enquiries have to go through our press officer,' he continued.

She had no doubts about which tactics to use on him.

'This is nothing to do with engineering,' she said cheerfully. 'There's something else I wanted to ask you about. You can speak freely, as I'll take care not to mention your name in connection with anything you tell me.' She chose her words carefully; if he came up with something hot, then she would use it in one way or another. All she had essentially promised was to not name him as a source.

She screwed up her courage to carry on. 'I know a lot about this matter already, so you're free to hang up if you like, but if you do, then there's no guarantee I'll keep your name out if it.'

'Listen …' he stammered. 'Is this about Snorri? Or what?'

This was already too easy, she thought. 'That's right,' it is. I'm just trying to get an overview of events. I'm not interested …' she told him, then repeated herself to add emphasis. 'I'm *not interested* in bringing you into this without good reason. I can imagine you'd prefer to keep out of it?'

'Listen … I have nothing to do with it … I can't afford to get mixed up with news of some murder. They'd go crazy at work, you understand?'

'Of course, I understand perfectly. I'm trying to climb the ladder, just the same as you are. It's a hard world.'

'Exactly,' he agreed, a little calmer now.

'Is it true that you told Emil, the man who ran Snorri down, that Snorri had been involved in the assault on Emil's girlfriend two years ago?'

'Well, yes. I called the guy because I couldn't keep the secret of what had happened any longer, you understand? His wife, or girl-friend, had just died, after that horrible attack. He deserved to know who was behind it don't you think?' he asked in a desperate attempt to seek validation of what he had done.'

'Of course.'

'I … I …' he stammered. 'I had no idea he was going to murder Snorri!' He sighed. 'I'm really torn up after the news yesterday. I feel like it's my fault. But I did the only thing I could have done, don't you think?'

'Right,' Ísrún agreed, relieved that there was no struggle to get information out of this man. 'But how did you know it was Snorri who was behind the assault?'

'There was talk about it in the party at the time, not long after it happened.'

'And just as Ellert was about to form a government?'

'That's right. It couldn't have happened at a worse time. I didn't know Snorri myself, but we all knew he was a burden on the old man, and on the party. Of course, none of us suspected just how far down the road he had gone and nobody imagined that it could end so violently. We discussed it between ourselves and we were concerned that it could harm the party if it came out, especially if Ellert was the party chairman or even Prime Minister by then.'

'Who told you about this?'

'I don't know. I just heard that Snorri had been involved in the attack.'

'Was it your friend Lára?' Ísrún asked, firing a shot in the dark – a shot that hit its mark.

'Yes … she knew about it. She was the chair of the youth wing back then. I remember she asked us all to keep it to ourselves, and the next day she told us that Ellert had decided to stand down. So from then on it wasn't a party problem, well, not exactly. So we decided to not say a word to anyone,' he said. He paused, before continuing breathlessly. 'I was amazed that he got away with it. I don't think he was even arrested or anything. I can tell you, I thought it was deeply unfair. Maybe I have an unusually strong sense of right and wrong. It kept me awake night after night, and when I heard the poor woman was dead, I just couldn't keep quiet any longer.'

'You said it had been discussed within the party. Did many people know about this at the time?'

'Yeah, it was. But not many, I don't know …'

It was as Ísrún had suspected. There were probably only a very few people who had heard the rumour, but it was difficult for Nói to admit it, as it would make his guilt for having stayed silent even greater.

'You and Lára?'

'Yes. And one or two others. Just the top of the youth wing.'

'And Marteinn?'

'Marteinn?' he asked in surprise.

'Did he know about this?'

'I don't know. Or, well … maybe Lára mentioned that she had talked to him. They've always been close,' he said and Ísrún felt sure she could hear the innuendo in his voice.

'Why didn't you speak to the police? Either now or then?'

'I didn't want to get caught up in a formal investigation. You understand? I found the boyfriend's name easily enough and got through to him after a few calls. He lives with his parents. I reckoned it was the right thing to do, but hell, I regret it now. It's best to keep your mouth shut and not get involved in other people's affairs.'

'You're probably right,' Ísrún said.

44

'You make a lovely couple,' the old lady said with a sly smile at Ari Thór and Kristín.

He had taken Kristín's advice and checked out if the midwife from Ólafsfjördur had delivered Hédinn. To his astonishment, the old midwife, Björg, was still alive and well, and she had been the one who had helped bring Hédinn into the world.

They sat in her living room in a spacious house in Ólafsfjördur.

'It's good of you young people to visit an old woman like me, especially on such a chilly Saturday.'

Outside, the weather was worsening and it had rained without pause all day. Ari Thór had heard that, in some cases, excessive rain caused flooding in these parts; it did in Siglufjördur, when there was too much water for the mountain rivers to handle. It could certainly be said that the weather was unpredictable all year round, and even when it wasn't snowing, the forces of nature could wreak havoc.

Although well into her eighties, Björg was quick on her feet. She had been happy to meet and invited Ari Thór to pay her a visit. She offered them pancakes with jam and cream, and warm bottles of Appelsín soft drink. A vast crystal chandelier hung from the ceiling. The living room was lined with bookcases and the spaces between them were hung with paintings and photographs with no apparent order to them. The objective appeared to be to leave no wall space uncovered.

'You're not short of books,' Kristín observed. Ari Thór was relieved that she had come with him as his skills in maintaining small talk were limited.

'I hoard books,' Björg said. 'Just like my father. This was my parents' home and now it's mine. When I'm gone it'll most likely become a holiday home for some distant relatives in Reykjavík.'

'I can see you're in fine health,' Kristín said lightly. 'I'm a doctor, so I ought to know what I'm talking about.'

'Thanks for seeing us,' Ari Thór broke in. 'I was surprised ... Pleased, I mean ...'

'That I'm still alive?' Björg said with a smile that showed off a fine set of false teeth. 'I can well believe it. How long ago was it now? I'll have to work it out; mental arithmetic, like in school in the old days,' she said and frowned.

'Fifty-five years,' Ari Thór said. 'Hédinn will be fifty-five in May.'

'Good heavens,' Björg sighed. 'And it's as if it was yesterday. Time certainly flies. I must have been about thirty then and a prettier sight than I am now.' She ran her bony fingers through her shock of silver hair. 'And my hair was better back then.'

'You remember that day?' Ari Thór asked.

'Do I remember it? It's the only birth I attended in Hédinsfjördur and the place had been practically abandoned. The father radioed over to Ólafsfjördur. His wife was in labour and he asked me to come as soon as I could. He came to meet me as I came down the mountain. It was spring, so there was more light than in the winter. I'm not sure I'd be able to manage a trek like that now,' she giggled. 'I've been over to Hédinsfjördur a few times since the tunnel opened; I enjoy going over there on my way to Siglufjördur, or simply to stop there and enjoy the beauty of the place. I still have my driving licence and I can manage some driving, even if it's only slowly. My old Lada's in the garage. I used to have a Moskvitch in the old days, but that's long gone,' she said with a smile.

Ari Thór helped himself to a pancake and hoped that Björg would keep her narrative going, preferably continuing her story about

Hédinsfjördur. But she seemed to be waiting for more questions from him or Kristín.

'Was there anything odd or unusual that you noticed there?' he asked.

'No, nothing that comes to mind. They were anxious, as is normally the case, but I can't say I formed much of an opinion of the people there. I didn't know them at all and never saw any of them again. And in those days, it was a long way between Ólafsfjördur to Siglufjördur, and there was the usual rivalry between neighbours. Siglufjördur people had their own way of life and we had ours. Things are better now, of course. Times have changed and we've been united, which wasn't so painful after all.'

'Did the birth go well?' Kristín asked.

'No. It was difficult. The poor woman had to stay in bed all day. I didn't go home until the following day.' She sighed.

'It must have been unusual – staying the night in such a remote place,' Kristín said.

'Yes – and no. You get used to all kinds of things in my job. It was an experience to see Hédinsfjördur, and it was such a beautiful day. It was a good thing to do. You asked if I had noticed anything odd,' she said, turning to Ari Thór. 'I remember that I expected the fjord to be grim and lonely, but it wasn't that way at all. It was a bright, beautiful place and the sun shone. It wasn't until I went inside the house that I felt overwhelmed by the silence and the loneliness. It was very strange. I didn't feel at all happy in that house, I can tell you.'

Ari Thór thought of the ruins. They had had an eerie feel, especially when he had gone close to them. If Jórunn had taken her own life due to depression, as seemed to be the case, was it the fjord that had affected her so badly, or the house and the people living there?

'I remember that what I missed there was music, as strange as that may sound,' Björg said suddenly.

She stood up and went over to an old-fashioned record player in a corner of the room. There were no records anywhere, but there was one to be seen on the turntable as she lifted the lid. She dropped the needle onto the record and an old tune – an English ballad from the war years – filled the room.

'Vera Lynn?' Kristín asked.

'Clever girl,' Björg said, sitting down again. 'I've lived through changing times: a World War and then a Cold War, and I don't know what else.' She sighed again, as if there were too many memories crowding in on her.

'Do you remember the people living there at the time?' Ari Thór asked, his interest in ballads low at that moment. 'Do you know how many of them there were?'

'There were four people. Two couples. I remember the news of the death there the following year. There wasn't much said about it publicly, but I have the feeling it was a dreadful tragedy.'

'No workman there? A young man?' Ari Thór asked, knowing, after his conversation with Thorvaldur, what answer to expect.

'No, I don't recall seeing anyone else there, and it certainly wouldn't have passed me by. Why do you ask?'

Ari Thór wasn't keen to go into explanations and posed another question instead. 'Do you know why they didn't contact the midwife in Siglufjördur?'

'Sigurlaug? She was a few years older and probably wouldn't have trusted herself to make her way over there. It wasn't easy, I can tell you.'

'But it's just as well you were able to go there,' Kristín said. 'She had a healthy boy with your help.'

'That's quite right, my dear,' Björg replied. 'It was a job that brought me a great deal of joy. Helping others is a wonderful thing. You understand that, surely. Didn't you say you're a doctor?'

Kristín nodded but didn't comment directly. 'Maybe you'd like to meet the boy you delivered there?' she suggested; Ari Thór had the impression that she wanted to change the subject.

'A fine idea,' Björg said, glowing with pleasure. 'If you see him, then you can tell him he's always welcome here.'

*

Ari Thór and Kristín dissected the visit on the way back to Siglufjördur, although they didn't mention Björg's comment they made a
lovely couple.

The rain had stopped, so Ari Thór agreed to stop in Hédinsfjördur, as Kristín's interest in the place had been piqued and she wanted
to see the ruins of the farm.

'I hope you're wearing good shoes,' he said.

They briskly walked in silence under the heavy clouds. It was only
when they reached the ruins that an idea came to Ari Thór's mind.
The last time he had been here he had wondered whether both Jórunn
and the young man had lost their lives in this place, but now he knew
that was not the case. Only Jórunn's spirit lay over the lagoon.

Part of Ari Thór would have liked to believe that being in close prox-
imity to where she had died had now led him on the trail to the truth
– that maybe Jórunn had whispered a solution to the mystery to him,
but he was too down-to-earth by nature to put his faith in that idea.
All the same, he shivered. Now he was in the fjord, it was as if he could
see everything more clearly than before, the facts and the narratives
beginning to slot into place. He would have to add to the information
he already had before being able to test his theory, however.

At the same moment, the heavens opened. Ari Thór and Kristín
grinned to each other and ran for the shelter of the car as if the devil
were on their tails. Kristín tried to start a light-hearted conversation
on the way back, but he just nodded absently. He would need to call
Ísrún and ask her to check Maríus's bankbooks carefully, and maybe
take a closer look at some other documents. Then he was going to
listen again to the recording of Ísrún's conversation with Nikulás,
and talk to Thorvaldur once more. After that he might need Ísrún to
ask Nikulás a few more questions.

Instead of starting the car and heading for Siglufjördur, he turned
to Kristín at his side, smiling at him through her wet hair.

'I want to tell you a strange story …' he began, '… a true story
that ends with a terrible death, right here in Hédinsfjördur over half
a century ago.'

45

'Thanks for coming,' Ísrún said.

Lára sat opposite her in a little coffee shop not far from the TV station's offices. Ísrún had chosen a corner table that would allow them to talk in peace and quiet, but for the moment they were the only customers in the place anyway. She had persuaded Lára to meet on the pretext of preparing for the interview with Marteinn.

'No problem, Ísrún,' Lára replied, appearing unusually nervous.

'I have to admit …' Ísrún began slowly, taking a sip of her cappuccino '… there's something else I wanted to talk to you about.'

'Talk to me about?' Lára asked, and Ísrún could see the fear in her eyes.

'I spoke to an old friend of yours earlier – Nói. He told me an interesting tale. Based on that, I've a theory that could … well, I suppose it could wreck the Prime Minister's career,' Ísrún said, not bothering to understate the drama of the revelation.

Lára sat petrified, her coffee untouched in front of her. This political fox was about to crack and Ísrún was ready to strike, and was not planning to show any mercy. She'd placed her cards on the table and was now waiting to see the reaction.

'You all lied about Snorri back then,' she said, 'that he'd been involved in that assault, and Marteinn was up to his neck in the rumour mill, clearing the way for himself to become party chairman and Prime Minister.'

'No!' Lára yelped, her voice quivering, looking up but not meeting

Ísrún's eyes. 'Marteinn had nothing to do with it. You can't pin any dirt on him! I refuse to allow the gutter press to drag him through the mud because of some unsubstantiated gossip.' Her hands shook so much, she had to pick up her cup in both hands to lift it to her lips.

'Marteinn had nothing to do with it?' Ísrún repeated. 'So it was your idea?'

Lára started. She swept the fire-red fringe away from her eyes. 'Well … yes.'

She had already said too much. Ísrún wondered if she was now turning over in her mind whether or not to shoulder the blame alone.

'Yes,' she said again, after a short pause. 'Yes.'

'So you started the rumour that Snorri had attacked that woman?'

'Yes.' Lára looked at the floor.

'Why?'

'It wasn't intended to turn out this way, you understand? Snorri was completely screwed up at that time, a bomb waiting to go off. And his father was about to become Prime Minister. He'd have dragged his father down sooner or later. I just speeded up the process.'

'To make sure of Marteinn's position?'

'And to save the party. We're in a fantastic position now. Marteinn has never been more popular and he's going to be leading the country for years to come. We'd be out by now if Ellert had taken office,' Lára gabbled.

'The ends justify the means.'

'Exactly,' she mumbled.

'Were you the one who let Ellert know about these rumours?'

Lára nodded, her face a picture of shame.

'And what about Snorri? He was murdered!' Ísrún barked, raising her voice without meaning to. 'Snorri was murdered because that poor man, Emil, believed he had attacked his wife.'

'I don't understand how that could have happened,' Lára wailed. 'We … I made sure it was all smoothed over once we had reached our goal of getting Ellert to step down.'

'Your friend Nói called Emil and told him the story. Nói believed what you had told him and his conscience was eating him up. He wanted Emil to know the truth. Not everyone's as strong as you are,' Ísrún sneered.

'Hell …! Then Snorri's death is Nói's responsibility. If he can't keep his mouth shut …'

'I'm not sure I can agree with you there,' Ísrún said. 'Why did you take such a far-reaching decision on Marteinn's behalf? Because you believed in him … or was there something more between you?'

'That's none of your business,' Lára said awkwardly.

'And he didn't have a clue about all this?'

'He had no idea!' Lára said heatedly. 'He's squeaky clean, an honest man. Those of us who are close to him sometimes have to take difficult decisions for the cause. That's the way it is.'

'How did you know that Snorri wouldn't simply deny it?'

'He … Well … Marteinn and Snorri were good friends back then. Marteinn knew, and he told me himself, that Snorri could sometimes be off his face for a week at a time – on booze or drugs. And the week that the assault took place, he was exactly that. I thought it was the perfect opportunity. The police hadn't arrested anyone, so it all seemed to work out – at least for long enough that Ellert could be persuaded it was time for him to retire.'

Ísrún was finding it difficult to believe that Marteinn had been as innocent as Lára was trying to portray him.

'Snorri never heard about this rumour?' she asked.

'I understand they discussed it, Snorri and Ellert. Marteinn heard about it. But Snorri couldn't remember a thing and was in no position to be able to say where he had been. He said he'd never done anyone any harm, but couldn't be certain. His father wasn't prepared to take a chance, and stepped back from politics right away. Everyone took care not to let the police get wind of it, of course. So there was no harm done. Ellert was getting on in years and Marteinn was just as popular as he was. It was obvious that under the circumstances Marteinn would be the one to lead the government. And that's what happened.'

'No harm done? Snorri is dead.'

'I didn't kill him!' Lára yelled. Then she paused, and said more quietly, 'You're going to use this, are you?'

'You can bet your life I will,' Ísrún said, getting to her feet.

'I'll resign. Marteinn had nothing to do with it.'

Ísrún paid for her cappuccino and left without a word.

46

María the news editor was doubling as the desk editor that Saturday.

Ísrún took a seat in her office.

'Spill the beans,' María told her. 'What's the latest scoop?'

'The full story of the abduction case,' Ísrún said, pleased with herself.

The story was already written and it would cause a stir. It was clear that now there would be no interview with the Prime Minister. His office had cancelled the appointment without giving a reason. For once Lára was not handling communications with the media, and there had been just a hint of an apology from the ministerial official.

'Something new?' María asked.

'You could say that,' Ísrún replied. 'It all started with the assault on Emil's wife, Bylgja.'

'Yeah, I know; she died not long ago, didn't she – never regained consciousness.'

'Precisely. So, when the assault occurred, two years ago, the culprit probably went to the wrong address. The police had Róbert as their main suspect but nothing was ever proved. Emil never recovered mentally from what happened. He knew that Róbert was guilty, but didn't do anything – at least, not right away. Around the same time as the attack, there were moves to establish a government of national unity under Ellert Snorrason. It was an open secret that his son Snorri was a hopeless alcoholic …'

'And probably a drug user,' María added.

'As you know, Marteinn was the party's crown prince. He was the deputy chairman and generally seen as a highly competent character. He was also an old friend of Snorri's, although he does his best these days to talk down their friendship. Snorri confided in him that he had been through a rough patch of drinking and presumably drug use, and that he lost a whole week of his life. By chance, the assault on Bylgja took place that same week, which is where things get interesting …'

Ísrún paused and saw that María was waiting anxiously for the rest of the story. This meant points in her favour.

'Someone had the bright idea of blaming Snorri for the assault, but not publicly – just whispers within the party. The story didn't go all that far, but it did reach Ellert. He spoke to his son, who confirmed that he had no idea what had happened to him that day. Ellert resigned quickly, for "personal reasons", and Marteinn took over and became the Prime Minister of the national unity government. And the rest is history, as they say. He's a young man who has already come far and will undoubtedly make an indelible mark on our political history.'

Ísrún took a deep breath.

María used the opportunity to ask the obvious question. 'So who had this bright idea?'

'Marteinn's adviser, Lára. She admitted to me earlier today that it was her idea and she made sure the lie reached Ellert. I'll certainly mention that in my piece. I'm under the impression that she'll resign. It wouldn't be a surprise if she and Marteinn make their relationship public some time soon, now that she's decided to sacrifice her career for the man she loves. He's bound to help her into some comfortable berth sometime later, when everyone's forgotten all this.'

'Sacrifice herself for Marteinn?' María was on her feet. 'Did he have some part in this?'

'She flatly denies he had anything to do with it,' Ísrún said. 'But I'm not convinced.'

María stood in silence. 'It's unbelievable,' she said. 'Do you think this could bring the government down?'

'It's hard to tell,' Ísrún said. 'Lára took care to stop the lie going too far, and Marteinn would naturally deny any knowledge of it.'

'How did you hear about all this?' María asked, now pacing the floor.

'From one of the party members; a guy Lára leaked the story to about Snorri's involvement in the assault. The man's name is Nói. Once Bylgja died in hospital, he couldn't keep his mouth shut any longer, so he contacted Emil and told him the whole story – that Snorri had assaulted Bylgja. Nói didn't know that it was a lie. Emil decided it was time for revenge; I suppose the hatred had been build-ing up inside him for two years.'

'Good grief,' María said. 'So he took it out on Snorri – when he had nothing to do with the assault?'

'It's not easy to tell how clearly he was thinking. He must have believed that Róbert and Snorri had both been behind the attack. He enticed Snorri to a place where nobody would see them and murdered him. It seems he borrowed his parents' car and ran down an innocent man. We know what he did to Róbert; and there's no way of telling how that could have ended if Emil hadn't been caught.'

María sat down with a sigh. 'This is all beyond belief. If I under-stand this right, an innocent man was murdered, while Róbert, the man who was probably behind that brutal assault, could still get away with it.'

'He probably will. But Emil himself will be charged. He'll be inside for years, or locked away in a psychiatric ward.'

'And Marteinn? Can we nail him?'

'I'm sure he was behind it, not Lára. It's obvious, don't you think?' Ísrún said. 'You know what he's like. He comes across as a great guy, but he's completely ruthless. There are good reasons why he's managed to get so far as quickly as he has.'

'So how are we going to approach this? Do you have anything that pins this on him?'

Ísrún side-stepped the question. 'I'd like to drop a hint in the news item,' she said. She knew, however, that if she did, she would be going against her own better judgement, giving way to her own anger and sense of justice.

'And what proof do you have that he had anything to do with this conspiracy?' María asked, excited now. 'If he had a hand in it, then this isn't just a massive scoop, but the biggest political scandal in years.'

Ísrún hesitated. 'I don't have any direct proof ... but it's so obvious ...'

'Are you out of your mind?' María roared – in disappointment more than anger. 'We don't broadcast accusations against the Prime Minister just because you've come up with a conspiracy theory, Ísrún; you know that. The news piece can be about corruption within his party and his adviser's admission of involvement in a terrible tragedy. We can let the viewers draw their own conclusions,' she decided. 'But it's a hell of a scoop, all the same,' she added, her composure returning.

Ísrún nodded.

She had known all along what María's reaction would be. And she also reckoned she knew Marteinn well enough to be sure that he would weather the storm.

47

It was evening in Siglufjördur and it was almost time to visit Delía. It was quite stormy, fresh northerly air blowing in from the ocean. Ari Thór had made full use of the day, gathering the information he felt he needed to support a concrete theory. He and Kristín had gone back to Ólafsfjördur to visit the retired midwife a second time. The result of their conversation was far from conclusive, but his theory was firm in his mind.

There was a knock on the door of his house in Eyrargata, and when he opened it, he was surprised to see Tómas standing outside. He hurried in without waiting to be asked, escaping the rain outside.

'Hello,' Ari Thór said with a smile. 'Do come in.'

'Sorry to disturb you,' Tómas said. 'Are you busy?'

'Not specially. Kristín and I are about to go out. We're going to meet Hédinn to see some old film of Hédinsfjördur,' he said, deciding to let that short explanation suffice.

'Sounds good,' Tómas said. 'I just need a quiet word.'

'Of course.' He showed Tómas into the living room. 'Kristín's upstairs getting herself ready,' he said and realised that Kristín and Tómas had never met. He felt it was probably better to keep it that way – preferring to keep the world of the rootless young man who had hooked Kristín separate from that of the Siglufjördur police officer who had wrecked every possible aspect of his personal life.

'I knocked earlier,' Tómas said when he had sat down.

'We went over to Ólafsfjördur,' Ari Thór said.

'Something happened today,' Tómas said gravely. 'I wanted to talk to you face to face about it.'

Ari Thór felt a wave of discomfort come over him and wondered what to expect.

'I had an offer on the house today,' Tómas said haltingly. 'An offer from a buyer – not a potential tenant, which is what I had been expecting.'

'Well … that didn't take long.'

'No. It's happened very fast – faster than I had imagined. As soon as it was advertised in fact. It's some doctor who lives in London but who has roots here. He's been on the lookout for a decent house up here and said that mine looks like his dream home. He made a good offer – above the asking price. Said he didn't want to miss the opportunity.'

'Well,' Ari Thór said. 'You'd best think it over carefully.'

Tómas looked away. 'We've already accepted the offer,' he said awkwardly.

'What?' Ari Thór stammered.

'That's right. My wife said we couldn't dare turn down an offer like that. It's not as if it's easy to sell property around here at such a decent price.'

'So are you taking leave?' Ari Thór asked, his heart pounding at the thought of the change about to come.

'No, my boy. I'm resigning,' Tómas said with an awkward smile. 'It's time to try my luck elsewhere. We're going to start again down south.'

Ari Thór said nothing.

'My job will be advertised and I'd like you to apply for it,' Tómas continued. 'It goes without saying that I'll recommend you for the position. I can't imagine that you'll be overlooked.'

It was exactly eight o'clock when Ari Thór and Kristín hurried from her car up to the little, corrugated-iron-clad house. The storm had gathered strength. The wind threatened to send them flying and the rain hammered down unmercifully. The streets were mostly deserted, few people were interested in braving the elements.

Ari Thór rang the bell. This time there was no need to hold a conversation through the letterbox. It didn't take Delía long to come to the door.

'Come inside,' she smiled. 'Dreadful weather, isn't it?'

'Thank you,' Ari Thór said. 'This is … This is Kristín.'

'Pleased to meet you, my dear,' Delía replied. 'The projector is ready in the kitchen. There isn't a lot of room, so we'll have to squeeze together, if nobody minds.'

Ari Thór and Kristín followed her into the kitchen, where he noticed that there were two chairs and one stool. Delía hadn't expected an extra guest.

'Do you have another chair?' Ari Thór asked.

Delía nodded, vanished from the room and returned with another stool.

The projector stood on the kitchen table with its green-and-white plastic cloth, alongside coffee cups and a plate of rolled pancakes. Two candles burned on the windowsill, giving the room a peaceful ambience while the storm raged outside. The rain was beating heavily on the windows and the wind managed to squeeze through gaps in the less-than-perfectly insulated windows of the old house. For a moment Ari almost had the feeling that the house might collapse.

Ari Thór took one stool and Kristín took a seat beside him on the other.

'I do hope Hédinn enjoys watching the film,' Delía said from the doorway. 'I ought to get it transferred to a video tape for him one day.'

'That's a good idea,' Ari Thór agreed, refraining from pointing out that the golden age of video tapes was long over.

Delía was on her feet to answer the door as soon as the bell chimed. She showed Hédinn into the kitchen. Ari Thór stood up to greet him.

Hédinn nodded and mumbled something indistinct. He was

dressed in his best – a checked suit that he filled out with no room to spare; a white shirt and a red tie. It was easy to imagine that these clothes had been acquired at a time when Hédinn had been both a few years younger and a few kilos lighter.

Kristín stood, introduced herself and shook Hédinn's hand.

'Good evening. My name's Hédinn,' he said, his voice clearer.

'Sit yourselves down. There's coffee in the pot,' Delía said. 'It makes a change to have visitors, especially in weather like this.'

Hédinn silently took a seat at the table, apparently unaffected by Delía's cheerful demeanour.

Delía poured coffee into the cups, offered milk and sugar, and urged her guests to sample the pancakes.

'Should we start the show?' she asked, switching on the projector.

'Absolutely,' Ari Thór agreed, and turned to Hédinn. 'As you know, I've been going over the case over the last few days. A lot has happened since I spoke to you last that casts some light on what happened. When the film has been shown, I'd like to share with all of you my theory about the circumstances around Jórunn's death.'

'Theory?' Hédinn asked in surprise. 'You mean …?' His breathing came shallow and fast, and he seemed to be struggling to find the right words.

'It's difficult to say with certainty what happened all those years ago,' Ari Thór said, trying not to sound too authoritative. 'But I think I know what took place that winter in Hédinsfjördur.'

Delía clicked off the kitchen lights. The lights in the living room were also off, so the only light came from the candles in the window and the projector itself. There was the feeling of anticipation normally found in a cinema just as the film begins. The atmosphere in the room was thick with tension, with the storm outside adding to the gloomy, almost sinister ambiance. Hédinn muttered something to himself and his heavy breathing almost drowned out the projector's clatter. But he sat in silence as images began to appear on the kitchen wall and Jórunn appeared, smiling at them. This evening would maybe reveal just why she had died so suddenly.

Ari Thór had seen the footage before, but the film had the same overwhelming effect on him. The spirit of a long-gone age filled the kitchen, and the beauty of the remote fjord, resplendent in its white winter finery, was almost tangible.

Ari Thór heard Hédinn gasp as the young man appeared on the screen. Kristín also seemed to feel far from comfortable when she saw him, and fumbled to clasp Ari Thór's hand tightly.

'Well, I'll be … That's Dad there,' Hédinn mumbled as Gudmundur was seen in the distance. 'Remarkable, quite remarkable.'

There was silence in the little kitchen as the film came to an end, as if all those present needed a moment's quiet to make their way back to the twenty-first century from the black-and-white Hédinsfjördur winter of more than fifty years before.

A heavy gust of wind battered the walls of the iron-clad house, bringing them all back to reality.

'Well,' Ari Thór said, speaking into the half-darkness. 'Hédinn, you don't mind if I explain briefly the theory about the young man and Jórunn's death?'

'Of course not … There's nothing to hide. Feel free. I'm intrigued to know what you have to say. I'd just ask that none of this goes further than this room,' he said, with an awkward glance at Delía.

'You can trust me, Hédinn,' she said.

Ari Thór turned his stool so that he was facing Hédinn rather than the wall.

'My suggestion is that Jórunn's death is linked to something that was a sensitive subject at that time, and which some people feel is still controversial today. But it's best to begin at the beginning. We need to go back further, to around 1950.'

'When Jórunn's and Maríus's son was born?' Hédinn asked.

'Exactly. The evidence is that they had a son. He would be in his sixties now, if he's alive. I haven't been able to find out anything about what became of him, though. Jórunn and Maríus were both about twenty at the time. I understand that Maríus's brother, Nikulás, encouraged them to put the child up for adoption. Maríus was out of work and they certainly didn't trust themselves to support a family.'

'That's interesting,' Delía observed. 'Hédinn, you'll have to try and find the man.'

Hédinn mumbled something.

'Maríus has been described as having been easily led; immature, even,' Ari Thór continued. 'Maybe he wasn't ready for parenthood at that time, but the descriptions cast a little light on what happened later on,' he said and paused.

'That fits perfectly with my memories of my uncle Maríus,' Hédinn said in a low voice, hardly louder than the whistling of the wind outside. 'He was a kindly soul, but not a strong man. He was quiet and retiring – I thought he had become like that after his wife passed away, but it may well be that he had always been that way. People don't change that much as they get older.'

'You're damned right there,' Delía broke in. 'I still feel like I'm twenty. The only change is what I see in the mirror,' she said, and her observation lightened the mood somewhat.

'It's interesting to compare these descriptions of the man with those of his brother-in-law, Gudmundur,' Ari Thór said. 'Most people agree that Gudmundur was the complete opposite: a strong, decisive man who was used to getting his own way.'

'That's true. Nobody pushed the old man about. He always got what he wanted and never gave an inch,' Hédinn said with pride.

'That's right,' Ari Thór said. 'All the same, it seems he had a thoughtful side that doesn't sit comfortably with the image of the man that I have.'

'What do you mean by that?' Hédinn asked in a sharp voice.

'I mean that he appears to have gone out of his way to look after his brother- and sister-in-law.'

'And is there anything odd about that?'

'Not necessarily.'

'So what did Gudmundur do?' Delía asked cautiously, as if hardly daring to break the tension that had built up between Ari Thór and Hédinn.

'To begin with, he found work for Maríus in Siglufjördur; and then he invited the couple to join in on the Hédinsfjördur adventure, which I assume he must have paid for,' Ari Thór said. 'As well as that, he also offered to take in their little boy, before he was put up for adoption. A letter has come to light in which he makes that possibility plain. But as far as I can ascertain, the upshot was that strangers from elsewhere in the country adopted him. Jórunn was unwilling to run the risk of meeting her son by chance. I can imagine that she never saw him after she gave him away, and most likely Maríus never saw him either.'

'Do I get to see this letter?' Hédinn asked, determination in his voice.

'We can sort that out,' Ari Thór said. 'But let's return to Hédinsfjördur.' He glanced at the wall where the film from Hédinsfjördur had brought the scene of his narrative to such vivid life. Now there was only a square of light from the projector.

'It's 1955; Hédinsfjördur is uninhabited, but Gudmundur, Gudfinna, Maríus and Jórunn decide to try their luck and move into the farmhouse on the western side of the lagoon. It's a beautiful place, but dangerous, right at the foot of a towering mountain. I haven't heard any reasons for this venture, other than a simple desire to strike out and try something new. Gudmundur appears to have been fairly well off, so maybe it was a wealthy man's need for adventure. I'm not so sure of that, however; I think the reasons are quite different, and behind them is the solution to the mystery.'

Ari Thór looked down, paused and then looked directly at Hédinn.

'You were born a year later, in 1956.' Hédinn nodded and Ari Thór continued. 'That autumn a workman was engaged to help with the farm work – a teenage lad from Húsavík. His name was Anton.'

'Anton? That's the lad I met in Hédinsfjördur?' Delía asked.

'That's right.'

'His name *was* Anton?' Hédinn asked, his voice dropping. 'He's dead?'

'He is.'

'Is that connected to … Did he die in Hédinsfjördur?' Hédinn asked.

'Don't worry,' Ari Thór said. 'Your family had nothing whatsoever to do with Anton's death. Quite the opposite, as your father treated him very well and paid for him to study abroad.'

'Well, I'll be damned!' Hédinn said in clear astonishment, about to get to his feet but then sitting back down. 'He did that, did he? Why?'

'I think he had good reason to send the lad away to study; and the same applies to his generosity to Maríus and Jórunn,' Ari Thór said, his voice becoming grave. 'That winter Maríus took the photograph that set all this off. As you know now, that's Anton holding you as a baby, Hédinn. There were questions to start with as to why an unknown man was holding the baby, but since Anton was a workman at the farm, there's nothing particularly out of place there. We can presume that, by the time the photograph was taken, he had been part of the household for some time. Then, around Christmas, on a beautiful winter's day, a young woman hiked over the pass from Siglufjördur to take pictures,' Ari Thór said with a sideways glance at Delía. 'She's the only one of us who met Anton.'

'So did Hédinn,' Kristín pointed out.

'True,' Ari Thór agreed, smiling. 'But Delía is the one who remembers meeting him.'

'That's right,' Delía said. 'That conversation with the boy, Anton … it's stayed in my mind all these years.' She lapsed into a thoughtful silence.

'Didn't you talk about how difficult it must have been to live in such a remote place?' Ari Thór asked, giving Delía an opportunity to tell her tale.

'Quite right,' she said. 'My feeling is that the place was haunted. There was something unearthly in the darkness there.'

'Ghosts?' Hédinn asked doubtfully. 'I don't believe it. My parents never mentioned anything like that. Not that they ever said much about the time they spent in Hédinsfjördur, if I'm completely honest.'

'The young man said he could feel something abnormal there,' Delía continued. 'I could see he was frightened. Then Gudmundur called to him; he clearly wasn't happy to see a visitor. That's my impression, at any rate.'

'I spoke to a close friend of Anton's and asked him about that. He recalled them talking about this, and said that there was a connection to breastfeeding, of all things.'

'What? And did you get an explanation?' Delía asked.

'Anton's friend couldn't tell me any more, although I feel it fits neatly in with my theory of what happened.'

'And what is your theory?' demanded Delía.

She seemed keener that Hédinn on reaching a satisfactory conclusion. Maybe he was feeling scared of the truth, Ari Thór thought, now that the narrative was unfolding, and would prefer not to hear the end of the story.

'I'll get to that in a moment,' Ari Thór said, enjoying being in the limelight.

He felt like a storyteller – someone who would disappear once the tale had been told. But then he realised that might not be a possibility. Since Tómas's visit, he had avoided thinking about the future, intending to relax for the evening and decide later whether or not to apply for the inspector's post in Siglufjördur. But the future had sneaked up on him again; he knew that a significant choice was waiting to be made. But that could wait a little longer. He tried to steer his thoughts elsewhere.

'First I'll tell you a little more about Anton,' he said, his mind once again focused on Hédinsfjördur. 'He wasn't there when Jórunn died, and it seems that Gudmundur ensured that as few people as possible knew that he had spent the winter there.'

Ari Thór heard Hédinn gasp for breath.

'I gather Anton left in January or February,' he continued. 'Gudmundur asked him to leave, but paid him his wages until the spring.'

'What had he done?' Hédinn asked.

'Nothing at all. Your father simply wanted him out of the way, and even paid for him to travel to Norway to study after Jórunn's death. He paid his sea passage and for his studies that winter,' Ari Thór replied.

There was complete silence, and even the wind seemed to be holding its breath.

'Gudmundur wanted to be rid of the workman?' Delía asked in a low voice.

'Exactly. First he was sent away from Hédinsfjördur, and after Jórunn's murder, there could be no half-measures. So he was sent far away, out of the country.'

Hédinn started in surprise and gripped the edge of the table.

'What did you say? Jórunn was murdered?' he asked sharply, a tremor in his voice.

'Yes. She was murdered. I'm sure of it.'

'And who was the murderer?' Hédinn asked, fear plain in his voice.

'I can tell you that, Hédinn,' he said, taking on the role of storyteller so wholeheartedly that he forgot that caution should be exercised around sensitive souls. 'At the very least I can tell you that your mother and father were entirely innocent of that terrible deed.'

48

There was a palpable tension in the air. Hédinn muttered something to himself and then fell silent. Delía said nothing. Kristín had let go of Ari Thór's hand, but now he felt for hers and squeezed it. Her fingers in his gave him the security that he felt a sudden need for.

Hédinn broke the silence, clearing his throat. 'Are you telling me that Marías murdered his wife?' he asked, astonishment and a note of relief in his voice.

Ari Thór let a few long seconds pass before he replied.

'No. Marías didn't murder her.'

'What the hell do you mean?' Hédinn asked, his anger rising. 'Are you insinuating that … that Anton came back to Hédinsfjördur and murdered Jórunn?'

'Not at all. He's completely innocent. He was just in the wrong place at the wrong time and knew too much.'

'Well … I don't understand,' Hédinn said. 'There wasn't anyone else there.'

'Only Hédinn himself,' Delía said slowly.

Hédinn got noisily to his feet, and as he did so a gust of wind hammered at the house, silencing them all.

'Damn it. I'm not listening to this nonsense. I wasn't even a year old then.'

Ari Thór stood up too and placed a hand on Hédinn's shoulder.

'Calm down. Of course I'm not suggesting that you could have committed a murder at only ten months old.'

Hédinn sat down again.

Ari Thór took his seat on the stool as Delía muttered under her breath. 'It must have been the ghost,' she said. Her voice shook.

Ari Thór paid her no attention. 'Let's go quickly over the facts that caught my attention,' he said firmly. 'When I started to look into the case, I spoke to the chairman of the Siglufjördur Association. His understanding was that the sisters, Jórunn and Gudfinna, had been alike in their nature, and not keen on dark fjords. They had both been brought up in Reykjavík. In general, whenever Jórunn's death is mentioned, the opinion seems to have been that she was in a delicate state of mind. I've listened to a recording of the conversation with Nikulás and my understanding to begin with was that he confirmed this. He said, and I can quote his exact words …'

Ari Thór took a notebook from his pocket and opened it at the page where he had made notes ahead of the evening's gathering.

'Nikulás was of the opinion that Jórunn had taken her own life,' he continued. 'He said he had been sure of it. To be precise, he said: "Marius often hinted at it when we talked. He said that the darkness had got to some of them very badly." After I started to look at this from a different angle, I decided to ask Nikulás about this. I contacted him today and was able to get one of the staff at the care home to ask him some questions, as the old man is too deaf to use the phone. He was able to give a clearer explanation. Marius had certainly spoken about how hard Jórunn had found it to adjust to their circumstances – but the same applied to Gudfinna.'

'Didn't she ever mention it to you?' Delía asked, her eyes on Hédinn.

Ari Thór sat in silence and waited.

'No, I can't say she ever did,' Hédinn replied, downcast.

'Living there affected her?' Delía asked Ari Thór. 'I can understand it. I wouldn't have wanted to live there.'

'Yes, Nikulás felt that living in Hédinsfjördur had been more of a trial for Gudfinna than for Jórunn. Gudfinna struggled to cope with the long darkness and the isolation, but that has hardly been mentioned. Maybe Gudmundur wanted to keep that quiet. Attitudes to mental illness were much more negative then than they are today.'

'That's very true,' Delía agreed. 'People didn't talk about that sort of thing.'

'My suspicion is that Anton knew about her state of mind. According to Anton's friend, Thorvaldur, "the lady of the house" had become increasingly peculiar by the day, and by that I assumed that Anton had meant Jórunn. So I spoke to Thorvaldur to make sure, and it turns out he had meant Gudfinna, as he had always seen *her* as "the lady of the house".'

'People can react badly to conditions like that,' Kristín said. 'It can even lead to clinical depression that needs to be treated quickly and properly.'

'So if that was the case,' Ari Thór continued. 'Gudmundur must have wanted to do everything he could to keep tongues from wagging.'

'You said he sent the boy to study in Norway?' Delía asked.

'Precisely,' Ari Thór said with a smile. 'The man could afford it, but Anton certainly knew more than just this, so Gudmundur had every reason to send him abroad.'

Hédinn again shot to his feet. 'What the hell are you insinuating about my father, boy? He was a good man.'

'Well, well,' Delía said, also standing up. 'More coffee, anyone?' she suggested, pouring it out into the cups on the table that had hardly been touched.

'Careful now,' Kristín whispered to Ari Thór.

'I suspect that Gudmundur had his own, good reasons for paying for Anton's studies and for supporting Jórunn and Maríus, who had been living in poverty until he pulled them out of it,' Ari Thór said.

He paused and there was a deafening silence in the kitchen. Delía looked ill at ease, as if she would prefer her guests to leave. Hédinn remained on his feet, his face thunderous.

'Let's see,' continued Ari Thór. Maríus owned his apartment

debt-free, plus he had money in a savings account that hadn't been touched for decades – money that inflation ate up. I had someone look more closely at the contents of Maríus's box of documents, checking his accounts and also all the available information about the purchase of his apartment. Two things stood out. One was the payment; the amount in Maríus's savings account, which was paid in during that summer of 1956. There's no way to see where that payment came from, but I suspect it came from Gudmundur.'

'No more. That's enough. These are endless unsubstantiated theories about my father,' Hédinn announced and set off towards the door. 'I'm leaving.'

'Wait a moment,' Ari Thór said.

Hédinn stopped and turned in the doorway.

'We were able to find the original documents concerning the sale of Maríus's apartment in Reykjavík. Originally it had been owned by a limited company in Siglufjördur, which passed the ownership to Maríus. This was after the Hédinsfjördur venture, and what's more, there's no indication that Maríus paid for the apartment.' Ari Thór looked down at his notebook and read out the name of the company.

'Hell,' Hédinn said the concern plain on his face. 'That was one of my father's companies.'

'I thought so,' Ari Thór said. 'Is there any way that your father owed such a debt to Maríus that he paid a significant amount of money to him? As far as I can see, this was a lot of money at the time; and he also transferred the ownership of the apartment to him. It's worth saying that Maríus appears never to have touched the money; he simply left it in the account and let inflation gradually make it worthless.'

Ari Thór paused to let this sink in before he continued.

'There are two more things that I'd like to draw attention to. I looked for Jórunn's obituary, but couldn't find one, just a simple death notice. There was no picture of the deceased on it, but that was usual at the time. On the other hand, there are no pictures of Jórunn anywhere to be found in connection with the reports of her death. That isn't especially suspicious in itself, but I have the feeling that this was convenient for Gudmundur. He presumably wanted to make sure no pictures of Jórunn appeared after her death.'

'Why on earth not?' Delía asked.

'Then there's what Björg told us,' Ari Thór said, with a glance at Kristín. 'We went to see her today in Ólafsfjördur. While I remember, Hédinn – she said she'd love to see you.'

'What? Me? Who is this woman?' he demanded, still standing in the doorway, but no longer on his way out of the house.

'She's the midwife from Ólafsfjördur who delivered you. She's still alive, and very active for her age.'

'Still alive? She must be ancient,' Hédinn said.

'She's as bright as a button,' Ari Thór replied. 'But why did Gudmundur go to her and not to the midwife in Siglufjördur? Why go the extra distance? Siglufjördur is closer and an easier journey over the mountains. Björg thought that the midwife from Siglufjördur didn't trust herself to trek over the Hestsskard pass, which is plausible, but as she died years ago, we'll never know for sure. There could be another explanation. I think the key to this is that Björg didn't know these people at all and never saw any of them again afterwards.'

Every eye was on Ari Thór and he felt his pulse start to beat faster.

'Gudmundur got in touch with Björg, telling her that his wife had gone into labour,' he said. 'Björg told us that it was a difficult birth, and that Hédinn's mother remained in bed all that day. Björg didn't go back to Ólafsfjördur until the following day. It took me a while to figure out how important that piece of information was, and then it all fell into place.'

Ari Thór caught Hédinn's eye. His expression remained stony, until the significance of Ari Thór's words dawned on him.

'No … That can't be right,' he said, thunderstruck.

'Exactly. It doesn't add up. It's possible that Björg isn't telling the truth, but why shouldn't she? She could have got mixed up, I suppose, but my impression is that she remembers the events of that day very clearly. Don't you agree?' Ari Thór said, turning to Kristín.

'Agreed,' Kristín said quietly.

'Now someone's going to have to explain all this to me,' Delía said sternly. 'Why doesn't it add up?'

'Are you going to tell her?' Ari Thór said, his eyes on Hédinn.

Hédinn hesitated before speaking. 'Yes … As I told Ari Thór when we met first, my name is linked to Hédinsfjördur. My mother used to say that the day I was born she walked down to the lagoon in Hédinsfjördur; it was a beautiful sunny day, so she decided that I should be called Hédinn.'

'Do you think she wasn't telling the truth?' Ari Thór asked. 'Because this doesn't fit Björg's account, which states that she had to stay in bed for the rest of the day having had a difficult birth.'

'No, it's true,' Hédinn said, although with hesitation. 'She often spoke of what a beautiful day it had been. I just don't understand …' he began, and lapsed into silence, his eyes blank.

'The simple answer is that Gudfinna wasn't your mother, Hédinn,' Ari Thór said bluntly, leaving those in the little kitchen stunned.

'What? No, that can't possibly be it,' he said, his voice hopeless. It can't be possible …' he added, his voice cracking.

'It's the only possible explanation,' Ari Thór said firmly. 'I said just now that this is linked to something that's a delicate matter today, and something that our Members of Parliament are even busy debating. By that I mean surrogate motherhood.'

'Surrogacy?' Delía said in amazement.' What on earth are you implying?'

'It's a term that has been coined relatively recently, but at its heart it's the same thing: making an agreement with a woman to carry someone else's child. Gudmundur and Gudfinna had no other children than Hédinn, which was unusual in those days. In addition, we have evidence that they offered to adopt Jórunn's and Maríus's child some years before Hédinn was born. Could this be because they had been unable to have children of their own, and not simply to make life easier for Jórunn and Maríus?'

'And Jórunn wanted that child to be adopted elsewhere?' Delía asked.

'That's right; she wanted him adopted by strangers so that she would not meet him later on. She had her own way that time, when she did not want her sister to adopt her child. Gudmundur and Gudfinna must have presumably continued to try for a child of their own without success. There was no fertility treatment at the time and they didn't have many other options,' he said, glancing at the doctor by his side for confirmation.

Kristín nodded her agreement.

'Maybe they went to a doctor and were told that the problem was with Gudfinna's fertility rather than Gudmundur's. Maybe that's when the idea came to Gudmundur; maybe before he invited Maríus and Jórunn to Siglufjördur. They were short of money, and Maríus was a character who was easily led. Maybe their financial situation worsened and Gudmundur saw an opportunity – helping them to move to Siglufjördur and finding work for Maríus, so that they were indebted to him. Then he was able to make them an offer they couldn't refuse. He asked Jórunn to bear a child for him and Gudfinna.'

'I don't believe it,' Hédinn said furiously.

'Jórunn and Maríus were to be paid handsomely, as the deposit into Maríus's account shows – the payment that wasn't to be made until after Hédinn's birth. Presumably the details were all agreed in advance, in case Jórunn changed her mind once the child had been born. But nobody could know the truth; nobody could see that it was in fact Jórunn who was pregnant and then breastfeeding for several months. Gudmundur's solution was to move to an abandoned fjord, on the pretext of making an attempt to make a living from farming there. Plenty of people thought it was a mad idea, but it provided ideal cover.'

'You must be out of your mind!' Hédinn said, his voice rising almost to a shout.

'So that's why I wasn't welcome when I went over there to take pictures?' Delía asked.

'I can well believe that that was the reason,' Ari Thór replied. 'But when it came to it, they needed more hands, and took on a young lad from Húsavík as a workman. But that turned out to be a mistake. I suspect that he noticed when Jórunn was breastfeeding the baby, which he must have thought was strange as Gudfinna was supposed to be the child's mother. Gudmundur can't have been happy about him seeing that.'

'But who …?' Delía stammered, and Ari Thór knew immediately where her question was heading. '… But who was the child's father? Who was Hédinn's dad?'

Ari Thór directed his answer to Hédinn. 'I believe that Gudmundur was your father,' he said.

'And how did that work?' Delía asked awkwardly.

'I doubt it was complicated. He probably got his sister-in-law pregnant the old-fashioned way, which was presumably part of the arrangement,' he said. 'Then they must have waited; she turned out to be pregnant, and finally the birth. Maybe they had hoped they could manage the birth by themselves. But in the end, they called for a midwife, probably because they didn't want to take any chances.'

'Which is why they asked for the midwife from Ólafsfjördur,' Delía said. 'Here in Siglufjördur everyone knows everyone else, and they wouldn't have been able to fool the midwife here.'

'Exactly,' Ari Thór said. 'Gudmundur presumably introduced Jórunn as Gudfinna and hoped to get away with the deception, plus the sisters were very alike, at least they are in the photograph that set all this off.'

He unfolded a photocopy of the photograph from his notebook.

'You can see that the principal difference between them is that one of the sisters is slimmer, and that's Gudfinna – the one who was supposed to have just given birth to a child. It's a detail, but just one more item that helps complete the puzzle. Incidentally, I went back to see Björg again and showed her the picture but, understandably, after all these years, she wasn't able to confirm which of the two woman had been the child's mother.'

'That's quite a tale,' Delía said, clearly overcome with emotion. 'So this was one of the reasons there were no pictures of Jórunn published when she died?'

'Precisely,' Ari Thór said cheerfully. 'They didn't want to take the risk that the midwife might recognise her later on, and realise that the dead woman was actually the mother of the little boy she had delivered, not the sister.'

'And who the hell murdered Jórunn?' Hédinn demanded, his voice laden with anguish.

'Gudfinna, of course,' Ari Thór replied.

'What the hell do you mean?' he snapped. 'You said just now that neither my mother nor father had anything to do with her death …' His voice faded away as he realised the implications of what he had just said.

Delía was quick to put the theory into words.

'You mean that Gudfinna was Hédinn's aunt, not his mother.'

'I can't listen to this any longer. Am I supposed to believe that my mother wasn't my mother at all?'

Ari Thór wondered for a moment whether or not to stop his narrative then and there, but decided to take a few minutes to give them the final pieces of the puzzle.

'What did your father say, Hédinn? That you had an aunt who had taken a life? I've wondered about those words and he was certainly referring to Gudfinna: your aunt who murdered your mother.'

'I told you that in confidence, damn you,' Hédinn said.

Delía got to her feet. 'It's late. That's enough, I think,' she decided.

But Hédinn had other ideas. 'And why did she murder Jórunn? Tell me that?'

'Of course, I can't say for certain, but there is reason to believe that the balance of Gudfinna's mind may well have been disturbed. We could say the same about both of them, in fact. Jórunn had carried a child for her sister, and saw that child every single day.'

'And Gudfinna had no choice but to live with the woman who had slept with her husband,' Delía added.

'It may well be that jealousy tipped the balance; or fear that Jórunn would take the child once they had left Hédinsfjördur. It's possible that Jórunn had threatened to do just that. At any rate, the isolation appears to have affected them both badly. Gudmundur's actions appear to support the theory that he was protecting someone close to him – such as his wife, a woman who had committed murder. He found an apartment in Reykjavík for Marius, putting distance between them and buying his silence to some extent. Marius appears to have believed that his wife committed suicide, according to his brother's recollections. Perhaps that's why he appears to have kept quiet and gone along with the lie that it was an accident. It had been a difficult time for Jórunn, so Gudmundur may have found it easy to convince Marius that it was suicide. In fact, it may well be that nobody but Gudmundur and Gudfinna knew the truth; but all three of them, Marius included, conspired to lie to the police, saying that Jórunn had told them that she had taken the poison by mistake. Gudmundur and Gudfinna did this to hide the truth, while Marius may have done it to hide what he *thought* was the truth.'

'And Gudmundur arranged for Anton to leave the country,' Delía added.

'The boy was probably fully aware that Gudfinna had been in a bad way that winter, and that there was a poisonous atmosphere between the sisters. Anton could have made people suspicious,' Ari Thór said. 'Maybe he knew the statement in the police report – that rat poison was kept in the kitchen in a similar jar to the one sugar was kept in – was a complete lie.'

He fell silent and looked around. He felt the kitchen was a darker place than it had been; then he noticed that one of the two candles in the window had burned out.

Nobody spoke, so he continued, filling the emptiness.

'The photograph tells its own tale,' he said, smoothing out the photocopy on the kitchen table. 'There's no joy in the faces of Gudmundur, Jórunn or Gudfinna, and it's noticeable how far apart the sisters are from each other. One of them is at either side of the group, neither of them holding the little boy.'

Kristín got to her feet. She had clearly had enough.

Ari Thór also stood up, but had not quite finished.

'It was an adventure that was never going to end well, and in fact it ended terribly. Maríus presumably accepted the apartment so that he had a roof over his head. But he never touched Gudmundur's blood money – the cash they had been promised for their part of the bargain and which had cost Jórunn her life. The only positive aspect of the whole thing was Hédinn's birth,' he said and tried unsuccessfully to send Hédinn a smile.

Hédinn glared back at him.

After an awkward pause, Ari Thór said, 'I'm afraid Kristín and I have to be on our way. She needs to get back to Akureyri before the weather gets any worse,' he lied.

Hédinn moved aside from where he stood in the kitchen doorway to let them past.

'It's up to you to decide whether or not to believe this theory or not. But I'm convinced that this was what happened,' Ari Thór said as his final offering.

He wasn't feeling too well, and asked himself why he wasn't delighted to have solved the mystery. Should he have let things lie? he asked himself as they stepped out into the rain. He had done his best to shine a light on the past, but by doing so he could have made things worse. Now Hédinn would have to live with the knowledge that the woman who had brought him up may have murdered his real mother, without ever being able to be entirely sure of the circumstances of the case. There could be an opportunity for him to find his half-brother, though, if Jórunn and Maríus's son could be found, and assuming the man was still living.

Ari Thór and Kristín hurried to the shelter of the car, leaving Hédinn and Delía behind in silence.

49

Ísrún's prediction that the scandal would force Lára to resign but would have no discernible effect on the Prime Minister was proved correct. He stayed firmly where he was, his usual urbane and trustworthy self. He had agreed to a single television interview on the subject – with another station, which didn't take Ísrún by surprise. She was hardly likely to be one of Marteinn's favourites after she had exposed the scandal.

Marteinn had come out of the interview well, having roundly condemned the actions of those who had started the rumours, without being overly critical of Lára. With a smile he had convincingly denied any involvement.

Two weeks had passed. Journalists and bloggers had already moved on, as had the general public. The story had disappeared from view.

Ísrún had, however, heard tell that Lára and Marteinn were dating, but nothing was confirmed. They were apparently managing to stay out of the spotlight. Lára would surely continue to stay by Marteinn's side, and she would certainly face no legal consequences for her actions; no one would be putting her behind bars for having started a rumour.

One week had passed since Ísrún had been called by her doctor.

'Hello, Ísrún,' he said warmly and her guts immediately knotted in anxiety. She was still waiting for the results of the MRI scan.

'Hello,' she replied, her mouth so dry that she could hardly form the word.

'I have some pictures,' the doctor said. 'It all looks good.'

She gasped for air. It was as if her heart had stopped beating for a moment. Had she heard right?

'What?' was all she could manage to say.

'It looks good,' the doctor repeated. 'Nothing to be seen; no tumour formation. It's all going in the right direction, Ísrún.'

They continued the conversation for a few minutes. Ísrún felt a kind of euphoria she could not describe. Although she knew her condition was unpredictable, this was certainly good news.

In the following days she wondered again whether or not to discuss this with her family and colleagues.

Her father, Orri, had finally given in and contacted Anna, who was still in the Faroes. Ísrún had heard from both of them, each interpreting their conversation in their own ways. At least the gap between them was narrower than it had been. She was sure they would be back together before the summer, so she felt it was best not to rock the boat with news of a medical condition that finally looked to be improving. She decided to keep it to herself for the moment.

The situation was the same at work. What would she gain by letting them know about it? It wasn't something she was anxious to share with anyone. She was in fierce competition for the choice of the best assignments and knew that it wouldn't be long before the news editor's job would be within her reach.

These were still minor considerations compared to the news from the doctor, though. She felt like she was walking on air.

'I'm very optimistic,' the doctor had said.

And this time she was inclined to believe him.

Róbert had tried calling Sunna quite a few times, but she never returned his calls. Then, one day, the number wasn't even working any more. Of course he knew he would never win her back, but it was worth a try. He wasn't a bad man, not really; or so he kept telling himself. It was just the drugs; he had been completely out of his mind on drugs.

After the reason behind the kidnapping had become public knowledge – the fact that Emil believed Róbert to be his girlfriend's killer – the court of public opinion had found him guilty. He had been called in for formal questioning once more, for the sake of formality, but the evidence just wasn't there. He would be free, in legal terms, but he would never be free of the images of the blood; of the poor girl, Bylgja, dying after he had struck her.

He had now left Iceland, given up on his studies, given up on everything. His parents acted as if they believed him, but he saw that they now knew the truth as well.

Now he had to try to make a fresh start abroad, but that was easier said than done.

The nightmares just kept coming.

Night after night after night.

50

Ari Thór and Kristín sat in the kitchen of the old house in Eyrargata. Ari Thór sipped his tea and gazed absently out of the window
towards the mountains. He had just taken a shower after going for a
run that morning instead of going to the pool; now he felt renewed
in mind and body. There was a hint of rain in the air, making it
perfect running weather. And it seemed that spring was on its way.

Kristín had been a regular visitor to Siglufjördur once the quarantine restrictions had been lifted, and Ari Thór had made several trips
to see her in Akureyri.

Now he had won her back, he had no intention of making any
more wrong moves.

'Beautiful day?' she said.

'Very.'

'Maybe it's possible to get used to Siglufjördur after all,' she said
with the tinkling laugh that he loved so much.

'There's plenty of room in this house for you,' he replied.

'Careful, Ari Thór. We'll see. Now the tunnel is there it's no
problem to live in Akureyri and work in Siglufjördur. Maybe you
could move into my place?'

'Maybe,' he said. 'But there's no certainty I'll get the job.'

'Of course you'll get the job,' she said with a smile. 'Tómas recom-
mended you. And I have every faith in you.'

There was a comfortable rapport between them. Maybe it had
done them good to take a break from each other, even though it

hadn't been the result of the most pleasant of circumstances. Now, though, Ari Thór felt confident that their relationship would be a success.

Then the phone rang.

'Hello, Ari Thór.'

It was the girl from Blönduós. He was sure that she was calling with the results of the paternity test. He felt his heart pound and realised he was not entirely sure which result he was hoping for.

'Listen … I had a call about … the results of the test. You're not the father. I'm really sorry I had to put you through this,' she said in a subdued voice.

Ari Thór was taken by surprise and did not know how to react.

'No problem,' he said without thinking.

'You must be relieved,' she said.

'What? Well, yes. Your old boyfriend, is he the father?'

'He is. He was always going to be the most likely candidate. Our relationship has been rather sticky … I was sort of hoping it was going to be you.'

Ari Thór was again unsure how to take this or how to reply. All he knew was that he was desperate to end the call.

'I'm sorry, I have to run,' he lied. 'Good luck with everything. I'm sure it'll work out for the three of you.'

'Thanks. Maybe we'll see each other some time,' she said awkwardly.

Ari Thór returned her sentiment with no sincerity and finished the call as quickly as he could.

Kristín was beside him and he put his arms around her.

'So you're not the boy's father?' she said warmly.

'No, I'm not. That's good; it makes life a little easier,' he said, conscious of how unconvincing he sounded and how his words were mixed with regret.

'True enough,' she said affectionately, clearly not taken in and not likely to let him get away with the pretence that he was happy with the result.

She didn't ask if he had been looking forward to meeting the boy and having the chance to teach him the ways of the world – ensuring that he wouldn't grow up without a father, as Ari Thór had done himself.

The unasked questions hung in the air, needing neither to be asked nor answered. Instead Kristín suggested what he had been waiting for.

'Then we'd better work on making you a dad, hadn't we?'

Acknowledgements

Rupture is dedicated to the memory of my grandparents in Siglufjör-dur – Þ. Ragnar Jónasson and Guðrún Reykdal – who have now passed away, but lived there for decades in a house which is the inspiration behind Ari Thór's house. My grandfather was town treasurer of Siglufjördur, but he was always writing, and published five books on the history of Siglufjördur after his retirement. My grandmother collected and published folklore. Both of them encouraged me from an early age to keep writing, as did my parents, Jónas Ragnarsson and Katrín Guðjónsdóttir.

The journey from publication of my series in Iceland to publication in the UK took five years, and I wish to thank a few people who provided great help along the way. Barry Forshaw included me in his writings on Nordic Noir long before my books became available in the UK, and has been incredibly supportive ever since. Yrsa Sigurðardóttir introduced me to so many wonderful people related to the field of crime fiction abroad and encouraged me to attend crime festivals in the UK before I had a UK publisher. Quentin Bates, who subsequently became my translator, supported the books from day one and has been invaluable in the process. Ann Cleeves and William Ryan also proved instrumental in introducing me to my UK agent, David Headley, and encouraged him to take a leap of faith, which eventually led to the series being picked up by Karen Sullivan, my incredible publisher, who took a leap of faith of her own, for which I am forever grateful.

Thanks are of course also due to my excellent Icelandic publishers,

Pétur Már Ólafsson and Bjarni Þorsteinsson, and my wonderful international agent, Monica Gram at Copenhagen Literary Agency.

Last but not least, my family deserves all the thanks I can give, and more: María, Kira and Natalía.